KILL THE CRAWLIES!

(Well, maybe not....)

"I haven't been to the West Terrace before," Auria tells me.

"Very wise," I tell her. "The Clan avoids the West Terrace." She sees Red Tree standing in the debris of its prey. "What a pretty tree! What's all that chalky stuff about it?"

"Bones and shells of birds, sharpteeth, stinging moths and Crawlies," I explain. "Years of them."

"What's a Crawly?" she asks.

I take her arm and lead her across the Terrace to the edge, holding her as she leans forward and peers into the dimness. A Crawly runs along the web to find a better hiding place. She gasps and steps back in alarm.

"That was a Crawley," I explain, "and its ancestors were spiders before radiation poisoned the land."

"Radiation did that?" she exclaims.

"No," I tell her. "Radiation was destroying them and I interfered. I was very young and still learning. I was inept, so they developed too many eyes and legs and grew too large."

"It's all revolting, Saulus!" she tells me, as though angry. "You must kill the Crawlies before they become a menace to us all!"

"No," I explain, "because they eat the sharpteeth which come over the mountain in large numbers. I try to adjust balance, not kill things just because they aren't attractive to humans.

"You've created horrors, Saulus! What will you do about the Crawlies until the trees grow?"

I think it wiser not to tell her about the silver beetles. "I'll arrange matters," I assure her.

DANCE TO THE SUN

WILLIAM ESRAC

DANCE TO THE SUN

A Baen Books Original.

Baen Publishing Enterprises
P.O. Box 1403
Riverdale, N.Y. 10471

ISBN: 0-671-87784-4

Cover art by Stephen Hickman

First printing, June 1997

Distributed by
SIMON & SCHUSTER
1230 Avenue of the Americas
New York, N.Y. 10020

Printed in the United States of America

For Claire

and with sincere thanks to
Algis Budrys for being there.
Thanks are also due to Toni Weisskopf.

* ONE *

The sky was pale blue, very bright and unmarked by cloud. The landscape, diseased and tortured, was ocher and yellow, brown and black. The road curved over the plain, broken in parts by the huge cracks and craters. Parts were overgrown with the dry, yellow weed which had survived and spread after the normal balance of nature had been destroyed.

Insects seemed to dance and sing everywhere, the heat rousing them to a pitch of activity in the noon brightness. The light glanced from millions of tiny wings and pale bodies until it was sometimes difficult to tell where weed ended and insect life began above the immediate surface of that distorted land.

Here and there, the decayed remains of trees thrust spikily upward and, far less frequently, the remains of old buildings leaned crazily, burned by the heat of the holocaust which had come years before.

The man shambled drunkenly along the road, his feet disturbing the weed and insects. He leaned forward, his head lowered and his knees bent, as though he had reached the last stages of exhaustion. But he moved at a fairly regular speed, skirting the cracks and craters to follow the road with stubborn, painful tenacity. He was filthy with dust and pollen from the weed, his clothes sweat-stained and torn. He had lost one sandal and blood had caked over one swollen foot. As he shambled along, he hummed tunelessly. It was a sound of pain, misery and despair, an expression of hopelessness beyond weeping.

Behind him, the mountains were very distant and, before him, the broken plains stretched to the horizon. The heat of the day was at its most fierce when he was discovered by the aircar as it sped over the ruined land.

The men in the aircar monitored him for a few moments and then carefully shot him with a sedative dart. The dart caught him on one shoulder and, within seconds, he began to stagger. He fell heavily to the weed-thick road. He was barely breathing and his heart rate was alarmingly slow when they lifted him into the aircar and sped northward.

There had always been those with clairvoyant capacities within the human population but, during the past two centuries, the increase of these individuals and the appearance of remarkable and sometimes frightening gifts had reached a stage where the Psi-Orgs had become a real necessity.

Some blamed the slight change in background radiation from nuclear-fission experiments and usage, particularly after the Great Mistake, for the sudden and remarkable appearance and growth of such capacities, but there were others who argued that it was a natural evolution of the species. Still others blamed the introduction of gene therapies and chromosome manipulation among past populations for the development. Nobody could present any proof one way or the other. Whatever the reason for such developments, the

Psi-Orgs were the most efficient means of controlling these gifted individuals and providing a means of protection for the ungifted majority of the population and the social structures.

Callios LeMaitre was slightly embarrassed by the deferential treatment accorded him when he arrived at the Grenoble Center. It was one of the older, larger Psi-Org Centers, having been established late in the previous century. It provided research centers, training sections and the best security that planning and government finances could provide. It also provided confinement for those considered too dangerous to be allowed loose among ordinary mortals.

LeMaitre was at the top of his field as a Calculator and Analyst, but he was more used to being part of a Team than working as an individual. The VIP treatment made him uncomfortable, but he retired behind a dignified facade and tried to ignore the effusive welcome at Reception once Security had cleared him.

He remained dignified when the fluttering young assistant arrived, but relaxed when it became obvious that she was overanxious and a little frightened of him. She took him to his quarters and showed a pleasing efficiency in the way she managed his unpacking despite his protests. She then filled him in on some of the routines observed at the Center and found him a glass of pleasant-enough sherry.

Perhaps the sherry relaxed the hard lines of his face or, perhaps, she discovered that he was human and approachable after all, but she was no longer frightened of him by the time she had explained that her name was Arina and that she had been given the honor of acting as his secretary, organizer and guide during his stay.

He was impressed and allowed her to know it. She

was an A-Class Gamma with equal telepathic and tele-kinetic abilities, spoke four languages like a native, was an expert recorder and had the prettiest legs he had seen for months.

She left him to freshen up after his trip and was back in half an hour to show him to the Administration Block. He noted that she had adopted a more attractive hairstyle and prettier overalls and was flattered. A graying man in his fifties, he was unused to the personal interest of pretty young women, but was not averse to the idea.

His introduction to Louise Vestos was brisk and informal. She was in charge of the Study Center and would be his immediate superior while he worked at Grenoble.

She was a very attractive woman of middle years with magnificent auburn hair which she wore free about her shoulders. Despite her practical nature, she possessed considerable charm and exchanged the expected greetings with more warmth than he was prepared for.

"It was good of you to postpone your recreational leave to take on work here at such short notice. We're very grateful," she said, smiling and offering a welcoming hand.

She led him to a comfortable couch in her rather severe office, to emphasize the informality of the meeting. He dared a smile in return.

"I only hope I can manage whatever it is you want me to do. I usually work as an Analyst with a Team or as a consultant in remedial cases."

"It's an unusual case. You seem to have done good work in unusual cases before, including deep Analysis with Alphas who were non-Registered."

"Once or twice with some who came in voluntarily.

Not with any you could class as real Outlaws such as you have here. I'm rather intrigued that you should request my services. I would have thought you'd have plenty of people about with my capacities, particularly in a High Security Org and especially if it concerns an Outlaw."

It was her turn to smile. She found him attractive and was pleased that he seemed modest, also. The two did not always go together.

"Perhaps you underestimate your own value. We're well aware of your expertise in the field of Analysis. I'm not sure that you could class this case as a real Outlaw. But the potential is there. He seems willing enough to undergo Analysis, but you may find—I'll leave you to discover the difficulties for yourself. This is a Security One case so you'll have to submit to a Classified Conditioning, I'm afraid."

"Oh? Well, if I must. A Security One case? Isn't that usually reserved for real criminals?"

"Not always. But I feel it only fair to warn you that there could be an element of danger with this case. For a start, there'll be no Team to help you. We tried two Teams and the subject immediately became very uncooperative and refused to have anything to do with them. We tried several methods of Probe and got nowhere. To be honest, you're something in the nature of a last resort. We don't normally apply to other Orgs for assistance. And, in this case, you may already have an advantage."

"What can I do that your Analysts and Therapists can't do?"

"We're not sure. Perhaps nothing. But we're willing to try anything at this stage. He mentioned your name several times. It seemed to be the only thing he could remember. We think he knows you. Perhaps you'll recognize him."

"Oh? Who's the patient and what's the problem?"

"His name is Saulus. He has an Alpha psi-field, but he also presents some kind of barrier which even a Team couldn't breach. He's in a confused state and amnesiac, but he remembered your name and became very excited about it. Come, I'll take you to him."

The room where LeMaitre met Saulus was spacious and light and separated from the rest of the High Security wing by an electronically-controlled barrier and two dour-faced Controls. The High Security wing was not particularly attractive and could not be mistaken for anything other than a prison.

Saulus was a pleasant-looking young man, dark blonde and handsomely built. It was difficult to assess his age. He looked slightly Latin until one saw his eyes. They were dark-light, no-color gray, brilliant and penetrating, but without aggression. As LeMaitre and Louise Vestos entered, he stood up from the rest-couch and smiled at them vaguely, clutching the soft lounge-robe to himself in a mild anxiety reflex.

"Relax, Saulus," Louise said. "Here's someone you may know. This is your friend, Callios LeMaitre."

The brilliant eyes fixed on LeMaitre. With some hesitancy, the young man moved closer to peer at his visitor anxiously. The strange, gray eyes examined the older man's face for some moments with piercing intensity as LeMaitre waited calmly.

"Callios LeMaitre. Yes, that's Callios LeMaitre. I know his face—but I can't remember about him—I can't remember anything except his face—"

Tears brimmed suddenly, sparkling as they spilled down the tan-gold cheeks, to be hastily wiped away on the sleeve of his lounge-robe.

He said, on a rising note of hysteria, "I can't remember!"

LeMaitre said, "Don't be upset, Saulus. Let's sit down and talk, shall we? Often, a little bit of talking solves all our problems."

Later, back in Louise's office, LeMaitre was puzzled and slightly angry.

"I'll swear I've never seen him before in my life. And yet there is something familiar about him. It's the eyes, I think. They remind me of someone, but I can't place who. I think you might have warned me about his capacity. He's no Alpha! That psi-field belongs to a Super! Why hasn't Central ordered his Termination? How did he come to be here?"

"Not all Supers are Terminated. I know of several who are actively involved with the Psi-Orgs and so do you."

"But they've been with the Orgs since they were children and are rigidly conditioned. If this man's an Outlaw what hope would you have if he decided to turn that whole wing into a madhouse? What hope would I have with him if he should decide he doesn't like me?"

"You underestimate our safeguards. Of course it's a calculated risk having him here, but I think he'd have shown any aggressive tendencies long before this, particularly after the visits of the Teams we sent to examine him."

"But if, and it's a big if, I did succeed in helping to penetrate that barrier, who'd hold him then? He's big! The moment I tried to probe him I was aware of both telepathic and telekinetic abilities far beyond my control."

"Perhaps you'll be less worried when I tell you a little about him. We've known something of him for just over two years and our information came from one of the best operatives in Security Investigation."

Arina appeared magically with glasses of brandysub and euphowafers. LeMaitre accepted them gratefully. The women exchanged a brief glance and Arina departed tactfully. Louise waited until he had tasted the brandysub before continuing.

"Grenoble-Psi, being constantly on the alert for criminal activities of a clairvoyant nature, relies very much on Investigative agents," she began. "The Investigative Center had vague information about a group of Outlaws known as the Jonaas Clan for some years before anything useful turned up. Two 'kinetics of the Delta class, petty thieves and none too intelligent, were captured during a drug raid in Rome. They'd had some sort of inhibitive directive imposed to prevent them from revealing their secrets, but we have techniques that can be very useful for breaking those down, provided they are applied with care. These two Deltas gave out some useful information on the Clan which the Security Sector decided they could put to use. They selected one of their best operatives, a woman named Auria Shasti, and set her the task of making contact with the Clan and becoming involved with it."

"That sounds like dangerous work."

"It was, but she's an expert. She's a 'path, a Beta Calculator with a Lure Specialty, a clever woman and a lucky one. Within a few months, working with the names and contact points given by the two Deltas, she'd become involved with a certain Hubertus Aanensen. He was a key man with the Clan who worked with the Euroasian underworld from time to time. Some days after she met him, she and Hubertus vanished. No word was heard from her for half a year.

Then a message was received by one of her Security contacts. She had, it seemed, persuaded Hubertus to take her with him on one of his trips and seized the opportunity to get in touch very briefly. She gave some information on Jonaas and his Clan and she talked of a Super named Saulus. She talked mostly of Saulus. That was when Central Control became really interested. He sounded like something very special."

"Special and very dangerous."

She ignored the comment.

"She couldn't tell us the whereabouts of the Clan stronghold because all those traveling to and from it were taken by a secret route through tunnels that she thought may have been made by the Warlords last century. According to her, the stronghold had to be one of the old Warlord fortresses situated somewhere in one of the Contaminated Areas."

"I thought those were all cleaned up."

"Most are, but there are still pockets where radiation levels are considered unsafe. It's a large area. You can't know how ugly and dreadful some of it is. Those damned wars in the name of religion—the Clan's security was good. She couldn't even carry a pinpointer back with her. We didn't hear from her again for some time. Then she managed another brief contact, describing some of the more dangerous Outlaws in the Clan and giving more information about Saulus. The contact was too brief and too vague to act on but it was clear the Clan was far more active than we'd suspected."

"She gave no clue as to the hiding place?"

"She didn't get the chance before the contact ceased rather abruptly. We didn't hear from her again until very recently. She had been presumed lost, possibly dead, by then. But she escaped to Izmir and got

word out about the location of the stronghold. She
seemed very agitated, so Central Security staged one
of its biggest raids. But they were a little late. They
found a few minor members of the Clan in the tunnels and a few more in the surrounding countryside.
There'd been an immense landslide caused by some
sort of explosion and most of the place where they'd
lived was under a mountain of rock and rubble. Of
Hubertus, Jonaas and half a dozen more of the really
important Clan members, there was no sign. We presumed them dead under that mountain of rubble. It
was reported that Saulus and some of the other Outlaws were trying to make their way over the mountains into old Turkey, so operatives were sent out to
scan the area. It was two days before they found Saulus on the Plains of the Warlords in Anatolia. He was
physically exhausted and quite amnesiac. He can't or
won't communicate in any real way. You're the first
person he's recognized or spoken more than a few
words to."

"But I don't know him, I'm certain."

"As to the danger of being hurt by him—if Auria's
reports are to be relied on, he's as benign and lovable
as Jesus of Nazareth. She is, unfortunately, emotionally involved with him so we're not too certain about
the veracity of much that she claims. She swears that
he's the originator of the Solar Faith which is becoming so popular."

"The Solar Faith? Isn't that one of those new reli-
gions? I'm not too familiar with evangelistic groups."

"You will be. And it's no group. It's a massive movement, becoming the biggest religious influence in
Euroasia. Now, what will you need? We can give you
every back-up—Teams, Consultants, Therapists. You
have a free hand."

Her rich, auburn hair surged and swirled momentarily, reminding him that she was an Alpha-Plus 'kinetic.

He sipped his brandysub thoughtfully before replying.

"I don't know if I can do anything. If it's possible to erase that barrier I'll certainly try. Is there any specific information on him?"

"Not a great deal. Auria's reports don't make a lot of sense concerning Saulus, but you may find some key in them. She tried to help when we discovered he was amnesiac, but he didn't remember her, either. When will you begin?"

"Tomorrow. I'll need to have free access to his ward and I'd like some Controls with me in case I get into difficulties. A Therapist might be useful to have about. And I'd like to talk with Auria Shasti."

"I'll arrange it as soon as you've undergone Classified Conditioning. Anything else?"

LeMaitre thought of Arina. Having met Louise, Arina no longer seemed quite so desirable. He said, "No. I seem to have all I need to keep me comfortable, thanks."

Memo.

To: Louise Vestos, Director, Study Center.

From: Callios LeMaitre.

Two days of trying, but little response. I've been attempting several simple techniques to stimulate some kind of starting point. He drew me a picture which I enclose. It looks to me like a flower or a sun sign. He listens to me, but I'm not sure that he understands a thing I say to him.

—C. LeM.

Memo.

To: Louise Vestos, Director, Study Center.

From: Callios LeMaitre.

Another drawing enclosed, this time executed with great excitement. A face surrounded by yellow hair. Curiously childlike, but notice the sophisticated rendition of the eyes. When I asked him who it was a picture of, he said, "The lady."

I've decided to move into the ward with him since I get slight flickers of response through the barrier at unexpected times. I receive impressions of growing plants, faces and scents, but too briefly to make anything of. I've had a bed and a few things brought in and Arina will see to recorders and the standard monitoring.

—C. LeM.

Memo.

To: Louise Vestos, Director, Study Center.

From: Callios LeMaitre.

Have had some sort of breakthrough. Saulus is talking. In fact, it's difficult to stop him talking and I've stopped trying. I'm recording everything.

His talking may sound like gibberish, but I think it could be a form of the old French language. Could you find someone who can translate the recordings in a hurry, please?

What started him off was the name "Auria." He kept drawing pictures of the "lady" so I kept hammering at her identity. I mentioned "Auria" and he said, "Yes, Auria," as though discovering something. I suggested he tell me about Auria and about himself and he immediately had some sort of hysterical seizure, screaming out about the fire burning the earth and his dear one and something about everything being destroyed. I sent for the medics, but he recovered and began talking long before they arrived. I don't interfere with the flow of his talking because I think he's remembering.

—C. LeM.

Memo.

To: Louise Vestos, Director, Study Center.
From: Callios LeMaitre.

Thank you for the translations. He *is* remembering, and very lucidly. Now he is speaking in well-educated Universal.

I think, and the Therapist agrees, that it's a form of catharsis. He remembers days and talks about them in maddening detail, as though they were happening right now. "Auria" was the initial key, but now he talks on regardless of anything I might say.

The psi-barrier is still in place. I suspect it may be a form of punishment which he has inflicted on himself, rather than a defensive device.

He talks, he eats and then talks again. There's no apparent routine to it. Sometimes he stares at the wall for long periods of silence and nothing will stir him, but when he talks he focuses on me and talks with a will.

The tapes grow. They'll need editing. Some of what he says has no bearing on events and is merely loving description of a day, an object or a feeling. I've become very good at waking when he begins.

His memory is extraordinary, directed and detailed. This is often the case when a subject enters a semi-trance state as he does. The detail maddens me, but it's certainly not boring!

—C. LeM.

Most Secret.

Security S2—14
To: Colin Helm, Director, Security Central.
From: Louise Vestos, Study Center.

Colin, I am enclosing physical data on the patient known as "Saulus," an edited manuscript of the data compiled from 32 recorded capsules and the said 32 recorded capsules marked in order.

LeMaitre did remarkably well, managing to direct Saulus into catharsis-mode and so producing these recordings. His patience and intelligence about the matter have been very impressive. Despite the patient having remembered his name, LeMaitre cannot recall having any previous contact with him.

Since Saulus is technically an Outlaw and obviously a Super, his Termination would be automatic under normal circumstances. However, while his telepathic ability is unusually powerful, it is his allied 'kinetic ability which is so unique and of undoubted value.

The decisions regarding his future must be made by Council and soon. I am hoping for a speedy decision on the case so that all concerned in the Security Quarantine may be released to pursue normal duties once more. Plus there are many in the Research Facilities who wish to examine his Secondary and put it to use.

—L.V.

Most Secret

Security S2—14
From: Joseph Thorenson, Semantics Division.

I have reduced the original manuscript by almost two-thirds, editing out much of the extraneous comment and lengthy dissertations which have little point in the narrative. I have given dates where they could be positively established.

Since the tapes cover almost two years, with some gaps, much of what Saulus thought, felt or did is often of little interest to anyone but himself. I have, therefore, taken some liberties in the compilation and editing of this second manuscript and I have also included some information to point out important occurrences beyond the narrative. This may clarify certain areas where Saulus is vague or uninformed.

The manuscript is, wherever possible, given as Saulus spoke it. He was speaking to Callios LeMaitre in part but, at other times, was speaking aloud to himself and becoming introspective, sometimes entering a trancelike state as he spoke.

Auria Shasti seems to have had a profound effect on him. She is a remarkable young woman in many ways.

In the early stages, Saulus speaks in a very poor form of the old French language and colloquial slang. In translating this, I have removed some grammatical errors and distortions for the sake of clarity and easier reading.

It is not until the third tape that Saulus begins speaking in highly educated Universal. What is remarkable is his ability to comprehend and apply the education that, as becomes clear, he was given so rapidly by Shasti and other members of the Jonaas Clan.

—J.T.

* TWO *

I wake up and it is a good day. My life-pulses are full again and I feel delight in being. I go out and do my dance to Sun-over-the-mountains. Yo-Yo laughs and tries to dance, too, but falls down and cries until I give him cuddles.

My hands are complete again so I am able to feed Yo-Yo and myself on the fruit stored away behind the ferns. He is greedy and forgets that he hurt himself. I go down to the pool and wash myself carefully as the lady says is necessary. She is slightly wrong about the need for much washing, but I do it for her. The water is cold, but I feel good afterwards.

I do a think-change so that I will not smell bad and the Lady will not be displeased. She is very particular about smells. I comb my hair and put on my wrap-around, then I sweep out my cave and tidy it so that she will think it pleasant. She is very particular about tidiness, too. The old vine is not a good curtain, but the new one is growing quickly and well and my cave will be secret again soon. I like that word "secret." Secret—

I go out and make sure that all the pretty blue flowers are open because she likes them so much.

16

The carpet of grasses is so beautiful and the scents on the air are delightful that my excitement shivers in my senses. The whole world is beautiful on this day.

She comes early today and smiles so pleasantly. She says, "Hello, Saulus, I see that your hands are better." I am glad they are better, too. She think-teaches me a pleasant lesson today. It is about words and why not words and I speak better in the Universal speaking.

I like the way of her thinking. She is strange and different to others I am friends with. She does not spill her thoughts carelessly as do my friends. Others regard her as being cold and cal-cu-lating but I do not find this to be true. But she is sad, I think. Hubertus is not the correct mate for her, perhaps. He is my good friend, but I see that he might not be right for the Lady.

Or is she sad because of the directive Hubertus has put in her brain so that she cannot run away from him and the valley? Noni says she tried to do this after the bad mistake she did with Outside work for the Clan. Hubertus would not like her to run away. Hubertus is my good friend, but I see that he is foolish in some ways.

She brings me a new tunic so that I may hide my bare skin. She says my wraparound is dis-gus-ting-ly dirty and that I should wash it. When I take it off to put on the new tunic she says it is not polite to show some male parts even when they are nice. Only sometimes, she says, but does not say when. I pretend I do not understand, but I know. Sometimes it is wise to seem foolish before her.

When she goes I feel sad. She is so pretty and so nice. And what Hubertus calls intelligent. It is strange that she can be intelligent and yet make such a mistake in the Clan-Work Outside. Noni says she will not be allowed Outside again because Jonaas is angry about the mistake. But I think Jonaas wishes to take her from Hubertus to be his woman and this is a way to keep her close. I have seen Jonaas look at her and have felt traces of the emotion he feels.

Carolus comes for a think-change of his face and fingertip patterns. He does not like to come to me for this, but comes because Jonaas says he must. Carolus is afraid of me like some others are afraid, but he is more afraid of Jonaas. I fix a wrong place inside Carolus's heart, but I do not tell him because he would become more frightened of me if I did. He is very foolish.

When he goes, I play with the little snake and feed her while I think on how Carolus smells like the way the Lady says is bad. Then I take Yo-Yo down to the pool and wash him while he yells and cries. He goes to sulk among the big ferns on the little terrace while I wash his tunic and my wraparound and spread them to dry on the rocks.

A think-call comes from Noni, so I go quickly to the South Wing where the wall pictures are so pretty. Noni thinks my new tunic is very suitable. She wants a change to breasts and face again, but I tell her no more until new balances establish. She is very cross, but does not argue. She is my good friend, but I see that she can be foolish about some things.

She puts on lots of smell from a bottle and I feel like giving her a good wash like I did with Yo-Yo.

She says Jonaas will be sending more people for face-change and fingertip-pattern change later. She says the Clan has big work coming.

She says Hubertus does not like the Lady coming to my cave so much and she wants to know why the Lady comes. I explain about the lessons, but she says

Hubertus wonders because he is jealous in the mating-way. I think Hubertus has asked Noni to question me about this so I pretend not to understand.

She says that Jonaas is still angry because I will not make his body-changes. This makes me angry and afraid and spoils my pleasure in the day.

I go quickly to the West Terrace where no one else goes so that I can look at Red Tree and forget my fear of Jonaas. I know he will hurt me badly again if I do not give him the body-changes soon. But I am more angry than afraid of him.

Red Tree is growing big and pretty since I changed his food needs. It is a pity I did not discover the right way of his food needs when he was younger. The hot-sickness in the ground is now no problem to him. His leaves are now bigger and he whispers to me with his life-pulse. He sucks a little of my blood, but only for an identification and not a hungriness. He ate many birds yesterday, the nasty brown killer-birds that try to eat his fruit.

I ask him for fruit and he gives me plenty until I cannot eat any more. He is very full of life-pulse now, but next year he may begin to fail. I must make his seeds fertile next year so that there will be more Red Trees. It will be easy to train them about ignoring the hot-sickness in the ground now that I know the way.

All the little mosses and the tiny purple flowers on the West Terrace now grow thickly and smell so pretty. All whisper to me with their life-pulse and eat many bad insects. But not bees. The bees are failing again because of the hot-sickness, so I must make corrections soon. The valley needs the bees. I must also look at the stinging-moths again soon because they breed too readily and have too many legs.

I go up to High-on-the-Mountain-Spur and look

into Deep Crack. Big Crawly-Thing is frightened and waves wiggly legs at me. I make a pleasure-think to him and he stops his chittering noises. I like him because he makes the soft bed stuff for Yo-Yo and me to rest on, and he does not hurt anything but the sharp teeth and stinging-moths which come to the West Terrace. He has so many eyes and legs that I want to laugh. He is all wrong, but funny.

The big vines on Fallen-Down Rocks are covered with flowers now—

(*A lengthy dissertation on the rights and wrongs of plant growth follows. The terminology and theories are garbled, however, and are impossible to understand.*

—*J.T. Semantics Division*)

A think-call comes from Noni so I run down to my cave. There are five men and two women waiting with Noni. Some of them are very frightened of me and roll their eyes or make fear-smiles. Noni manages them well and I get busy.

It takes a long time because they wish to look good and their ideas of this are sometimes strange. They look in Noni's mirror again and again and make frightened, wondering sounds. They go away with Noni, leaving meat and cheese and bread for payment and it is already midafternoon.

Yo-Yo comes for his tunic so I dress him, give him cuddles and feed him. I tell him there will be washings every day from now on and he squeals. I wish he could think better. He plays games very well and is happier since the last time I fixed his back and legs. I would make him grow bigger, but Jonaas might notice him more so it is better to leave him small. When he is finished eating we play Bob-Up Bob-Down in the long grass until he is tired. Then I sing songs for him until it gets dark.

I feed him the milk which Noni brought and put him to bed, then I go to High-on-the-Mountain again and work at the steel door that is hidden there. This must be the fourth year-cycle of working at it. Soon the stone which holds it will be chipped away enough to open it. What is inside? I am always excited to think on it, especially as it is my secret.

Secret—

I go down to the pools and swim for a long time. Water is so wonderful—

(At this point, Saulus goes into lengthy ponderings concerning water, body functions pertaining to the elimination of body wastes and then to very basic sexual matters. The ideas are concise and well-ordered, but seem to me unnecessary to the narrative.
—J.T. Semantics Division)

I go to the cave and light the candle that Noni left me, then I read the book that the Lady brought me. Many of the Universal words are strange to me and the things written are sometimes a puzzle. None of the other Clan ever had such a book. Tomorrow I must ask many questions. I am tired. I must sleep. I call Yo-Yo, tuck him into the soft bed and snuggle down beside him.

(Saulus himself makes the following jump in time. Days or possibly weeks have passed. He speaks in excellent Universal from here.
—J.T. Semantics Division)

I awake, full of energy and life-pulse and dance to the sunrise. It's very good and I feel wonderful after. I lift Yo-Yo from his warm bed and take him down to the pools, ignoring his squealing and kicking. I wash him and myself, then dry us with the towel that I swapped for Red Tree's fruit with Mario. I tickle Yo-Yo until he laughs again. He's getting very fat and

pot-bellied so I do some little changes to his insides
and adjust his hunger-need. "Adjust" is an uncomfortable word. I adjust my ideas, but not so easily as I
adjust Yo-Yo's insides.

I wash our tunics and we run up to the cave to
spread them on the rocks. Then I go to Red Tree
and to the vegetable garden on Low Terrace for our
breakfast. I collect milk from the kitchen before
Mario awakes and Yo-Yo and I eat very well. I think
I'll steal some bread and cheese later.

I clean my cave very carefully and throw out the
Crawly-Thing bedding to make rope from later. My
new bed, brought here by Noni and the Lady, is very
fine and Hubertus has promised me blankets. Yo-Yo
and I will sleep very well.

It is a long time since we had a proper bed with
blankets. Not that I have missed them so much. But
I have accepted the bed and blankets because
Hubertus feels so guilty that he did not think about
them before this. Why should he think of them? He
has never come to my cave before. The Lady has
caused him to think about me. He has always presumed things before. Hubertus is clever, but he pre-
sumes wrongly sometimes.

It's a hot day so our tunics dry very quickly. I dress
us, put Yo-Yo on my shoulders and go quickly up
to High-on-the-Mountain. Such a wonderful secret to
have! The door is almost hidden by the new vines
now. I put Yo-Yo down to open the door and we
creep into the darkness.

I find the candles stolen from Carolus's supply box,
light them and close the door carefully. Yo-Yo likes
the little gold box with the pretty jewels in it so I
leave him to play with them while I look in the big,
wooden chests again. They are full of wonderful

things. "Treasures" is the word, I think. So many
beautiful clothes! They are made of beautiful synthetic
fabrics and are not damaged at all!

Now I have beautiful new clothes which are strange
and good. I had to look at them carefully before I
realized what they were. They are what Mahmud calls
"kaftans" of the old style, used when the Warlord
was here. Perhaps they belonged to him. They are
beautifully embroidered and made in wonderful colors. I like to feel the smoothness and see the shine
of them. They are big and loose, so I like them better
than tunics.

Poor Warlord. I wonder if he was one of those who
made the terrible war in the name of religion and
helped to destroy all the fertility beyond the valley?
The Lady says that the religion was only part of the
excuse for so much destruction, that politics were also
important, but I don't understand some of what she
tried to explain. Religion seems to be an excuse for
many bad things. I must find out about politics.

I look at the large, soft couches with the beautiful
cushions, at the carved benches and the bright hangings on the walls. There is a box with a necklace of
heavy gold pieces in it and I put that on because it
pleases me. I put on a kaftan of green and gold and
decide to wear it today. I find a beautiful piece of
fabric which I wrap about Yo-Yo and pin with a gold
butterfly so that he's pleased, too. He likes pretty
things. So do I.

We put the rest of the things away carefully, blow
out the candles and go outside again. I close the door
tight and then look about the little courtyard. There
were once gardens here, I think. This would be a
pleasant place to live in. I must consider that. It would
be pleasant to have a garden here again.

I take Yo-Yo back to the cave and find the Lady there. She has brought me more books. She is very beautiful to me and excitement quivers in my senses. I send Yo-Yo to play in the meadow.

She think-talks to me, "You look very handsome, like one of the old Warlords."

I tell her what Noni keeps saying about her visiting and that Hubertus grows angry about it. But she shrugs, as though not caring.

She quickens my life-pulse powerfully today because she is so pretty and golden and has such a scent of woman. I let her see that I am desirous.

She pretends disapproval and tells me, "No, I belong with Hubertus," but her body is interested and I persuade it unfairly with my special-think despite her wish not to be persuaded. It is a wonderful mating. She is beautiful and I am beautiful and we stay touching and looking for a long time.

She asks, "How old are you, Saulus?"

I am not truly certain, but I tell her I remember seventeen years and am probably twenty years old.

I ask her a little about where she came from on the Outside, but she does not answer very much. Noni says she was a petty thief found by Hubertus in Rome. I wonder why? She is surely intelligent enough to have found easier ways to live. She never talks of her Outside life. She is a woman of secrets. Perhaps her secrets concern crimes which no one knows of. Perhaps there were crimes of which she is ashamed. She is sensitive and refined, unlike most of the Clan.

She gives me a very long and very good think-lesson about many things I wished to know and then says she must go. I give her the necklace of gold pieces and she thinks it is very fine. When she asks where it came from, I tell her it is payment from the Clan for what I do and she believes me.

I ask, "Why do you make your hair this wrong color?"

She tells me, "Hubertus likes it and it helps to make me look younger."

I tell her, "I'll make the color real if you wish it. And thirty years isn't old."

She says, "I'm twenty-five."

I say, "I know you are thirty years. Your body tells me so."

She does not like it that I can tell about these things.

She says to me, "Hubertus likes to be with a younger woman. You must keep my secret. For how long have you lived in this cave?"

I tell her, "When I was unripe I lived with Mario. He took care of me because Jonaas said he must. But Mario is a bully and he dislikes Yo-Yo being about him. So, when I was older, I brought us to this cave and we're happier. Yo-Yo likes it that nobody yells at him. No one is afraid of me while I'm here and I feel safer away from Jonaas."

I am looking at her insides and outsides with my special-think and see how she can be made more youthful without pain because it is important to her. She is healthy, but too fat a little. I make adjustments for slow changes.

She says, "All are afraid of Jonaas. Why does he hate you so?"

I show her with my mind and she says, "Jealousy? Of his own son?"

I say, "I'm not his son. Yo-Yo is his son. Our mother was the same woman."

I show her the place where our mother is buried behind the rocks in the cave. I say, "She died when

Yo-Yo was born, eleven years ago, but she didn't die of Yo-Yo as Jonaas says. She died because of the hot-sickness in the ground. I tried to help her when she became sick, but I was too young to understand and my special-think was not strong then. She coached me in mindspeaking. But my special-think was something I learned the beginnings about from one who died in work for the Clan. He was a Healer. And the enlarging and refining of those things I learned for myself."

She says, "Do you know what a Super-Talent is?"

I say, "Yes. Noni is a Super, not with mindspeaking but because she has such a great ability for lifting things. Noni helped me to cover the hot-sickness of the north side by pulling down parts of the mountains. And Hubertus is a Super, a Calculator who thinks of how and why better than others and because he's so powerful as a mindspeaker. And Jonaas is a Super, a Charismatic and a Firethrower."

She asks, "And what are you, Saulus?"

I say, "You know. I'm a Super with a big ability to mindspeak and a special-think which is to do with the telekinetic."

She says, "And you are more intelligent than most people here. You are stronger than Jonaas in your own way. Why don't you fight him when he hurts you?"

I like it that she calls me intelligent.

I say, "I don't like the hurt he gives, but he's the Big Boss. He keeps us all organized, united and safe from the Outside. There must be a Big Boss or the Clan would run about like ants without a nest. He's hurt me only twice. My hands were the worst—but they took little time to heal and restore."

She says, "Jonaas becomes increasingly unstable.

Someday he will have to be fought and you could do it."

I say nothing. I've never considered such an idea before. The idea of fighting Jonaas makes me shivery inside.

She says, "You learn very quickly. Who taught you things before me?"

I say, "Many people. My mother, Hubertus, Torros and Mario were some. But you teach me things that are interesting and make other thinking clearer. Hubertus teaches me much since you began teaching me, but I enjoy the learning with you more. You are so beautiful and have the manner of secrets which I like."

She says, "What secrets?" and becomes full of fear inside.

I say, "I don't know your secrets. It is your manner which is secret and I like it. Meriem calls it enigmatic. That is a good word, I think. You sometimes give a feeling of sadness in your thinking, so I wonder if this is because of what you hide from others."

She says, "We all have our secrets. Like you and me being with each other today. It mustn't happen again or I won't give you more lessons. And Hubertus must not know."

I allow her to think I agree about no more mating, but I don't promise. I should feel shame at my unfair persuasion, though. It was not a fair thing. I must not do it again. Maybe.

When she goes I'm so hungry that I call Yo-Yo from the little meadow and take him hunting for the sharpteeth in the valley. They are such nasty, destructive creatures with too many teeth and voracious— that's a lovely word—appetites. But they are delicious—another lovely word—to eat.

The air in the valley is good and the grass is green, green, green because there is no hot-sickness in the ground. There are pretty flowers all over the valley. It is such a beautiful place.

We find a little herd of sharpteeth near the white rocks. I tuck up my kaftan. Yo-Yo makes loud noises, so I leave him and run and run until I catch a fat male and kill him with my special-think. I pick Yo-Yo up and run back to the cave, peel the sharpteeth of his dirty skin with my knife and then we eat him. The meat is delicious, not spoiled by cooking and putting things on it to change the taste.

I bury the fur and bones, wash us both, then I take Yo-Yo up to High-on-the-mountain again.

We play with the treasures again and then I begin a deciding. We will live here. There are two good rooms and plenty of space. Outside, the court is in good condition and there is soil for a garden. Noni might repair the bowl where water was once piped from the pure stream and, perhaps, Angelo may know where to find a pump.

There's no hot-sickness up here and it feels secret and calm. I'll start a garden with ferns, blue flowers, some purple moss and vines and the pretty flowers which Meriem calls roses. And some feathery little trees such as I've seen down in the valley. I like it.

Mario sends a think-call, so I pick Yo-Yo up, close the door, and go down to the kitchen of the Red Palace very fast.

Mario says, "Jonaas wants you in the Big Room."

I smooth my kaftan and my hair and wish I had my shoes on. I leave Yo-Yo playing with some bread dough and go quickly to the Big Room. Some others of the Clan are there. Meriem, Carolus, Noni, Hubertus, the Twins, Angelo, Fatimah and some new people.

And Jonaas. His radiance-of-fascination is strong today, but I'm not influenced by it any more. Not since he burned my hands so badly.

He looks at me and says, "Chaos! You look almost respectable for once! Such pretty clothes! Where did you find them, imbecile?"

He says it loud and growling, with his black brows pinching his nose and his brown eyes glaring. He is thinner and sicker than when I last saw him.

I say, "In a hole," then I hold up my hands and say, "I made new flesh and bone," so that he knows I'm not crushed down by him any longer. But I'm afraid. He looks at me with anger and pretends not to recognize that I'm no longer crushed down.

He says, "These people are new to the Clan. Examine them," and I notice that his teeth are decaying again because of the drugs and other substances he uses.

The new people don't know me, so are not afraid. But they are puzzled. One man has a chest sickness, two women have sickness caused by drugs, one woman has a growing-wrong in her womb and the last two men are healthy in the usual half-possible way of some people. I mindspeak this to Jonaas.

His mindspeak is not strong but he tells me, "Hubertus will bring the sick ones to you for treatment."

I tell him, "Find a treating place here. I don't want people at my cave. It is my private place."

Jonaas smiles his nasty, how-you-disgust-me smile and mindspeaks, "Is your cave too exclusive for the Clan, then? Anything you have here is because I say you may have it, imbecile. Get out of my sight."

I tell him, "Don't call me 'imbecile.' I will not have them in my cave."

I mindspeak with Hubertus about not treating people at my cave and he nods. I like Hubertus very much, even when he has his I-am-very-important-and-you-are-nothing-to-me manner.

I go back to the kitchen where Yo-Yo is eating bread dough and making himself sick. I'm about to pick him up when Jonaas mindspeaks at the full extent of his capacity.

"When do you intend giving me the attention I need? I am ill! Must I punish you again, imbecile?" he demands.

I tell him, "I want no people at my cave and don't call me 'imbecile.'"

He tells me, "You dare to bargain with me? You are as imbecile as your brother!"

I tell him, "He's only half my brother. I ask nothing of you but respect as a Clan-member."

I feel his anger flare and shove Yo-Yo away from me.

I feel the pain coming and I fall down, rolling wildly and screaming. Aah! Aah! The pain! My hair is afire, my skin burns and blisters in agony! My face, my neck, my scalp! Aah! Aah! The heat and flame! Aah! From some small reasoning-place in my mind I think of the Lady's words, "Why don't you fight him when he hurts you?" I open my mind-power big, bigger, bigger again and turn it on Jonaas, sweeping him away like a stick in the flood! Then all is pain and I feel myself fall into the blackness. . . .

I awake. Oh, the pain is bad, bad! I cry out until I can block off the little paths which send feel-messages to my brain. The Lady's voice is saying something and I hear Hubertus and Noni, too. Yo-Yo is crying somewhere.

I force my eyelids open against the swollen, half-dead flesh and see them. Hubertus is holding Yo-Yo and patting him, the Lady is so pretty even when she weeps and Noni is scowling so very angrily. And there is the woman who hasn't been at the Palace for very long—what's her name? Jazalu.

I use my special-think to look. My hair is gone and my scalp, face and neck are red-black-wet and bubbling. One ear is cooked and must be entirely replaced. My mouth is all blubber so I mindspeak to them, "Go away and I'll remake myself."

The Lady mindspeaks, "Oh, Saulus, I'm so sorry!"

Hubertus says, "Come away. Best not to interfere with him. Saulus knows best."

It is Noni who picks me up with her mind and carries me. I am so grateful for her help. I close my eyes and become busy with the remaking, excluding all other awareness.

When I open my eyes again I find I'm in the cave. The woman, Jazalu, is close. She is big and heavy-boned and strong, but shaped very well. She has orange-red hair which is not true and she wears much cosmetics on her face. She has no mindspeaking ability—it is something 'kinetic.

I manage to croak, "Please get me water."

She says, "Very well, wonderman."

She has a voice like crunching rocks.

I have drawn energy and fuel from areas of my body where it is not needed immediately, but I need water badly. When she returns, she holds my newly healed head so that I'm able to drink. She is very careful.

She says, "I didn't believe what they told me about you until now. It's horrible but wonderful. Do you hurt now?"

I say, "Not now. Will you get me some food, please? I need materials from eggs, cheese, fruit and bread."

She leaves me and I finish rebuilding my eyelids so that they open properly. All my skin is restored and the ear replaced.

I am suddenly angry. I don't get angry often. I think on how Jonaas could have damaged my brain with his fire. He has never attacked me so seriously before. This time it is more than just because he is angry that I don't bow down to him. It is his madness which he begins to show.

I also think on how I swept him away. This is an interesting thing to think on. Very interesting. I never tried anything like that before.

I sit up and Yo-Yo comes, making squeaking noises to tell me he's frightened. I give him cuddles and tuck him down beside me so that he feels safe.

When Jazalu returns I eat greedily for the materials I need. She squats down and is intent on my scalp hair as it grows.

She says, "Don't grow hair on your face. You're too handsome to hide it."

She touches eyelashes and brows delicately.

I say, "Are you afraid of me?"

She says, "Should I be?"

"No," I say, "but some people are."

I get up slowly, take the dead tissue to bury beneath the vines and then I go down to the pools to wash. The kaftan is burned and ruined, but clings to me still. Jazalu comes with me, helps me to remove the kaftan and wash, then follows me back to the cave. I put my tunic on and she takes her comb and tidies my curly hair kindly.

I say, "Do I look pleasing?"

She stares in a strange way and says, "Very pleasing. When I went to fetch the food for you, Meriem told me that you did something to Jonaas. Every 'path felt it. He screamed for some time before he passed out. You must be a Super."

"Yes," I say. "Did I hurt any other among the mind-speakers?"

"No," she says. "Only Jonaas. I must say you're taking what happened very calmly. Does it happen regularly or only once or twice in a month?"

I think this is a kind of joke so I smile. I like her a lot. She is afraid of me, but bold enough to be interested beyond fear.

I say, "I'm not calm in what I think about what Jonaas did. My body is calm because I make it so."

She says, "Do you really live in this awful cave? And who's the ugly dwarf?"

"He's called Yo-Yo," I say and tell her about Yo-Yo and me and Jonaas and my mother. Yo-Yo finds the snake in the bed and picks it up. Jazalu squeals at it and Yo-Yo begins to cry.

I say, "Yo-Yo is frightened of you. Give him pats and hugs and he won't be afraid. He is what the Clan call imbecile, but I love him and he needs me. The snake won't hurt you."

She pats Yo-Yo carefully and says soothing things to him so that he smiles and offers her the snake. I take it and put it outside.

Jonaas's weak mindspeak comes to me. I let him know that I'll do what I did to him again if he tries to hurt me. He is afraid, but tries to hide it from me.

He tells me, "I could have killed you, but I didn't."

I tell him, "Keep people away from my cave. I'll do a body-changing for you tomorrow. And if you ever try to hurt me again I'll hurt you far more."

He tells me that I may use the Long Room to treat people in, calls me "imbecile" and is gone from my mind quickly.

I shake with fear and anger and must calm my body again. Water is on my face and runs down my ribs.

Jazalu comes and takes my arm.

"What is it?" she asks. "You look ill."

"I need sleep," I say. "I'll be better then."

She helps me to stretch out on the bed, although I need no help. I drift into sleep quickly.

When I wake she is gone. Yo-Yo sleeps against me and the snake is curled against my neck. I think on Jazalu and her kindness for a while. She will lose her fear of me quickly, I hope. She is a strong person in her emotions.

I close my eyes and go back to sleep.

* THREE *

(There is a lengthy, rambling and rather incomprehensible talk on the seasons following this. Autumn worries him for some unspecified reason. It also becomes obvious that there is another time gap in the narrative. A mention is made of a "body-change" for Jonaas. He ponders, at length, on the problems concerning Jonaas physically and wonders about his mental stability.

One also gathers that a rather casual but intimate relationship has been established with Jazalu.

—J.T. Semantics Division)

I wake and dance to the sunrise. Its light is soon hidden by the heavy clouds which come from the south and a cold wind sweeps the valley. Driving rain comes so I take Yo-Yo out in it and wash us while he squeals loudly.

We are having breakfast of fruit and bread when Jazalu comes. She's very wet and her hair hangs in orange strings. She has brought vegetables, bread, cheese and meat which she drops on the bed.

She growls, "Why haven't you got a fire? It's freezing in here!"

"I don't need a fire," I tell her. "I make Yo-Yo and myself warm from the inside. Shall I do it for you?"

"You leave me alone," she says. "This is ridiculous! You live like a savage! There are dozens of empty rooms in that warren of a Palace! There are apartments with good furniture and handsome rooms and fine carpets on the floors. You could be very comfortable there."

"I'm comfortable here," I say.

"Well, I'm not!" she shouts. "I won't put up with it! And put some clothes on! I don't like it when you loll about naked for everyone to see!"

"Who sees me but you and Yo-Yo?" I ask.

She's very angry and leaves me to run back to the Red Palace. I'm sorry I've made her angry. She becomes angry very easily. She doesn't reason well and becomes frustrated when she cannot make things as she wishes them to be. Perhaps I should conform to her wishes more since she has been so kind in her way. Perhaps the time to move to High-on-the-mountain has come.

I leave Yo-Yo playing with his collection of stones and go up past Red Tree to the dimness and gray webbing of the Crack. The rain pours down but Crawly-Thing comes running up to me when I touch his ropes. I send him pleasure-feelings and he stops chittering, but doesn't go away.

The yellow weed which attracts the birds to the Crack is dying off so he's probably not so well-fed as he was. His eyes watch me as I climb down his main ropes, avoiding the sticky ones. There are skeletons of birds and even a few sharpteeth caught in those ropes. I keep sending him pleasure-feelings, but he continues to watch me until I reach the ledges which lead to the secret rooms.

I adjust my sight as I go because I know that Crawly-Thing now has a mate. I can see her in a crevice with her eggs, guarding them with ferocious chitterings at me. She settles when I send her pleasure-feelings. She has many eggs, but only a few are fertile.

I climb around the sacks of chemicals and powdered metals and find the old rooms where the maps and machines cover the walls. This is the Warlord's Computer and it still lives a little bit. This is where the power generator still works and provides electricity for the Red Palace below, thanks to Torros being so clever with the electronics after the original power sources ceased to function.

"Lights," I say and adjust my sight as the lights come on dimly. Everything is just as Torros and I left it in our last visit two years ago, although I notice that water is staining one wall badly where a new crack has appeared. I take two powerpaks and four of the permalamps and one of the cleaner-bugs. I tie them to my body with the rope made from Crawly-Thing's old web and they are quite heavy.

"Lights off," I say and adjust my sight again as they fade. The load is so heavy that some of Crawly-Thing's ropes stretch alarmingly as I climb up them. He and his mate make little runs at me, chittering noisily, until I send pleasure-feelings so strongly that they curl up their legs in ecstasy. It is still raining when I climb out of the Crack, but my body is already dripping wet with sweat.

I go up to High-on-the-mountain. The garden in the court is pretty now and the roses and the feathery trees have established themselves with a little help from me and the rains. All the work of removing the concrete covers from the windows set into the mountainside was worth it because, when I open the door, it's all beautiful to see.

I never thought that Noni and Angelo would keep

my secret but they have. And I'd never have done it without their help. The rich carpet, the big couches and the carved chests, the embroidered hangings, the big tables and chairs secreted up here from the Red Palace and all the facilities bargained for with the Clan should make this attractive enough to Jazalu. Even the water basin works again and the pump is an automatic one.

The second room is dark but, when I put up the two permalamps and switch them on, it is as light as day. The big bed and mattress, the blankets and cushions in here all come from the crumbling ruins beyond the Red Palace and the chests look well with them.

I'm quite pleased with the shower cubicle and body-waste stool built into what must have been a big closet of some kind. Both Noni and Angelo are to be thanked for their help and Angelo for his knowledge of plumbing. I put up the remaining permalamps and then attach the powerpaks to the hot water tank and the stove as Angelo instructed. The benches and basins that he put in look very fine and solid.

I've kept the further door concealed with a heavy hanging. Someday I'll get through that, too.

At the moment, all I need is a refrigeration unit. Perhaps I can negotiate with Mario for the small one, which he never uses, in the Red Palace kitchen. I wonder what he would like me to do to his body?

The rain is easing off as I go back down to the cave. I dress in my red kaftan and then take Yo-Yo with me to my lesson with Auria and Hubertus. It is very interesting, all about the way people live Outside. I'm glad I'm not there. It sounds to be very strange and uncomfortable. So many rules to obey and so

many customs to follow. We eat lunch after and then
I go looking for Jazalu.

She has a small but painful burn mark on her arm.

"Why did Jonaas do that?" I ask.

She looks close to tears so I hold her. Jonaas and
I haven't set eyes on each other or even made mind-
contact since I made the last corrections to his body.
I don't interfere in Red Palace business and he sends
people to me through Hubertus.

"It's my own fault," she says. "I argued about the
Rome operation."

I ease the pain of the burn and stimulate the healing processes as I hold her.

"I have a surprise," I tell her.

We go up to High-on-the-mountain.

*(There are lengthy descriptions of Jazalu's reactions
to the newly prepared dwelling, some of these being
sexual in nature.*

—J.T. Semantics Division)

We use the shower together and then wash Yo-Yo,
too, because he wants to be with us.

"We can try it for a while," she says, "but I'm not
sure about any long-term living together, Saulus.
You're too peculiar for comfort at times."

She looks at her unmarked arm where the burn
had been and says, "You're useful sometimes, though.
But I won't have Yo-Yo in our bed, you hear me?"

So I shall have to make a little bed for Yo-Yo and
think-talk him to sleep. He is so used to sleeping
against me for warmth and comfort.

"What kind of work will you be doing in this Rome
operation?" I ask.

"Deactivating alarm units so that a certain storage
center may be broken into, for one thing, and tampering with recording apparatus so that identities won't

be caught by camera eyes," she says. "Quite easy for me. I can delineate small objects and handle them with a skill that makes Noni seem like an elephant crocheting fine lace."

Jazalu is jealous of Noni's value to the Clan and often boasts of her own skill.

"What is an elephant?" I ask. "And crocheting?"

"Sometimes you're very stupid, Saulus," she says, but she's being patronizing, not nasty. There is a difference sometimes.

It takes time to move her belongings to High-on-the-mountain. Jazalu calls it the Blue Place. I suppose that's as good a name for it as any, although only the walls are blue. We spend a long time putting away her things and shifting things about pointlessly before she is satisfied. She says it's very basic but better than the cave.

She cooks a dinner which is horrible, the meat spoiled with other flavorings and the vegetables all soft and with half their nourishment cooked out. But she's happy, so I pretend to enjoy it. Yo-Yo will eat anything he's given, but I adjust his digestion to cope with the food.

He cries when I make him a bed on a couch, so I tell Jazalu that I'll sleep with him because he needs me and she doesn't. This make her very cross and she calls me "imbecile," knowing how I hate that.

(Here Saulus skips days or perhaps weeks in the narrative. When he resumes, it is interesting to note that he now speaks Universal with Auria Shasti's impeccable Central Euroasian accent. We must presume that he has an excellent and analytic ear for subtleties of sound.

*　　　　　　　　　　—J.T. Semantics Division)*

I awake and Jazalu is warm against my front while Yo-Yo is snug against my back. I ease myself from between them and go out to do my dance to the rising sun. Despite the coldness of the season, the garden is full of strong life-pulses. I run across to the West Terrace, skirting the Crack, and go to Red Tree. He has no fruit at this time of year and his life-pulse is slow, but he acknowledges me by brushing my shoulder.

When I go back, Jazalu has bathed and put on an orange-colored gown which is very pretty. I'm glad she's back from Rome.

"Are you still running about without clothes?" she says in a mock-scolding voice and I hug her hard. I take Yo-Yo into the shower and bathe us both, dry us and dress him in his new tunic. He looks better with the new haircut which Noni gave him. It makes his head appear less large. He has such beautiful, trusting eyes.

I feed Yo-Yo and myself on raw eggs and Mario's lovely, rough bread. Jazalu makes a face when I offer her the same and goes to cook meat. She also scorches Mario's bread slightly and puts sugar on it, which is such a pity.

I go to dress in my red kaftan and sandals. The red shows off my experiment with darker-blonde hair and warmer colored skin which Jazalu finds pleasing.

While I dress she comes in and sits before the mirror to use her cosmetics. She is about to cover her skin with a powdery stuff when she sees, touches her face and then looks angry.

"What have you done?" she says fiercely.

"I made you healthy," I tell her.

She screams, "You've been tampering, changing me!"

I say, "Yes, but not in any wrong way. This is what you should look like when you're perfectly healthy.

Look at your skin. Beautiful, clear, smooth. Look at
your eyes. Sparkling and not reddened in the lids.
Look at your breasts. Firm and full. Look at your belly.
Flat and taut. I merely made your body systems more
efficient and tightened muscles which need exercise."

She screams, runs at me and strikes me about the head
in a frenzy until I grip her hard and hold her tightly.

"I've made things as they should be, not created
anything new," I tell her. "This is the body you should
have when it isn't abused with drugs, alcohol and poor
food. I did nothing that was a wrong thing. You worry
about age and decay and yet you do such terrible
things to yourself in the name of pleasure, things
which make age and decay come sooner than they
should. Now you are as you should be, full of energy
and youth. No saggings, no puffiness, no sallow color
which needs to be hidden. Look at yourself carefully
and then tell me if I did a wrong thing."

I release her and she runs to the long mirror, pulling off her pretty dress. She is truly red-haired now.
She stares at her reflection and then screams, "You
tampered with me! You made me different!"

I go out quickly and Yo-Yo runs to me in fear.

"We will go down and look at the valley," I tell
him and pick him up. I'm not in the mood to endure
her lack of reason.

So we go and look at the winter daisies and the
rock pools and the red mosses. We play Bob-Up Bob-
Down in the long grasses and run and jump and play
in the cold day until I feel less upset about Jazalu's
reaction to something which I intended as a pleasing
gift. Then I pick Yo-Yo up and go to have my lesson.

My lesson has grown from receiving information
from Auria and Hubertus. Now Angelo, Noni, Carolus, Mahmud, Meriem and even Gino come along

when they aren't out of the valley because they enjoy to socialize. So it's not really a lesson at all, although I learn a great many things. It's more like a regular social occasion, with my learning as the excuse. I wonder why they think they need such an excuse?

They talk of a great many things concerning the Outside. Some of it is very interesting, but some of what they say is very puzzling. I don't query things too much because I feel foolish when I'm always asking questions which make some laugh at my ignorance.

It's strange how my view of these people, some of whom I've known all my life, has changed since Auria came. Jonaas was so very angry when Hubertus found this stranger to the Clan and brought her back to join those who hide in the valley. He said that Hubertus wasn't discreet in accepting her so swiftly. Yet now he, too, finds her of greater interest than she or Hubertus care for. She has her own charismatic influence, although it is not the same as his. She is like an exotic bird among the sparrows. Why would such a woman choose to come amongst us? But how glad I am that she did!

She has changed my perceptions of things and stimulated me to observe in a way that I wasn't capable of before. She has made sense of many puzzles. She has made me aware of things which I'd forgotten or, perhaps, ignored. Or perhaps I isolated myself too much from the Clan and simply lost contact with them as people. Or could it be that she has alerted them to the fact that I'm another person and not just a valuable kind of monster to have about?

I no longer see Hubertus as pompous and self-important. He is a grave man who is anxious to preserve his dignity and standing as second-in-command to Jonaas. He fears being laughed at since he has no ability to laugh at himself. He has self-doubts which make him anxious to conceal his gentler nature.

Angelo, too, whom I've always accepted as being rather callous and self-indulgent, hides behind an image which he's made so that people won't realize he's not clever or very brave.

Noni, whom I've categorized as selfish, sulky and obsessed with her own sexuality, is really insecure and what Auria calls "romantic" to the point where her dreams obscure reality. And Auria, too, much as she seems so self-confident and decisive, so charming and calm, is a person who lives with strange fears and often conceals a cold anger which I don't understand.

They are my friends and I should know them better, but I've never really tried to understand their difficulties before. I've always been too concerned with my own problems. Meriem says that we all tend to live in little worlds of our own making because we can't always face the truth about the real world. Perhaps this is so.

They talk of their activities Outside so casually, pretending cynicism to hide fear. They make it sound as though life is a kind of war between Outside and the Clan. They talk of money and drugs, frauds and robberies, murders and manipulations as though that's the normal world and the other isn't.

Torros had a more realistic view of it, I suspect. He said that it is the Clan who are the scum of life, the enemies of a better world. Life for the Clan doesn't seem very satisfying or happy for them if one listens to what they say. They hate the valley as much as they hate the Outside. They are like prisoners no matter where they exist. I seem to be the only one who loves this place and really wants to stay here.

It's almost midday when I pick Yo-Yo up and go

back to the West Terrace. This is the bleakest time of the year in the valley but, standing there and looking out over it all, it seems a very beautiful place to me. The mountains which rise all about don't seem imprisoning as much as protective to me. I wonder if it was so much more beautiful when the Warlord was here, before the insane war which put an end to his world and destroyed the lands about it, beyond the mountains? I can't conceive of it being so.

Far below, the Red Palace stretches along the Low Terrace, all softly rosy and imposing. Beyond it, the old ruins of buildings and fountains, pillars and unkempt gardens are mysterious and lovely. And down in the basin of the valley the little lakes and the river shine as they nestle among the pretty forests and rocky outcrops, the lush meadows and the expanses of alpine daisies. It is wonderful.

The buildings which rose up the mountainside to the West Terrace are gone into rubble, but I can still see places where the old gardens were. All the West Terrace was a garden once. Now it's covered in wild grasses and only Red Tree survives. It's only on and about the West Terrace that the hot-sickness still exists. Down in the valley and on the mountains the water is pure and the soil is fertile. We could make gardens and farms here and be content if the Clan could only see it.

Below the West Terrace are the hidden places where the Computer and the machineries, the chemicals and some of the weaponry still exist. Is it more strange weaponry and such things that are hidden beyond the Blue Place further up the mountain? I must investigate that door further when next Jazalu goes Outside—

Yo-Yo is hungry, so we go up to the Blue Place.

Jazalu has been playing with the new clothes and adornments which she brought back from Rome and they are spread everywhere. She has calmed down and thought about what I did, it seems, because she comes to embrace and kiss me.

"I'm sorry I was cross," she says, "but, in future, you must tell me if you intend such things. And I think my eyelashes could be darker and longer. Could you do that?"

"Yes," I say, wondering if that will be the end of it. I don't like the thought that she might become like Noni, always asking for changes and what she imagines are improvements to her looks.

She shows me all her pretty things and then we eat. Jazalu is anxious that she hasn't upset me with her anger earlier. We send Yo-Yo off to play in the meadow and it's all lovely between us until Yo-Yo returns with the snake. Jazalu still dislikes the snake but accepts it because it eats the "field mice" when they invade the terrace. I daren't tell her that the "field mice" are baby sharpteeth which grow so large and savage but which taste so good to eat.

Jazalu goes down to the Red Palace to show off some of her clothes to Noni and Meriem and I work at the door for a while. Then Yo-Yo wants to sit on my lap while I read aloud from a book which Auria has given me. It's a book about travels in the Outside and very interesting. Yo-Yo doesn't understand a word, of course, but he likes to hear my voice and see the pages turned and becomes excited if there are pictures to look at.

Late in the afternoon, Jazalu returns with Noni who has carried up the refrigeration unit that I bartered for with Mario. He has new teeth and we can now keep our food preserved for longer.

Both Noni and Jazalu return to Rome soon and are full of plans that don't interest me. It's a strange thing that, although they dislike each other, they are drawn together because of their work within the Clan and their 'kinetic abilities. They argue rather than talk.

They cook a huge meal which I pretend to enjoy and we all talk until very late.

I've set up the necessary balances to make Jazalu's eyelashes grow dark and longer as she wanted, but I think they'll look strange. And I notice that she's covered the clear skin of her face with that cosmetic stuff again. Habits govern us all, I suppose.

(Here there is another unexplained gap in the narrative, possibly of months, since Saulus talks of new growth and the return of leaves to the trees. However, when he resumes the narrative, he is very conscious of dates and times.

—J.T. Semantics Division)

I awake and the calendar which Pearlman gave me says 20th Day of the 4th Month of the Year 2280 A.D. I must ask Auria what A.D. means. The sun has not yet risen over the mountains so I move carefully from Jazalu and Yo-Yo and go out into the garden. There is a chill in the air against my body, but I think today will become warm.

The scents of the garden fill my nostrils. Fresh, clean, damp with dew. The light fills the east and the garden is stirring. The new growth is wonderful and I watch the mosses unfold and blush deeper purple, the blue flowers open and seek the light, the bamboos rustle their silver-gold leaves expectantly and the young rosebushes move, so slowly, on their dagger-thorned branches.

All the young trees are rich with new leaves and Red Tree's Daughter grows swiftly. She brushes my thigh and takes a token of blood, her fragrance already obvious. That same fragrance attracts the killer-birds and stinging-moths to her and I quickly brush away the empty carcasses before Jazalu sees them.

She calls the Red Tree and his Daughter monsters although I've tried to explain that all plants move. Red Tree and his Daughter are merely quicker to do so than most because they are now carnivores as well as plants, living things which are the results of my long-ago experiments and development from many hybrids down in the valley. The vines and the rose-bushes move quite quickly, too, but she is not so aware of that movement, never having sat for an hour watching them seek and shift. My garden is full of life-pulse and wonder. I regret that Jazalu doesn't like it.

Yo-Yo comes scampering, not seeing me. He pees on the mosses and I growl so that he gets a fright and runs in again. I repair damage to the mosses and then watch as the light floods the valley. The urge to dance comes, but I repress it since Jazalu says it's primitive and ridiculous and that I must be more "mature" in my behavior. I go indoors to bathe.

As I dry myself I look at the changes I've made to myself and approve. Having devised the Modes, I'm getting quicker with such changes and expend less energy on them. The heavier muscularity of Dark Mode feels good to me. Jazalu doesn't like the night-dark skin and tightly-curled black hair for no very clear reason. Perhaps my Dark Mode features are too heavy for her tastes, but they give me confidence. I must change to Blonde-Gold Mode before I go down to the Red Palace.

I put on the black and gold kaftan and the new sandals which Jazalu bought me in Rome. The sandals are made from plastex and are beautifully fashioned to hug my feet, no matter which Mode I've chosen to assume. I waste some time growing a black mustache to suit my face and realize that I look very like Pearlman. I wonder if he'd mind if he knew I could look very like him? It might be amusing to make myself look like others and deceive all their friends. But perhaps not. They might not appreciate my joke.

I go out and begin breakfast. Jazalu comes, yawning and sleepy-eyed, as I lightly scorch bread and make the nasty coffex drink for her. Yo-Yo, poorly dried from his shower, comes to be dressed and demands a morning cuddle on my lap. He's very hungry this morning and eats half my fruit as well as his own.

Jazalu says crossly, "You spoil him."

I say, "It's so easy to make him happy. What else is there for him but his senses and affection and security?"

I send him to play in the meadow.

Jazalu has taken over the organizing of my work from Noni and she does it very well.

She says, "I've set out a schedule for your visit to the Palace today. Radley and Paul need new faces and fingerprints and Gino is complaining of headaches again. They're all involved with the drug run from Turin tomorrow night, so they come first. Lacy is back from Paris, so you'd better check him for alcohol damage. Do you think you should look at Fatimah's knife wounds again?"

"They'll be healed by now," I say. "Who is the new Lifter she brought in?"

"An Epsilon named Guiseppe. You'll have to do something about his drug problem," she says. "What of Hubertus?"

"I'll finish rebuilding the arm today," I say, remembering the horrible mess I worked on last night. "How did it happen?"

"He and Angelo were on that Allied Chemicals sabotage job and the new explosive went off too soon," she says. "I warned them about that explosive! Did you know that the Clan lost Danielle and Ray to the Law Enforcers? How Hubertus escaped I'll never know. It's a miracle that Pearlman and Gino got him back here before he bled to death!"

She sounds angry and disgusted. I know she wanted to be included in that enterprise, but Jonaas rejected her and I'm very glad he did.

"Oh," she says, "Pearlman's willing to get us a room heater in exchange for cosmetic services. Cosmetic services! There's no need for his face to be changed that I know of!"

But I know what he wants. Having become involved with the highly-sexed and lively Foster Twins, he has already broached the subject to me.

"Jonaas is having conferences with Auria, Gino and Angelo later this afternoon so keep away from the Long Room," she says. "Something big is in the wind, I think. I know that Jonaas has been away negotiating with the Arabs in Haifa, so it's probably to do with drugs."

I change to Blonde-Gold Mode, which is what everyone recognizes as "me," call Yo-Yo from the meadow and go to visit Paul, Radley and Gino. They take little time and seem satisfied with their new appearances. I help Lacy over the aftermath of his alcohol binge. Fatimah is up and about, her wounds healed. She tells me all about the fight between her and the woman she caught with her lover, Guiseppe. He's drug-hazed, so I set up the process of clearing his systems of the narcotics and Fatimah promises to keep him away from them.

Hubertus takes longer but soon has a whole arm again. He tries to thank me, but I won't have that. I put him into restful sleep, then go to see Pearlman and rebalance his glandular system to increase his libido and sexual capacity. He promises to bring the room heater back from Outside.

In the hallway leading to the White Court, I catch sight of Auria as she enters the Long Room. She has on a flowing yellow gown which shows off her lovely body, flowers in her hair and—I stare, disbelieving— her hair is dyed black and shines like a raven's wing! She has gold paint on her long eyelids, her lips are artificially reddened and her brows are darkened with cosmetic.

This is the first time I have seen her in person since she left Hubertus and became companion to Jonaas. I don't understand her at all. I always thought she hated Jonaas. And yet she has gone to be his woman. Poor Hubertus. He is still very hurt about it, but he gives in to Jonaas because Jonaas has been the Big Boss for so long. I think it will be a long time before he forgives Auria.

I slip away through the colonnades to see Meriem, who is cooking sweetmeats and gives some to Yo-Yo. I make changes to eradicate her arthritis.

As I take Yo-Yo out through the colonnades I pass Angelo. He whispers to me, "I must meet you secretly to discuss something important. Meet me here this evening at 20th hour."

I nod and go on, wondering. It's probably about Torros. I have a conviction that Jonaas won't allow Torros back into the valley after what happened between them last year, although Angelo has been trying to persuade him. I remember how badly Torros was burned and how I had to work on him to preserve his life and restore him.

Angelo is worried about his brother and has been trying to persuade me to intercede with Jonaas on Torros's behalf. I miss Torros. He was my closest friend. But Jonaas hates me and we avoid each other since that awful time when he burned me about the head. I'm not sure that I'm brave enough to face him yet.

We go to visit Red Tree and then wave at Crawly-Thing who lurks at the top of the Crack. Some of his mate's eggs hatched and there are now several young Crawly-Things in the Crack. Yo-Yo clings to me hard. He's very frightened of this place after his narrow escape last month and that's a very good thing. I show him the skeletons of sharpteeth and birds on the purple mosses and warn him again. He rolls his eyes and clings even harder. I may have to do something about the tenants at the Crack if they continue to emerge from it.

Back at the Blue Place, I find that Jazalu is out and about on her own visits. I pull the hanging aside and work at the door until I'm tired of scraping stones. I tidy up and then go out to look at the valley. A warm breeze blows but rain will come soon. I work in my garden until late.

Yo-Yo comes squealing for food, so I feed both of us and then begin cooking Jazalu's evening meal. Yo-Yo and I always eat before she does now because she shudders at the sight of us eating raw food.

Outside, the clouds have rolled across the sky and obscured the last of the sunlight. A sad breeze moans about the garden.

Jazalu returns and eats. She's excited about the

meeting in the Long Room this afternoon and I only half-listen until she tells me that Jonaas wishes me to do some work Outside. Me working Outside!

She says, "When Hubertus is well enough, he and Gino will attend to the organizing and try you out with some carefully selected people. You'll be working as a proper part of the Clan, Saulus! You'll be paid like everyone else instead of having to barter for things! I did the bargaining for you. I'll look after your earnings and see to it that you aren't cheated. Are you pleased?"

I'm afraid. I've never been out of the valley before. But I'm curious, too. I'd like to see what is beyond.

"Yes, I'm pleased," I say, but I don't know if I am or not.

It's dark now and nearing 20th hour. I tell Jazalu that I must look at Hubertus's arm again and leave her with Yo-Yo for company. The rain is very near and the wind has grown strong. Lightning flashes and thunder rumbles as I hurry past the West Terrace and down to the Red Palace.

The colonnades are in darkness and I adjust my sight before walking the length of them. There's no sign of Angelo, so I find a sheltered recess and wait.

Presently the wind drops slightly and the rain comes down in torrents. The walkway is soon flooded and water runs like a river over the sunken part of the colonnades. Lightning flashes brightly and thunder cracks deafeningly. Despite my protected recess, I'm soon so wet that I decide to go back to the Blue Place. It seems obvious that Angelo isn't coming.

Then, in a flash of lightning, I see Angelo sitting against one of the pillars. I run to him, yelling, "Let's get out of the rain!" And then there's another flash of lightning.

Angelo is dead, his face and scalp half-burned away. From the processes going on in his body I can tell that he's been dead for almost an hour. Jonaas had killed again.

Horror and disgust fill me. Then anger comes. I pick up the wet, lifeless shell that was Angelo and stagger through the colonnades in the pouring fury of the rain. The body is very heavy. When I come to the door of the West Wing I heave it open with my shoulder and walk into the softly lit hallway. Trailing water onto the old mosaics, I move along the corridor until I come to Auria's door. I thump it several times with a foot.

When she opens the door I push past her without words and walk into the richly decorated salon. I place Angelo's body down on a brocaded couch and wipe my face with my hands. She is shocked by what she sees—I can feel her distress emanate—but she keeps her calm manner. Even at this time, with my emotions in turmoil, I see how beautiful she is. She drags a richly embroidered cloth from a table and covers Angelo's body with it.

"How horrible," she mindspeaks.

I reply with some violence, "Death isn't the horrible part. It was the way it came to him! This shell is nothing. It will return to the soil. But Angelo is no more and he was destroyed by Jonaas, the man you choose to partner! Why was it done? How could you let it happen? You have more influence with Jonaas than any of the vermin in this place! How could you let it happen?"

She mindspeaks, "I knew nothing, Saulus. They had an argument this afternoon, but I don't know what it was about. Where did you find him?"

"I was to meet him at the colonnades," I tell her.

"He said it was to be secret. I presumed that he had some news of Torros or, perhaps, hoped to persuade me to front up to Jonaas about Torros being allowed to return. And I found him dead."

"But why would Jonaas put him in the colonnades?" she asks.

I think about that, then I go and look at Angelo's body more closely. Seeing his head in the light and examining it in detail, I begin to see how it might have happened as it did.

"Perhaps the burning wasn't intended to kill Angelo," I wonder. "Perhaps Angelo was alive when they parted—perhaps Angelo managed to drag himself to the colonnades before he died, hoping I would find him. Now that I look more carefully, I realize that it must have been shock that killed him. The skull is intact, but heat could penetrate to the brain—"

"Don't tell me about it," she mindspeaks, shuddering.

"You must have heard something—screams from Angelo—"

"I heard nothing," she tells me. "Don't blame me for this."

"I don't blame you for Angelo's death," I reply, "but it hurts me that you could tolerate living with such a man as Jonaas. I can't believe that you would allow yourself to be caught up in the web of his charismatic broadcast. Well, it seems I must confront Jonaas myself, after all. I can't simply accept Angelo's death and walk away—"

"No!" she tells me. "You mustn't confront him. Let me handle this. Remember that although you may be able to protect yourself from Jonaas, the rest of us aren't so fortunate. And the Clan need to gather about someone. Don't involve yourself, please."

I can't quell my anger. I pick up Angelo's body in its embroidered shroud and carry it out into the hallway, Auria following. I go to the Long Room, sit Angelo in the heavy chair which Jonaas uses at meetings and arrange the shroud so that the burned head is shown in all its ugliness.

"Where is Jonaas?" I ask.

"Saulus," she mindspeaks, "you must not confront him—"

I catch something from her mind, an agony and a terror which threatens to escape her control, but which she fights to conceal. It concerns me in some way—is she really afraid for me?

The high table where discussions are held is slightly dusty. With a wet hand I write "Jonaas, the Killer" across it.

"Open your mind and allow me to put a barrier there," I tell her. "When the gathering is held here tomorrow there'll be too many telepaths to conceal something of your distress from. It should appear that you know nothing. If they think you know something about this they may probe for your secrets."

She is suddenly all defense.

"What secrets?" she says, terrified that I may take them.

"I don't know," I tell her. "I wouldn't take them from you."

She hesitates and then opens her mind. I take her gently, filling her with myself as I once filled Torros to keep him alive with my strength. I impose the barrier such as I'd impose on anyone who suffered from extreme shock and add pleasure-pulse so that she becomes faint. I lift her and carry her back to her room, the wetness from my kaftan soaking her thin gown. I put her on the bed and draw the cover over her.

"Sleep," I instruct her and she relaxes.

I run out into the night and into the drenching rain. Angelo was not a close friend as Torros was, but I find myself weeping for the waste of him as a human being who was never disloyal to the Clan. He didn't deserve to die as he did. What was it they argued about that caused Jonaas to do such a thing? Jonaas isn't always stable emotionally, but he's not a fool. Or is he?

Jazalu and Yo-Yo are asleep when I return to the Blue Place. I strip and go to the shower before I creep into bed with them. My thoughts go around and around for a long time, my anguish and anger difficult to put aside. Perhaps I have put too many things aside in the past instead of thinking on them and trying to do something about them.

✳ FOUR ✳

I awake and it's the 21st Day of the 4th Month of Year 2280 A.D.

Jazalu is already awake and dressed and preparing breakfast, although the sun has barely risen behind the thick clouds. I kiss her and then prepare Yo-Yo and myself for the day, remembering Angelo and feeling the return of anger.

The rain still comes in short bursts and the wind sweeps the slopes. My garden seeks the sun in vain.

Breakfast is a concoction of dead cereals, dried fruit and milk substitute. There's little nourishment in it, but I hide my distaste, smile thanks to Jazalu and eat it. Yo-Yo follows my lead, but then, I think he would eat anything that looked like food.

She says, "I leave for Paris with the Twins today. I should be back within a week."

"Is it a drug run or the stock forgeries?" I ask.

"Forgeries, of course. What would they want with me for a drug run? I'm the best copyist in the business. A few bonds and signatures and the Clan will have a nice little income for a couple of years. We'll bring in supplies when we return. Is there anything you'd like me to bring you?"

"Could you get another picture book for Yo-Yo?" I ask. "He's almost worn the other one out."

She shrugs. Yo-Yo is still an irritation to her.

I kiss her good-bye and she leaves. Yo-Yo and I help the cleaner-bug to tidy up and then I put Yo-Yo's waterproof jacket on him and send him out to the meadow to play. I am working on the secret door when Auria mindspeaks.

"We gathered in the Long Room a few minutes ago," she tells me. "There was no body and the table had been cleaned."

"Jonaas must have removed it," I tell her. "Now he'll be suspicious and insecure with everyone and that'll keep him quiet for a while. I know him very well and now you can learn from me. Do you find him a good lover?"

"Things aren't always what they seem, Saulus," she tells me. "Don't despise me."

"I don't despise you," I tell her. "But I don't understand you either."

She ends the contact, but not before I experience a moment of her unhappiness.

I try to imagine Jonaas's reaction to finding Angelo's body and the writing on the table. How many of the Clan has Jonaas killed over the years? I know of three for certain. And Torros would be dead if I hadn't been about. I wonder how he'll hide the body? Probably it'll be buried among the ruins.

Angelo was popular with the Clan. Knowing that Jonaas killed him would make for hostility. And Auria is right. Jonaas holds the Clan together, keeps things organized and sees that the valley is safe. But, by not opposing him, I place myself in the same debased position as the rest of the Clan. I'm no better than they. I don't know what to do.

I wish I'd been born to be clever like Hubertus is. Clan-members come and go, some die of the drugs which are so profitable, one or two are caught by the Law Enforcers and some—the truly fortunate—find ways of escaping the criminal life. But, when attacks come from inside the Clan itself, it shatters the fragile camaraderie and sense of security on which so many depend.

The Clan stays strong because it has people like Hubertus, Noni, Carolus, Angelo, Jazalu and Pearlman to keep it secure, profitable and organized but Jonaas is the one who leads because he possesses the ideas, the drive, the authority and the attraction to bind the others to him. If he no longer led the Clan it would split apart and then what would happen to all of them?

No matter how much I hate him I see that he's very necessary. But, oh, the thought of Angelo's death makes me angry still! I wish I knew the reason for it.

I try to read some of the book that Hubertus gave me. It tells of the times before the Warlords, but there are a great many references to things I don't understand and I can't concentrate.

I collect the big chisel and the hammer that I stole from Carolus's workshop and attack the stone surrounds of the secret door with a will. My persistence over the months and my anger today begin to have an effect at last. The place where the big tongue of the lock thrusts into the stone is suddenly freed and the door moves! My heart races! I drop the tools and pull hard at the tongue and the door swings open!

Beyond is darkness and air which has a strange, dry smell. I run to collect one of the permalamps and move into the new place cautiously, peering about.

Beyond the door is wonder! I can't help but cry out at the strange magnificence of it! The Blue Place is only a tiny part of a complex built inside the solid granite of the mountain in the same way as the Computer and the machineries were built below the West Terrace!

The first room is a vast cavern and the permalamp shines on rich brocades, lovely statues and ornaments. The carpets laid on the tiled floors are so thick that my footsteps are silent. The dryness of the air has preserved everything perfectly. There are strange pictures on the walls, great swags and hangings of wonderful materials and lamps which hang from the high vault above. And then, as I move further into the cavern, the lights come on and strange, lovely music plays softly!

I stand very still for some moments, but nothing moves. Cautiously, I switch the permalamp off and continue exploring. The lights come on wherever I go and the air, which was so dry, begins to move gently, becoming fresh and faintly scented of the valley.

This is a palace of many rooms, all of which are wonderful and filled with amazing treasures. Some rooms are for relaxing or eating in, some are sleeping places and some are for utility purposes. There are rooms for cooking in, rooms for bathing and even a room for exercising in. All so beautiful and rich! All so large and graceful!

Perhaps the Red Palace, too, looked as this palace does when the Warlord lived. There are the same kinds of shapes in doorways and the same kinds of decoration on the tiles. This secret place must have been tenanted by many before the Great Mistake destroyed the Warlord and his minions.

I start in fright as a voice speaks! It speaks in Universal but with strange inflexions and says, "Intruder, identify yourself!"

I realize that it's a voice like that of the Computer below the West Terrace. I know that if I don't do the correct thing it may try to destroy me, as the other Computer tried to destroy the first of the Clan who discovered it.

"Where is the handplate?" I say, already changing my fingerprints to those which Torros discovered on the handplate in the Crack and which I always use if the power for the Red Palace needs checking.

"By the entry door," says the voice.

I don't know which way to go. There was no handplate on the door by which I entered.

"I am the Master," I say firmly, fear-sweat prickling my skin. "Light my way."

The lights go out everywhere but in a corridor, so I go there. And I see, at the other end, one of those big sphincter-doors which Torros once showed me a picture of. I walk slowly toward it to give me time to change my fingerprints. There is the handplate, shining silver in the light.

The plate is warm as I press my hand and fingertips to it.

"Master, you are recognized," says the voice and I breathe a sigh of relief.

I say, "Open the door."

The sphincter swirls and recedes into the walls. A cloud of dust and chips of muddy soil make a mess since dirt has built up on the other side over the years. Cleaner-bugs, delicate and silver, like huge, strangely made arachnids, run from the rooms and begin busily tidying the doorway.

Beyond is rain and gusty wind and the wonder of the valley. As I step out I see that I'm on the overgrown East Terrace. Below, and far to the left, part of the Red Palace can be seen, a few minutes' walk instead of the long way to the Blue Place. I've never been much interested in the East Terrace since it seemed to be a dead end. I see now that the exterior handplate is hidden behind thickly growing yellow weed and small vines. I step inside again, touch the interior plate and the door closes.

"Master," says the voice, "shall I have the servomechs prepare the Love Palace for you?"

The Love Palace. How wonderful. I like that.

"No," I say, "but continue to maintain it. What of the other entry to the palace? Why was it locked?"

The voice says, "You locked it, Master. I have discovered damage there. Shall I repair it?"

"Yes," I say, "but make it so that I may enter there. Another handplate will be needed. What name does the Master go by?"

"His Most High Rajawen Ali Hannis Kobeeyah of Serenel," it tells me.

"Serenel?" I say. "What is Serenel?"

"Serenel is the title given to the estate, Master," it says.

Serenel! The valley is named Serenel! A magical name.

I say, "The Master is now Saulus of Serenel and you must call me Saulus."

"Acknowledged, Saulus," it says.

I stay for a long time, exploring and examining. What seems to be the Master's sleeping room has a vast and magnificent bed, its own body freshener and closets jammed with clothes and jewels. The statues are what Hubertus calls very erotic and the ceiling lights up with myriad lightpoints like stars in a deep-blue firmament. The carvings and metal decorations are wonderful and I deduce that the Warlord used the sun sign as his own since it's everywhere.

In all the outer rooms there are windows sealed by steel shutters. I remember seeing the inaccessible ledges covered in vines when I explored outside as a child. The Master Rajawen Ali certainly camouflaged his living place very well.

(Ali Hannis Kobeeyah was one of the obscure, minor Warlords and is mentioned only briefly in old records. Born in 2112 A.D., he appears to have been a man of considerable wealth. After the Great Mistake of 2162 A.D. no more is heard of him. Serenel can be pinpointed in the Pontine Mountains, to the west of the Contaminated Area—M.V. 22.

—J.T. Semantics Division)

It's late in the afternoon when I leave the palace by the sphincter-door and walk the long way around to the Blue Place, arriving very wet because the rain still drives across the valley. The door remains closed when I push it firm against the opening. I clean up the debris and pull the hanging over it again. It will remain my secret, to be hugged to me until I decide otherwise. Secret, lovely secret.

I go out and call Yo-Yo. When he comes running up from the little meadow he's incredibly dirty. We shower and dress and I make us a meal.

We've almost finished eating when Hubertus mind-speaks to me from the Red Palace.

"Arrange for Yo-Yo to be looked after by Meriem," he tells me. "Tonight, Pearlman, you and I leave the valley. We must be in Rome by morning. Tomorrow you'll treat a very important man, one of those who are allied with the Clan. Come down now and I'll see if I have clothes to fit you."

I'm very afraid, but excited, too. I pack some clothes in a carryall for Yo-Yo, close up the Blue Place and take him down to Meriem. I give him a big cuddle and tell him to be good with Meriem, give her his clothes and tell her that he needs plenty of fruit. She loves Yo-Yo and I know he'll be well cared for, but I feel bad when he cries because I'm leaving him. Meriem gives him a little sweetcake and I slip away while he's distracted.

Then I go to Hubertus. He looks a much grimmer man since Auria left him and went to Jonaas. That must have hurt his pride deeply and I'm very sorry. Hubertus needs his pride to maintain his outer dignity.

His clothes fit Blonde-Gold Mode well enough but, oh, the discomfort of them! Trousers with tight legs, undershirts and a tight jacket and hose and tight shoes! I hate them! He tells me to grow a beard and mustache, ties back my hair with a colored lace and promises me toiletries—whatever they are—when we get to Rome. He then gives me an identidisc and a lot of instruction on how to behave. This last frightens and confuses me, but I don't dare question him because he's in an impatient mood and I don't wish to seem stupid.

"And," he mindspeaks, "no mental linking or using your Secondary unless I say so. It only needs one slip and the Psi-Orgs will be among us like a deadly disease. If you must speak, use Universal. And don't gape about at everything like a fool."

We got to the Long Room and find Pearlman, Auria and Jonaas there. I hear Auria murmuring to Jonaas about danger and not liking it but Jonaas ignores her and gives me his sneering look.

He says to me, "You do exactly as Hubertus says, you understand? And, if Cassim demands two heads, you give him two heads! No arguments or playing about or I'll see to it that the Psi-Orgs pick you up before you can blink twice! Understand?"

I give him my biggest smile and he doesn't know what to make of that.

To Hubertus, he says, "And a bit of hocus might be a good idea. I want Cassim Odemi impressed and very grateful!"

(Cassim Odemi, reputed to be a major figure in the Afrodet underworld, was reported killed in a warehouse fire on 22-4-80. Law Enforcers were seeking him to arrest him on drug charges at that time. If Saulus is to be believed, Cassim Odemi is still very much alive.

—J.T. Semantics Division)

Hubertus and Jonaas move away to talk together and Auria gives me a look which speaks of worry for me. This pleases me very much.

Minutes later, Hubertus, Pearlman and I walk through the colonnades, which still show puddles of rain, and I think of Angelo sitting there, dying as he waited for me. We walk across the rocks to the old tunnel.

The sky is already dark and a few stars show between breaks in the clouds. I'm reminded of the ceiling in that lovely sleeping room in the Love Palace and this refreshes my spirits.

In the tunnel, the security system recognizes Hubertus and allows the gates to be opened. The air is cool and stale and the monorail car looks more battered and dirtier than I remembered. We climb inside and Pearlman seals the door while Hubertus fiddles with the controls. I sit down on one of the very worn seats as the car jerks and moves off. It gains speed steadily. I don't like the sensation at all. Outside, it's very dark, but I can see the tunnel walls speeding by. I look for a few moments and that's enough. I wedge myself against the car wall and put my head on my knees so that I can't know about the speed.

Pearlman says, "Don't be scared, Saulus. Nothing bad will happen! This car's good for another fifty years at least!"

But I don't move. After a time, I feel Pearlman sit beside me and put a hand on my shoulder. I calm myself and sit up, but I don't look at the speeding walls again. The car goes on and on, the air squealing softly about it and the vibrations running up through my legs. The time seems endless before we slow down. Then we stop and Pearlman unseals the door.

We climb out into a dark, flat place and Hubertus alerts the security system to allow us through. The deadly gas-ejectors high on the walls retract. The air is thick and odorous and horrible. I follow Hubertus and Pearlman in the darkness and almost fall when we begin to climb some stairs. We go up and up and then we come into another tunnel where the air is fresher. This tunnel is very long but, at last, we come to more stairs, climb up and up again and suddenly come into the open. I can see the sky and the air is very sweet.

We are now on a mountainside and the vast waters of what Hubertus says is the Aegean Sea are before us. I stare at it in wonder.

To the left, not so very far away, are tiny lights which Hubertus says come from the remains of a city called Izmir. But I have no time to look further. Pearlman calls me and when I go to him, I see another strange vehicle hidden in a place among the rocks.

We climb into it and the door closes so that we are

encased in a little room full of seats, not unlike the monorail car. But this is all clean and smooth and metallic, with padded seats and big windows which are curved. Hubertus seats himself at the controls, then looks and fiddles with many little dials and levers. Pearlman pulls me onto a seat.

"We're going to fly now, Saulus," he says.

Jazalu has told me about the aircar. I don't care for the idea of flying above the world.

I quickly close off my senses and go into the sleep-state where I won't know about it.

Someone tugs at me and I awake. It's the 22nd Day of the 4th Month of the Year 2280 A.D.

It's almost dawn and the aircar is on a big flat place of rocks with sea to one side. Pearlman is opening the door and Hubertus, looking very tired, mindspeaks to me.

"This is a place called Bari, which is in Italy. We go to Rome from here. Come along, quickly."

I follow him from the aircar, seeing the first paling of the sky in the east. There's another car here, one which has wheels for moving it along the road. There are also people I don't know waiting. We climb into the car and it moves off very silently. My clothes are so uncomfortable that I can't relax—

(I have deleted part of the narrative here since it concerns a jumble of impressions regarding the land-scape, the plant life, the people in the car and, finally, Rome. The entry into Rome confuses him but he takes in most of the landmarks. He also comments, very disapprovingly and at great length, on the strangeness of so many people living in such crowded conditions among buildings which he finds very ugly. He comments on the terrible "abuses" which humans impose

on themselves. They are taken to the Imperiatrix International and his opinions of the novelties and arrangements in their apartment are very acid.

—J.T. Semantics Division)

—and sprays me with an awful, cloying perfume which is so disgusting that I have to shower all over again! I don't wait for the air dryer this time, but get out and use the little tissue towel to dry myself as best I can.

I dress and comb my hair, tie it back and then comb my beard which needs trimming. Then I sit on the sleeping-couch because I don't like those peculiar chairs that shape themselves to support one.

I look at a sort of book called a magfile, but I don't understand a lot of it. There are many pictures of naked women in positions which I think are intended to be erotic. I think Pearlman bought it because of these. Then I go to look at the view which is very interesting, but as ugly as ever.

Hubertus gets our breakfasts from a little slot in the wall and he and Pearlman seem to like it. It's like cheese, but sweet and of poor nutritional value. There's stuff like coffex but Hubertus says it's real "coffee." I taste it, but find it very nasty, so I go and drink water and put the rest of my breakfast in the disposal chute. Then I go to the table-on-wheels and eat some of the tasteless but nourishing concentrates which Hubertus bought for Cassim's body-change.

Pearlman and I cover the long table with a plastex sheet and put a pillow there while Hubertus goes away to collect the man. When I say I'll need cloths to clean Cassim with and to soak up the messes, Pearlman sighs irritably, but goes and collects a pile of the tissue towels. He helped me with a body-change once before and knows what to expect. It's a long wait and I'm tired of looking at the view by the time Hubertus brings the man.

Cassim is a man of fifty years, very overweight and with physical damages in several areas, particularly his heart and kidneys. His skin color seems almost totally black, even darker than Pearlman's, and he has a balding skull. He's a blustering man, appearing very confident, but really full of fear. I'm so interested in the color of his skin that I forget to speak when Hubertus introduces me as the Solar. Cassim is only mildly Talented with what one could liken to Jonaas's charismatic ability—but to a far lesser degree and not strong enough to be termed Talent.

Hubertus and Pearlman handle him well, asking the questions to find out his wishes, reassuring him and making little suggestions which I agree to with Hubertus in mindspeak. What he wants is simple enough, but it'll take time. They all talk for far too long. I suppose that's part of the hocus.

I finally become impatient and put Cassim into trance state, instructing him verbally before Hubertus can stop me. Hubertus is annoyed. I think he was enjoying the hocus.

They help me to strip Cassim and lift him onto the table, then Hubertus gets more pillows to settle the man comfortably, despite me telling him that Cassim won't know the difference. Hubertus is very curious, never having seen me do a body-change before.

I repair the heart and kidneys first so there's very little for Hubertus to see. He's always wondering what I "see" and how I "change" things. I've tried explaining that it's like I become part of the patient's physical self and that I experience the purpose of the patterns and the possible alterations to them. I don't make miracles. The "miracles" are already there, waiting to be activated. But when I say that, it always annoys Hubertus because he has a passion to know how things work in the mechanical sense.

He has more to observe when I begin utilizing some of the fatty tissue for its energy value and removing the excess from Cassim's system. Messes he understands. He looks quite nauseous after a few of these, so I tell him to go away and leave things to me and Pearlman.

In a way I become like two people, the one directing and the other being a more intimate part of the procedure. One of me sees the necessities, the other sees the possibilities and they both manage the completion. From my point of view it's a very practical matter, like Angelo with the plumbing for the Blue Place. One can't create what there isn't material to create with, but one can persuade other materials to unite and become what's needed if one is very careful and has the skill.

That's why it's easier to utilize food and chemical concentrates together rather than using food by itself. Ordinary food has to be digested and broken down into its elements, but the concentrates are already broken down, so it's only a matter of speeding up the patient's metabolism and making the digestive systems work faster for a time. And there's less body waste with concentrates. Maybe Hubertus will appreciate that better in future and not complain so much when I ask for them.

The easiest means of making body-changes is simply to make adjustments and new balances to the patterns and then allow the patient's own body to do what it must in its own time. That's how I correct Jonaas's problems. But this time it has to be done

quickly, so I'm more involved as a stimulator, a manip-
ulator and a persuader. Like I had to be when
Hubertus's arm needed to be rebuilt and restored.

I'm never aware of time itself when I need to apply
myself fully to a patient. When I relax and look to
Pearlman he's looking very grimly at me and
Hubertus is gone. I glance at the chronometer and
discover it to be past 14th hour. Almost four hours.
Pearlman must be tired.

Pearlman says, "Have you done with him then?"

I look at Cassim, still in his trance-state. I'm quite
tired myself, but not unpleasantly so.

"Yes," I say. "Help me to get him into the freshener. He needs bathing."

So we carry him in, give him a thorough wash, dry
him carefully, comb his hair and then carry him to
one of the chairs.

The plastex sheet and the pillows are in a very
messy state and the tissue towels are all used and
reused. We drag the plastex sheet into the freshener
and scrub it, push the stained pillows down the laundry chute, dispose of the tissue towels in the rubbish-
disposal unit and then go to bathe. By the time we've
dressed again and I've washed the stains from my
shirt, the air conditioning has removed the worst of
the odors from the apartment.

As I put the jacket on, minus the wet shirt, I say,
"Where's Hubertus?"

"Outside," he says. "In the corridor. He felt a little nauseous."

He goes to collect Hubertus, who avoids my eyes
when he comes in.

"Should we dress him?" Pearlman asks, indicating
Cassim.

Hubertus stares and is very impressed.

"No," says Hubertus. "Let him see all of the miracle."

I put Cassim into normal sleep and tell Hubertus, "You can finish your hocus now." He laughs at that and gives Cassim's shoulder a light shake.

Cassim awakes, feeling refreshed and well. He blinks up at Hubertus, then at me, then at his hands and body. He sees himself in the mirror and his eyes become wide and wondering and half-afraid.

"Oh," he says, breathing strangely. "Oh—"

I go into the other room and look at that ugly view again. So many huge buildings and no trees or grass anywhere! And so many people! How can they tolerate such a place? I'm aware of a multitude of life-pulses and it's so unpleasant that I have to exclude them from my sensitivities.

There's a great deal of noise from the other room. Hubertus and Pearlman are talking and Cassim is laughing, exclaiming and shouting with excitement. It continues for some minutes before Hubertus mind-speaks to me.

"Cassim wishes to speak with you before he leaves. He's very pleased and there'll be big benefits for the Clan, Saulus. He has contacts and knowledge and he's paid a great deal of money for this. You don't need to talk. Just be dignified and blank-faced, as you usually are."

Dignified and blank-faced? Is that how Hubertus thinks about me?

I go into the room again and find that Cassim has dressed. His clothes are now loose on his solid and compact body. The color scheme of red and yellow, which looked so well against his black skin, seems too bright now that he's pale-skinned like Hubertus and has such a wealth of golden-brown hair. His appearance is that of a man twenty years younger, as it should be. He laughs a lot, showing off his beautiful new teeth, and his blue eyes are alight with happiness. He looks very handsome with the features which Pearlman calls "patrician." I gave him new fingerprints and retinal patterns and his health should be excellent until he abuses his body once more. He sees me and comes forward, half bowing to me.

"Solar," he says, "I'll be grateful forever! It's a miracle! I'm reborn! My life's renewed and clean! I feel such joy as I've never known before! You are the divine gift to humanity, my saviour!"

I don't know what I could possibly say to that. I nod and allow him to take my hand. He kisses it! I'm embarrassed and go back into the other room to escape his effusion. Hubertus and Pearlman talk to him some more and it's a relief when he finally leaves. I go back and Hubertus gives me a beaming smile.

"Will Jonaas be pleased?" I ask.

Hubertus laughs and says, "Jonaas will be as fond of you as Yo-Yo is when he hears the results! I think we should celebrate."

"I'm truly hungry for some good food," I say.

"Saulus," says Pearlman, "we'll take you out, buy you some new clothes and show you a slice of life such as you've never imagined before!"

(Following this, the narrative becomes somewhat garbled and confused, sometimes disapproving and sometimes outraged. As near as can be deciphered, Hubertus and Pearlman bought him clothes, took him to a restaurant, a sensie-house and a brothel before the night was done. His views of the "civilized" life of Rome are inclined to be puritanical, he disliked the food which he classed as ruined with flavorings and

strange cooking, the sensie-house puzzled him and the
brothel was dismissed as being both crude and
disappointing.

                                    —J.T. Semantics Division)

I climb into bed after jamming the mechanism
which causes the vibrations and I think about Yo-Yo,
about Jazalu, about Auria, about Angelo and Torros,
about Jonaas and about Serenel.

Hubertus says that we won't be going home to
Serenel for a while, that we have further business
here in the Outside, something to do with an idea
that Cassim discussed with Jonaas and which
Hubertus finds exciting. Something to do with some
kind of religious movement and making a lot of
money. Tomorrow I'm to be instructed about what
they want me to do.

I don't think I like Outside. It's all so strange and
unpleasant. I'm very depressed.

✳ FIVE ✳

(Another jump in narrative follows, this time a gap of some four months.

—*J.T. Semantics Division)*

I awake and it's the 11th Day of the 8th Month, 2280 A.D.

The weather is cooling and the deciduous trees will begin changing color soon, but the valley is green and my garden is lovely. I watch the sun rise and Red Tree's Daughter, now almost as tall as I am, caresses my shoulder and takes her tiny token of blood. The air is chill and feels good against my naked body, but Jazalu looks out through the window and shouts at me to cover myself. She truly detests Dark Mode's Cassim-black skin.

It's so good to be home again. I'm tired of all the traveling and I missed Serenel terribly. I go inside, bathe Yo-Yo and myself and get ready for the day. I dress in my old red kaftan and sandals and exult at the comfort after so many months of wearing tight clothes. We have a good breakfast and Jazalu doesn't seem to care about Yo-Yo's and my food being raw now that I'm so much the success as a moneymaker.

I run down to the West Terrace to see Red Tree

and Crawly-Thing. Red Tree shakes his empty seed-pods and I don't think he'll live for much longer. There are at least four young Crawlies in the Crack and I see a large dry husk which was Crawly-Thing. I feel a foolish regret at his passing.

I go down to the colonnades and sit there until signs of life begin to show in the Red Palace. Then I go to visit Meriem, Mario and the Foster Twins. They are the same, but I'm becoming different and that's sadder than the passing of Crawly-Thing.

Hubertus and Pearlman are still asleep because of our late arrival last night. Noni is grumbling as she lifts and carries supplies from the monorail car, so I avoid her. Auria, all groomed and beautiful, opens her door to me.

She dares not invite me into her room because Jonaas would not like that, but moves out into the corridor to greet me. She mindspeaks, "Did all go well?"

I tell her, "Jonaas will think so. Cassim and Barbier arranged the meetings cleverly and I made thirty-six 'miracles.' Cassim calls himself Diam Ennio now, enjoys his role as the Solar and has survived the governmental investigations without difficulty. The Solar Faith is now officially recognized as a religious body and plenty of funds seem to be pouring into the coffers. The Psi-Orgs haven't shown any interest as yet and the sceptics put it all down to hysteria. The Faith now has at least thirty thousand members! Isn't that amazing? Besides the 'miracles' I treated about three hundred others, all of them stupid people who should have been treated at the Med-Centers. So, yes, it all went well."

(The "Solar Faith Organization" made its appearance in Naples on 18-5-80 at an open air rally in the *regional stadium. There was a great deal of publicity leading up to the first meeting and the local media also made much of it as a novelty item. Its second rally took place in a positive blaze of attention six nights later. It was at this second rally that the Faith was proclaimed as a religious body. Led by a so-called mystic named Diam Ennio and an entrepreneur named Barbier Fugerio, the organization survived the usual governmental investigations and was recognized officially on 29-5-80.*

The Faith's declared aims were much as they are now—"Purity of mind through the perfection and recognition of the body"—and its methods are similar to the evangelical meetings of the now-defunct "Callers of the Lord." It is of interest to note that Cassim Odemi was also much-involved with the "Callers of the Lord" and is suspected of having used it as a cover for criminal activities before its collapse.

The first "miracles" attributed to the Solar Faith were thought to be spontaneous cures of the type often recorded among devotees of faith healing. Six more meetings were held on successive nights, two of them in Fiorenza, one in Bologna, one in Perugia and two in Rome. Diam Ennio, the "Solar," became a well known figure in the media from that time on.

—J.T. Semantics Division)

"It's dangerous," Auria worries. "One little slip and the Psi-Orgs will be among you like sharks among the salmon! You realize what would happen to you if you're caught?"

"Yes," I say. "Hubertus and I would be terminated."

"Yes," she tells me, "you'd be terminated as sociological menaces under the Psi-Org Pact of '02. The Psi-Orgs are well organized and powerful and they protect the public. And they're right, Saulus. Can you imagine the horrors which must have taken place before the Talent-Fighters and the Anti-Psi Riots forced the Orgs into existence and the Psi-Laws into fact? Ordinary non-Talents, ninety-nine percent of the world population, could have been at the mercy of one percent of the Talents, some of whom were too greedy and ambitious to be tolerated! Narnia of Syracuse, the Cohen Tribe, Foscio the Twister and the Belles Mysterieux were Outlaws, vicious animals who might have enslaved millions had they been allowed to survive! The Psi-Orgs are needed and they take their responsibilities very seriously, Saulus."

"But I don't want to enslave anyone!" I protest.

"But Jonaas does and he's using you as an instrument. Don't you see that?" she asks.

I tell her, "I only know that I help people. I have my abilities and the desire to use them in a way that I find satisfying. I don't hurt anyone."

"The Psi-Orgs don't consider intent when they discover Supers, my dear. They consider capability," she tells me.

"Then what hope is there for me other than in doing what I do now?" I tell her. "Should I have remained here, happy amid the ruins of Serenel, used and pushed about by anyone who wished to make use of me?"

"I don't know the answer, my dear," she tells me. "But you were safer then than you are now. I'm afraid for you."

She's so beautiful and I find myself wanting her so badly that I leave her quickly and go to see Hubertus.

He's dressing and eyes me grumpily, but says nothing when I make a hot drink of coffex. I sometimes wonder if he still desires Auria and resents her departure to Jonaas's domain.

"Auria seems very concerned that we could be caught by the Psi-Orgs," I tell him. "Perhaps she doesn't understand the precautions we take."

He tells me, "She's worried about her own pretty neck, that's all. None of us would escape Termination if some silly mistake led the Psi-Orgs here. This Solar Faith scam is a big thing, Saulus. If all continues to go well Jonaas thinks we could make enough money to leave this hole."

I'm shocked at this last statement.

"Leave this valley?" I say. "Where would we go?"

He says, "With enough money we could go to many places. But Jonaas is particularly interested in an island off the coast of Greece, a good buy if all continues to go well. We'd need someone to front as an owner, a non-Talent, someone like one of those wealthy politicians who seem to own everything in that area. We'd be safe and also close to the world again. And a good part of that will be your doing, my innocent friend."

I feel more and more horrified. My doing! To leave Serenel! I couldn't bear it! The beautiful valley, the Love Palace, Red Tree, and his Daughter, my garden! No! The others dislike this place because their attitudes make it a prison to them, but to me it's home.

Perhaps they'd leave me here with Yo-Yo? No— Jonaas would find a way to make me go. Like when he threatened to burn Yo-Yo if I didn't renew his youth, like when he burned my hands because I stopped him from killing Torros. He needs me to take money and to look after him and the Clan.

Hubertus goes to see Noni. I leave, my head pounding and sweat running coldly down my ribs. My insides ache. I run all the way up the mountain to the East Terrace and the door of the Love Palace. I touch the doorplate and it opens. I run in through the entry hall and into the beautiful main salon as the lights come on and the music begins playing.

"The Mozart music," I say and the Piano Concerto Number 19 begins. I touch the ornaments and the furniture. I look at the lovely pictures. I go to the big sleeping room where the statues make love eternally and I climb onto the bed. The lights fragment as the unwanted tears fill my eyes.

"Be quiet!" I shout and the music stops.

I curl up small, cutting off all my senses—

I awake and all is soft darkness except for a tiny glow from the goddess who holds back the bed curtains and the myriad stars of the ceiling.

"What time is it?" I ask.

"Fourteen point five hours," says the Computer.

I've slept for almost five hours. Jonaas expects me at the meeting at 15th Hour! I begin changing back to First Mode as I shower, the dark hair gathering on the floor of the cubicle. I dry myself, dispose of the dark hair in the converter-chute and go to the closets.

I choose a plain blue robe, slit to the knees at the sides, and choose a wide belt of bronze and jet pieces to go with it. I comb my hair, neaten my beard and mustache, choose some ornate sandals with bronze pieces in them and I'm ready. I leave the Love Palace and walk down to the Red Palace, meeting Jazalu at the colonnades.

"Where do you find such old-fashioned clothes?" she says, but she's pleased that I've returned to First Mode and kisses me.

The Clan, now fifteen in number, are in the Long Room. Some stare at my robe. Jonaas, broadcasting his charismatic attraction powerfully, raises his psi-barrier at sight of me. He always does this now. He makes a sneering face at me.

"You look more eccentric each time I see you!" he says. "I remember fashions like that from forty years ago!"

I say, "I'm comfortable. Obviously, the fashions were more sensible forty years ago."

He says, "Go somewhere out of my sight, imbecile!" and I'm so annoyed by this that I sit at the table next to Mario where I'm directly in Jonaas's line of sight. I smile hugely at him. He pretends not to notice.

Hubertus, Carolus and Jazalu do all the talking about the percentages of money, the meetings and negotiations with contacts Outside, the risks taken and plans for future activities. Jonaas is clever, makes good suggestions, ties up loose ends, gives quick decisions and makes praises to all but me. He has such a gift for praising and organizing and planning that one must admire. His perceptions of people are keen and accurate.

Perhaps that's one reason why he hates me, because he can't calculate my responses to events and circumstances. I'm alien to him, a threat and an unknown but valuable quantity. Perhaps he really does regard me as an imbecile because I demand nothing except privacy and because I keep my thoughts to myself.

I examine Auria's long, graceful throat and clean profile. Now that I've made her a natural brunette again she wears her hair simply and it suits her. In her she carries calm strength, strong will and warmth. She's so beautiful that I ache. What can it be that attracts her to Jonaas? Already his addiction to drugs and excesses of eating are showing again.

The talk goes on. Cassim, it seems, has become genuinely fanatical about the Faith and its principles and infects Barbier with his unhappiness about the criminal connections. They may not be completely trustworthy any longer. Jonaas suggests that I might become the Solar sometime in the future but, before I can say "No," Hubertus is talking about possible interest from the Psi-Orgs. Jonaas drops the subject and I'm very relieved. What a terrible thought!

The Paris forgeries, Jazalu's project, are beginning to pay and she's complimented. The Turin drug run is being threatened by carelessness on the part of some silly woman who has become addicted. Mahmud is given the task of resolving the difficulty—which means she'll be assassinated. Mahmud is an expert at assassinations that appear to be accidents. Jazalu complains about the new type of identidiscs being produced because she finds it difficult to alter their discharge patterns. Some people in the casinos are demanding too much money, so it's decided that Carolus must "discipline" them. Rumors that an Outlaw group of Talents were captured in Berne by the Psi-Orgs are discussed.

The tunnel needs attention, so Noni and Gino are ordered to look at it. Noni protests but is ignored. Auria asks to be allowed to go to Rome to do some shopping but is refused as usual. Jonaas is still angry at the way she ruined the robbery in Tel-Aviv last month, her second mistake since she joined the Clan. Mario complains about the condition of some food supplies and Meriem hotly defends her handling of the buying. It's decided that the Foster Twins will do it next time and Meriem is deeply offended. The Twins will have to soothe her later or she'll never forgive them.

A Chino state-minister and his two mistresses wish to have their identities altered and Hubertus is ordered to arrange it for next week when we're in Genoa. I've never had Chino patients before.

The drug runs are discussed in detail but I find the subject boring and difficult to understand. Money is handed out to Hubertus, Jazalu, Meriem, Noni, Pearlman, Colas, Harrison and Dundas. The meeting begins to break up.

Jonaas says, "You'll wait, Saulus."

Auria gives me a be-careful look and Hubertus looks worried. I sit and wait until only Jonaas remains.

He scowls at me and says, "You look ridiculous."

I nod and shrug, smiling hugely at him again.

"I'm putting on weight again and I have some pain here," he says, pressing his back.

"It's because you overeat and take drugs," I say. "And I should tell you that you'll have cancer of the bowel if you don't watch your diet."

"So," he says, "fix the damage."

I smile at him again.

"If you allow Torros back without hurting him," I say.

He looks angry and a scorch mark appears on my sleeve.

He growls, "You never learn, do you! One of these days I'll discipline you so hard—!"

Still smiling, I interrupt with, "You burned my head last time. If you had damaged my brain there would be no Solar Faith, no grateful people paying fees for body-changes, no disguises for the Clan and you'd be dead by now. Think on it. I want Torros back here."

"Blackmail," he says.

"Bargaining power," I parry. "Noni needs him and he's my friend. And don't think on destroying him as you did his brother or I'll let the entire Clan know what you did."

He's startled by that. Another scorch mark appears on my sleeve.

"And," I say, "next time you burn me or my clothes I'll wipe you senseless. If you don't believe I can do it then try me. Why did you kill Angelo?"

"Nobody killed Angelo. He abandoned the Clan and ran off," he says warily.

"Ah, that's the story is it?" I say. "But, you see, I was the one who found him. I want to know."

He thinks on that, shocked by what I've said. How he must have wondered about the body and the writing for all this time! I'm pleased at shocking him.

"None of your business," he says, his eyes very fixed on me.

I tell him, "He managed to crawl out to the colonnades before he died. Would you have preferred it if someone other than me had found him and spread the news?"

I can feel the power of his Talent gather and I poise myself. He thinks about things and his power subsides.

"He was a traitor to the Clan," he says. "Carolus found out that Angelo intended to depart the Clan and join his brother in Paris. And Angelo had been cheating the Clan of money in his dealings for some time, I discovered, no doubt to finance himself and Torros in some other project. I thought he was dead but, when I went back for his body after finding a place to dump it, he'd gone. I'd kill any traitor who tried to cheat the Clan. Carolus and I found the money in his room. Ask Carolus if you don't believe me."

I see no reason to disbelieve him. Perhaps that's

what Angelo had been about to tell me. Perhaps he'd wanted an identity change—

"There was no need to kill him," I say. "You're too fond of killing. Anyway, I want Torros accepted back here. If you refuse you'll regret it."

"Are you threatening me?" he growls and I feel his power grow again.

"No, I'm not interested in hurting anyone. But I won't do a thing for your abused body unless you allow Torros to return. You'll be dead in a year or so without help from me and I won't care one way or another," I say. "Is it so much to ask? In what way could Torros harm you?"

He considers, his power subsiding again. I stare at the table, no longer capable of smiling.

"Very well," he says. "I won't prevent Torros from returning. But he won't be a member of the Clan. You'll have to support him and keep him well away from me. Any trouble with him and I'll hold you responsible. Agreed?"

"Yes, agreed," I say. "Sit still and I'll fix what ails you."

An hour later, I go out through the colonnades and up the slopes to the Blue Place where Jazalu's waiting. She eyes the scorch mark in alarm.

"Did he burn you?" she asks.

"No," I say, and then tell her about Torros.

This doesn't please her. She's angry that I took risks and angrier that my cut of the money, which she regards as her own, will support Torros.

She rails at me and, when I ignore this, she slaps my face. She's very shocked when I slap her back and runs away with a pretense of weeping. She expects me to follow her and make up, but my patience with her games is at an end. I go out and call Yo-Yo. When he comes out of the twilight I wash his hands and face and make a meal for him.

Then I pick him up and carry him the long way around to the East Terrace and into the Love Palace.

I say, "We'll sleep here tonight," and he runs about, looking at the pretty things and squealing with excitement before he comes to me for cuddles.

I examine his brain, as I've done so often in the past. I trace the limited pathways and consider the whys of it all. It's as though I see some things for the first time and I enlarge my perceptions as I've never done before. The brain can't be interfered with in the same way that the rest of the body can, but I see interesting possibilities.

Is it right to interfere here? I look at the combinations, the patterns, the groupings and make-up of the cells and the messageways for a long time. He goes to sleep in my arms, trusting me and happy with me. I think and wonder and study until I'm too tired to think properly, then I take him to the big bed and rest.

I awake and it's the 12th Day of the 8th Month. I wake Yo-Yo and take him to the freshener. When we leave the Love Palace the sun is not yet risen. At the Blue Place I get him and myself breakfast. Jazalu comes from the bed as we're finishing.

She says, "Where were you? I was worried!"

I say, "I was where I was welcome."

"You are difficult," she says. "A little spat and you go off in a huff! I suppose Torros won't cost much . . . Where will he live? I won't have him here!"

"He'll live with Noni," I say.

She makes breakfast and eats. Then she adopts her

seductive manner. Jazalu likes to imagine that her physical charms can be used as a weapon.

"I missed you," she says, pouting.

I send Yo-Yo out to play and we make love. I suspect she likes it that I asserted myself, although I don't understand why. She calls me "a dreadful brute" in a way that's like a compliment. Very strange.

Later we collect Yo-Yo and go for a pleasant walk down into the valley where I haven't been for months. Jazalu is happy and sings and we play chasing games with Yo-Yo. I enjoy it very much. I wish we were like this more often. At midday we come back to the Blue Place and eat. Jazalu says such funny things that I laugh and laugh.

She goes down to the Red Palace while Yo-Yo and I clean up the dishes. It's then that Hubertus mindspeaks with me.

He complains, "Jonaas says you want Torros back in the valley! How should I know where he's skulking now? He was in Paris last I knew."

"You know people in Paris. Could they find him?" I ask.

"Torros is cunning," he tells me. "No non-Talent will ever find him. Why do you want him here? He's a troublemaker and Jonaas doesn't like him! He'll make for more problems."

I tell him, "You used to regard him as a friend. He's still my friend and Noni needs him. I don't like to feel that he's abandoned. He likes the valley, too."

"I'll do my best," he tells me, "but it won't be easy to find him."

Outside, the day becomes dim as stormclouds roll across the sky. The Foster Twins arrive to talk and, a little later, Noni and Meriem and Gino come, too. Jazalu arrives with Mahmud in the midafternoon and the Twins take their music-wheels from their belts. Outside, the rain pours down, but in the Blue Place we sing and talk and play with Yo-Yo and are happy with each other.

(Examinations of reports from the Security Section on interrogations of minor members of the Clan, captured in the raid on "Serenel," make it clear that Saulus had a strong influence on the domestic and personal lives of Clan-members. In Auria Shasti's reports she indicates that he was highly regarded for his sympathetic ear and his efforts to help individuals of the miniature society. Yet there is little in his narrative to point out his popularity. Any help he gives is mentioned by him very casually or not at all. Saulus displays a naive outlook at times and was regarded as an "innocent" by most of the Clan, yet he drew their affection and was a person they could talk to and trust. Considering his potential danger to others, it is of interest to note that he never considered harming others or using his abilities for personal power.

—J.T. Semantics Division)

The burn on Noni's leg has healed and the Foster Twins no longer have any signs of the radiation rash.

Noni says she'll examine the possibility of redirecting the flow of water from the poisoned West Peak so that it flows down the other side if I show her where the radiation is. Then all the valley's water, apart from that which runs across the West Terrace, would be pure.

They all stay to eat. That's difficult, but we manage. Jazalu loves company and is wonderfully entertaining. I sit Yo-Yo on my lap and he enjoys the noise. I spend a little time sorting out his brain patterns again and am tempted to make one tiny change. He begins to watch people in a slightly different way. I don't dare do more yet. If he begins to learn I'll study the possibilities further.

Everyone leaves late and the rain has stopped so I walk halfway down the slopes with them. The thickets which conceal the Crack from the walkway have grown huge and now cut off the entire West Terrace from the Palace below. Not that anyone but me ever goes to the West Terrace because of the sharpteeth. But I'm glad of the thickets which keep the unwary safe.

When they've gone I stand at the spur and look at the dark basin of the valley. After such a happy day I'm suddenly sad. They all wish to leave this lovely Serenel and I don't. Am I the one who's wrong? I know the valley and find it enough. The little I've seen of the Outside seems strange, dangerous and often unattractive. Am I being blind to the benefits of an island near Greece?

Jazalu has tidied up and we bathe Yo-Yo and take him to bed with us. She's very affectionate towards me.

"Saulus," she says, "I think we should have a child."

I'm startled and show it.

"We've already started one," she says, snuggling against me.

I hold her lovingly, but I'm puzzled. I examine her and there is a foetus, already six weeks developed and very healthy.

"Are you sure you want a child?" I ask.

"Yes, I'm sure," she says. "Don't you want one?"

"A child will be wonderful," I say and she seems relieved.

She goes to sleep in my arms. I examine the foetus again. Such a wonderful thing. But not a part of me. I made myself sterile long before I met Jazalu because other women who accepted me as a lover didn't want children in a place like Serenel. Jazalu obviously wishes me to think it's mine. I wonder why? Does she think I wouldn't want her with me because it isn't mine?

Our relationship is excitingly sexual and we get along quite well, but I've never pretended to myself that she or I are deeply in love. Should I tell her that I know it isn't mine or accept the responsibility? I'll wait and see. I wonder who the real sire is?

Six weeks—she was in Paris when she conceived. . . .

✳ SIX ✳

(No date given.—J.T.)

I awake slowly, a sense of danger shrilling delicately in me. It's dawn—

There's a peculiar, faint scrabbling sound close to the bed, then a soft chittering. I sit up slowly, tense with a realization. I carefully, slowly, lean across Yo-Yo's sleeping body and peer at the floor, adjusting my sight.

Two of Crawly-Thing's children, half-grown and already dangerous, are exploring cautiously. I see their shining black bodies and many-eyed heads with the mandibles and full poison sacs, the waving fronds behind their heads lifted to detect movement. I must have left the door open! They hear my movement and turn quickly, ready for attack, their many-legs braced to spring.

I thrust pleasure-pulse at them and they lift their front legs, then begin to sway, half ecstatic and half paralyzed. I climb from the bed very carefully and move to the door. I "call" them and they stagger towards me, chittering noisily. Yo-Yo wakes at the sound and sits up, his eyes growing round with terror as he sees.

"Stay there, Yo-Yo," I say softly and move through the doorway with the Crawlies following. The outer door is half open. What a fool I am not to have checked it! I walk slowly outside and into the garden.

There are six more of Crawley-Thing's children in my garden. Two are dead in Red Tree's Daughter's clutches, another is struggling as the rosebushes grasp and pierce the fat body with deadly thorns. The other three are tearing at the purple mosses in a search for insects. A huge web hangs, thick and glistening, across the path and the remains of a bird hang in it.

The Crawlies assume defensive positions at my movement. I walk quickly to the steps, widening the ecstasy pattern until all are captive, then I "call" again. More Crawlies appear from higher up and join the others as I crawl carefully beneath the web and move down the path towards the thickets. I push through the thickets in some haste, scratching myself painfully, and move across in the direction of the Crack. By the time I'm halfway there, the Crawlies number eight and two more, caught by the pleasure-pulse, run from the Crack. Two more run from the crumbling ruins.

I see that Red Tree has grabbed two despite his weakness and is already devouring them. Twelve now seek my "call," the sounds of their chittering becoming shrill with excitement. I draw close to the Crack, keeping my distance from them. I pass the lip from which they usually emerge and then change tactics.

I cease the "call" and change the pleasure-pulse to a pulse of fear/danger/urgency with all my energy. The Crawlies stiffen with shock and then pandemonium reigns among them as they run and leap in a rush to get to the Crack and safety. I can hear the clatter of their legs, loud in the still air, as they vanish into the web-strung Crack and vanish from sight. I

wipe sweat from my ribs and stand there, healing my
scratches and thinking for a time.

I go and look at Red Tree. He may live for a few
months more, but his life-cycle is almost done. He
has feasted on killer birds and sharpteeth and kept
the Crawlies at bay for a long time, but his fragrance
is weak now and he bears no more fruit. He is almost
spent. His seedpods are empty, but I have the few
that were fertile stored away, one of which became
his beautiful Daughter.

I run back and climb through the thickets with
more care than before. When I reach the garden it's
to find that the rosebushes have finished their meal
and so has Red Tree's Daughter. She brushes my
shoulder for the token of blood and drops the empty
shell which was once a Crawly. I hastily collect the
remains and hurl them beneath the vines out of Jazalu's sight.

I go to the mosses, now torn and disfigured. The
silver beetles which live beneath them have almost
finished repairing their nests. I send them the
required message patterns and they swarm up my legs
excitedly to gather about my body. I walk to the
heavy, glistening web and they swarm over it, cutting
it to shreds and disposing of it as I move this way
and that. I return to the moss banks and they stream
down into their nests. I draw the torn mosses over
the gaps as best I can and look about.

The garden looks orderly enough now.

As I go into the Blue Place, Jazalu comes to the
door of the bedroom, sleepy-eyed and blinking at
the light.

"Yo-Yo is excited about something," she complains.

"I'll see to him. Go back to bed," I say as calmly
as I can.

I go in, pick Yo-Yo up from the bed and take him to the freshener. He quickly forgets his fright in the shower.

I dress us and get our breakfast, then I soak Red Tree's seeds, all eight of them, in warm water until the shells soften and crack. Yo-Yo goes to play in the meadow and I take the seeds and an eating-prong to the West Terrace where I plant all of them in the damp soil near the Crack. Within a few months, despite the season, they'll be big enough to take care of any too-adventurous Crawlies. In the meantime, I'll instill a directive in the silver beetles to protect the garden against any further invasions of the Crawly Tribe.

Oh, but the valley is so lovely this morning! The air is so fresh and clean and all the little red flowers are out near the woods in the far valley. Even from this distance I can see the sheet of scarlet surrounded by lush greenery. I would love to go down there and run and run and run—but there are too many other things to do.

I go back and make breakfast for Jazalu. While I do so, Hubertus mindspeaks to me from the Palace.

He tells me, "The railcar is back with the new people. Do you want to meet them now while they're off-balance?"

"Poor things," I reply. "You're all like sharpteeth, protecting your territories from intruders."

"My teeth are good for many a day," he tells me.

I take Jazalu's breakfast to her and then go down to the Red Palace. I find Auria inspecting the collapse of yet another pillar in the colonnades. Part of it now leans visibly to one side and there will be more pillars collapsing soon. It's sad—but we don't need pillars to live here.

"Aren't you welcoming the new arrivals?" I mindspeak.

"I'm escaping from the too-friendly posturing," she replies. "It's amazing how many of the Clan became early risers in order to meet the strangers."

"How many are there?" I ask.

"Five," she tells me. "An old woman who's a 'kinetic of Epsilon class I'd say, a seven-year-old boy who's a Beta 'path but mentally retarded, and an eighteen-year-old girl who's a Delta 'path. The other two are Gamma 'kinetics, savage men who need a bath badly. Was that you I saw up near the West Terrace this morning?"

"Yes," I tell her.

"Take me up there. I haven't been to the West Terrace before," she tells me.

"Very wise," I tell her. "The Clan avoids the West Terrace."

"Why?" she asks. "Everyone rolls their eyes and says it's a terrible place, but nobody tells me much more. They mention spiders and a strange tree that eats people. Is it true?"

"Come and I'll show you," I tell her. "You'll be safe with me, but never go there by yourself."

I take her arm, she gathers up her long gown and we climb up the steps and walkways to the path and then higher to the thickets. I pull the thornbushes apart and help her through.

"Is Jonaas with the newcomers?" I ask.

She tells me, "Yes, he's doing his kind-but-awesome-father-figure act to impress them. They've lived terrible lives in Paris. What a pretty tree! What's all that chalky stuff about it?"

"Bones and shells of birds, sharpteeth, stinging-moths and Crawlies," I explain. "Years of them."

"What's a Crawly?" she asks.

I take her arm and lead her across the expanse of the Terrace to the Crack. I take her to the edge, holding her as she leans forward to peer into the dimness. A Crawly runs along a web to find a better hiding place. She gasps and steps back in alarm.

"Saulus! What was that? It was horrible—like a gigantic spider!" she asks.

She's very pale and her heart is pounding. I put an arm about her and she's slender and warm. I lead her to where Red Tree stands twisted and majestic.

"That was a Crawly," I explain, "and its ancestors were spiders before radiation poisoned the land and affected genetic patterns."

"Radiation did *that?*" she exclaims.

"No," I tell her. "Radiation was destroying them and I interfered. I was very young and learning to use my Secondary. I was inept so they developed too many eyes and too many legs and grew too large."

So I tell her about the Crawlies, Red Tree and the experiments in changes and balances that I made when I was much younger, the things I did so that struggling creatures and plants could live despite the radiation.

She tries to move away from Red Tree, but I hold her.

"Red Tree doesn't eat humans," I explain. "He may take a tiny sample of my blood occasionally, but humans don't attract him because I made it so. Hubertus says that what I did was genetic programming. I did a great deal of genetic programming when I was younger and some of it didn't turn out as I hoped it might. I was very ignorant but I learned a lot from my experimenting."

"It's all revolting, Saulus! You were making monstrosities!" she tells me, as though angry. "You must kill the Crawlies before they become a menace to us all!"

"No," I explain, "because they eat the sharpteeth which come over the mountain in large numbers. Red Tree prevented the Crawlies from coming to this side of the Terrace and soon there'll be eight more Red Trees to attract predators with their scent. They'll catch the killer-birds that nest on the Peak and munch on poisonous moths and gobble up excess Crawlies. I try to adjust balances, not kill things just because they aren't attractive to humans. Humans are just as much a menace to the creatures and plants of this valley as some of them are to us. What makes you think we deserve to live any more than they do?"

"Don't tell me you don't believe in self-preservation!" she states. "You've created horrors, Saulus! What will you do about the Crawlies until the trees grow?"

I think it wiser not to tell her about the silver beetles.

"I'll arrange matters," I assure her.

She looks at me in a puzzled way.

She asks, "How can you love this place, this horrible valley, Saulus? The ecology is a nightmare in some areas! Did you do all that?"

"I started things and, sometimes, they became other than what I'd hoped. But there are worse nightmares Outside," I tell her. "You accept those because you're used to them. I'm used to the valley and find it beautiful because I understand its lifeforces and find fascination in its balances."

She tells me, "I don't like the fact that you created horrors. You're fond of saying that you like things to be right, that the balances must not be aberrated, and yet you did this."

"I was young when I did these things. I didn't know any better," I say.

"But you know better now," she tells me severely. "You should put things to rights, especially when they could be so dangerous to us!"

She may be right. I feel guilty about my mistakes. But should one destroy things that work simply because they don't fit the usual pattern? The ecologies are stable enough while I'm still able to keep an eye on them. And not everything turned out so dangerous as the Crawlies, the stinging-moths and the killer-birds. They also have their place in the ecologies I assisted. Getting rid of them may make for other problems which I doubt that Auria would understand. I must think on it.

She tells me, "Sometimes I wish I'd never come to this dreadful valley," and there's something so weary about her manner that I long to hold her and comfort her. But she pushes away and leads the way to the thicket. I help her through and she leaves me to walk down to the Red Palace, almost as though she needs to escape me.

It must be hard for her, remaining with Jonaas. I don't understand that. And she must grow so bored since the Clan voted her out of participating in Outside work. And she seems such a capable and efficient woman—how could she have turned both of her jobs Outside into such disasters?

"Careful, Saulus. Your tongue's hanging out," Noni mindspeaks.

I turn and she's standing higher up the path, wagging her head at me.

"I came to find you so that we could go up to the Peak and look at those watercourses," she tells me.

I nod and follow her as she sets off up the walkway. We pass the West Terrace and the Crack, then head up through the gorse and tangle of strangler vines to the high ridges. It takes us almost an hour to reach the Black Ridge and we both need to sit down and breathe hard while our tiredness passes.

From here one can see the wonderful valley, green and inviting, full of life and fertility and richness— and on the other side one looks out over a blistered and arid land, pockmarked with craters and mostly devoid of life, a contaminated area where radiation is still too dangerous for people to live with.

I show Noni where the watercourses flow into the valley, one of them passing over poisoned land on the valley side and affecting the higher slopes so that no trees or even grasses of the simplest kind can survive there. It's such a small area of radiation and the watercourse has only flowed over it since the big rockslide of four years ago.

Noni's Talent is rarely used to its full capacity. She lifts supplies from the railcar, moves furniture and helps keep the Red Palace's foundations from crumbling by bolstering them with stone. But there's not much else for her to be useful with except in the way of heavy work. She's not clever and she's not often useful Outside, so she usually lives on the charity provided by Hubertus and Carolus, who look after her because they were friends of Torros.

Two years ago she and Torros helped me carry out the building of those small terraces on the north side of the valley to cover the radiation patches. She did incredible things. I'll never forget those massive landslides. They took her a month to achieve, but how impressive they were!

She eyes the rockslide now and tells me, "I can't shift that, Saulus."

"Two years ago you brought down part of a mountain on the north side," I tell her.

"That was different," she tells me. "I had lines of stress to work on, natural tendencies in the strata to work with. Like those in the West Terrace and above it."

"The West Terrace?" I query.

"That whole area of the mountain will slide into the valley one day," she explains. "That's the reason for the Crack. But this rockslide is just a big, heavy weight. It would take me months to lift it away bit by bit."

We sit some more and I know that she's "feeling about" almost in the same way as I do before I make changes to anyone, only her "feeling" is on a large scale. I can feel her psi-field stretch out and she keeps looking up to the Peak.

She asks, "Do you remember how Torros planted the explosives to help with my pushing when we made the north terraces? The explosives did the big work while I pushed where the weaknesses were."

"I remember," I tell her.

She explains, "Part of the Peak up there is the same. If explosives were planted in the right way I could probably push a landslide that would bury this whole area and cover the radiation very deep."

I tell her, "But I don't know anything about the how and why of explosives. Do you?"

"No," she replies, "but Torros does. And I hear that you're organizing for him to come back—"

"He has to be found first," I tell her.

She looks at me with anxious eyes.

"But, if he comes back, Jonaas will kill him, Saulus!" she tells me and she's full of fear.

"No," I assure her. "I made a bargain with Jonaas. I won't let anything happen to Torros. All he has to do is to keep out of Jonaas's way. Between us, you and I could make sure of that."

She thinks about that and nods slowly.

"I think I know where he might be," she tells me.

"Then tell Hubertus. He'll find him and then we can look after Torros and keep him out of trouble," I tell her.

She weeps then because she has missed Torros for so long. I send her pleasure-pulse for comfort and she stops weeping.

"Oh, Saulus," she tells me, "I do love you," and I know how she means it.

"I love you, too, Noni," I reply and she knows how I mean it.

After a rest we walk down the mountainside again.

"Jazalu being pregnant—you don't mind?" she asks.

"She says it's my child but I know it isn't," I reply.

She looks relieved and tells me, "Oh, then you know about Diam! Well, I'm glad. I'd hate for you to feel upset about it, Saulus. Jazalu's no good for you. It'll be better when we move to the island and Jonaas releases her from the Clan to go off with Diam. There'll be other women for you. And what does the money matter? The Clan will always look after you."

"How did you know so much about it?" I ask.

"Why, most of the Clan knows," she tells me, "but we didn't realize that you did."

I say no more on the subject, but I have plenty to think about. I realize now why my cut is always given to Jazalu. She and Jonaas arranged that between them. Well, she's welcome to the money. What would I do with it, anyway? But it's the deception that stings.

"How do you think Auria will accept Cecile?" Noni asks.

"Who is Cecile?" I reply.

"Didn't you meet the new lot this morning?" she asks. "Cecile's the new bedmate Jonaas found in Paris. She's a sly thing, but quite pretty in her way and she knows a lot about men, believe me! Fancy Jonaas taking up with an eighteen-year-old girl! He may need some help from you with two women to occupy his free time!"

I say nothing to that. Noni talks on about a variety of things, asks me if I knew about the relationship between Radley and Paul and seems very shocked that Meriem has parted from poor old Gino. I murmur suitably, but I don't take in much of what she says. I have other things to think on.

We part at the Blue Place. Jazalu isn't there, but Yo-Yo is. He's tried to get lunch for himself and has spread food all over the table and much of his face. I clean up, wash him and get him a proper meal, but I'm not hungry myself. He tries to speak, not merely grunt, when he comes for a cuddle. I feel such a surge of pleasure at this that my depression goes. I examine the developing pathways in his brain and am delighted. He tries to speak again, poking at my face happily and saying "Thors, thors." I think he may be trying to say "Saulus."

He runs out to play with the new red ball that I bought him in Berne and I go down to the Red Palace to meet the new arrivals.

Christina is in her 70th year, has no teeth and very poor digestion. I arrange to treat her. The boy, Francois, isn't retarded but has a spastic condition which I could correct. The two Gamma men are drug-damaged and will need treatment. I dislike both of them because they are so aggressive and mean-spirited. Cecile is with Meriem and is a very attractive female, rounded and ripe and vivacious in manner. But she's stupid and not eighteen. She must be more in the region of fifteen but certainly looks older. She has a spiteful wit which is unpleasant. I correct her thyroid deficiency during the introductions.

All of them know about me and are afraid. I pleasure-pulse Christina and Francois so we'll be friends, but I don't care for the others at all.

I go to Hubertus to arrange the treatments and ask, "Did Noni tell you that she thinks she knows where Torros is?"

"Yes," he tells me. "It's possible he's in The Hand's Court."

"What's The Hand's Court?" I ask.

He tells me, in his giving-a-lesson way, "The Hand is a man, the King of the Paris Sewers. I met him once. He's an Alpha 'path, physically deformed and cunning as a rat. He and his followers have managed to avoid the Psi-Orgs and Enforcers for several years now."

He shows me his mind-pictures, his impressions, of a vile, frightening place where slime and darkness and cold stone reign. Then he shows me an ugly creature with one beautifully cared-for hand which has many rings on the fingers. And I catch a name—the Rue de Saint Marie.

"If Torros is there I'll find him," Hubertus promises.

He goes on to the subject of Genoa and waxes enthusiastic about the hysteria being generated there, ready to ensure success of the Faith. He talks of money and bribes and manipulations, but I don't understand much of it. I adopt an interested look while I think on other things and Hubertus is content.

Jonaas calls him. I leave and go to play ball with Yo-Yo in the meadow until twilight. We go to the Blue Place, have a good dinner and then I sing to him as he sits on my lap. He likes that and stares up at my face with his beautiful eyes, making mewling sounds which are a kind of singing. When he gets sleepy I put him to bed and go out into the darkness of the garden. I think on a great many things, but come to no sensible conclusions about any of them.

Jazalu must be enjoying herself down at the Red Palace.

I think on the changes and new balances I made in the valley so long ago and try to think how new directions could be made without destroying so much that functions well, but come to no decisions. I go and tidy the Blue Place and go to bed.

✳ SEVEN ✳

(Another gap in the narrative at this point.

*The Solar Faith held meetings at Genoa (17-8-80),
Bergamo (18-8-80), Milan (20-8-80), Turin (21-8-80),
Lyons (22-8-80), and Dijon (23-8-80). It is calculated
that one million followers were recruited during
this one brief tour! The media followed the trend of
public interest and reported "miracles" of enormous
quantity, far more than Saulus could possibly have had
any hand in.*

*Incredible amounts of money poured into the
Faith's coffers—impossible to estimate with any
degree of accuracy. The Psi-Orgs were alerted to
investigate the possibility of Talent interference and
had operatives attend the meetings of the 21st and
23rd. It says much for the Faith's strategy that no
trace of unusual psi-activity was discovered, yet
according to Saulus, he was among the crowds at all
meetings and remained unaffected.*

—J.T. Semantics Division)

It's the 23rd Day of the 8th Month and a beautiful
day, even in this overly luxurious prison. The sun
streams in through unpolarized windows and I climb
out of bed full of energy. Hubertus still sleeps, but

Barbier is already moving about in his room. I hear him using the callphone so he's very wide awake.

I've seen only brief views of all the places I've been in for the meetings, but from these windows I have a wonderful view of the city and the mountains. The city looks clean and graceful, there are lovely parks and the airlanes and groundlanes of traffic remind me of my industrious silver beetles going about their homing rituals.

My usher's uniform hangs untidily over a chair. That was the most successful disguise of all and enabled me to move about very easily without drawing attention. The fieldworker's costume in Milan was too conspicuous and the businessman's clothes with the strangling trousers were too uncomfortable. I'll suggest that I use the usher's uniform from now on.

I go to the freshener and then dress in my new gray tunic and loose black trousers. Pale Mode is quicker to assume than Dark Mode. No-color clothes suit his anonymous features and minimize his muscular appearance.

But I've used Pale Mode for all these meetings, perhaps too often. I'll return to First Mode tomorrow. The difficulty with First Mode is that it's noticeable and people find it attractive to look at. And Dark Mode is much too noticeable in these parts. I comb Pale Mode's short, mousy hair and lank mustache and am ready for breakfast.

I'm very hungry and it's difficult to order from the servex because there's no way of knowing the nourishment content of the food before it arrives. I settle for fresh fruit, milk and coffee. Strange to think that I didn't like coffee a few months ago and now I like it so much. Not that I've changed my mind about the value of it, but a little vice won't hurt me.

Hubertus goes to the freshener and I'm finishing breakfast when he comes in, all dressed and neat. Barbier is usually one of the first to breakfast, but not this morning.

Hubertus slaps my shoulder and is very cheerful for him.

"Quite a night," he mindspeaks. "You really excelled yourself so I hear. Did you know there were Psi-Investigators about?"

"Yes," I reply.

He tells me, "I wish I could do that trick of yours. Could you teach me?"

"I don't think so," I tell him. "It's just a thing I can do. May I continue to use the usher's uniform? It made the moving about less conspicuous."

"If you wish," he replies. "Have you packed your things yet? Pearlman should be here in a few minutes."

I go and pack my things in my carryall and am surprised to see Barbier suddenly hurry past my door, already dressed and with his carryall. I hear the outer door of the apartment open and close. I wonder where he's gone? I thought he was leaving with the rest of us. I hurry to finish my packing and run out to Hubertus.

"You were quick!" he tells me, surprised.

"I saw Barbier leave and thought we must be going." I explain.

"Barbier's gone?" Hubertus wonders. "But we were to wait for Pearlman—" and he looks very puzzled.

The door buzzer sounds and I go to open the door. Pearlman bursts in, shouting, "They're in the elevator tube!"

"Who?" I say, smelling his fear.

"Investigators! They brushed my psi-field as I got into the elevator! Three, I think!" he shouts.

Hubertus, at the door of his room, curses and runs to grab the case with the money in it and his wallet. He runs back, saying, "Quick! With me!" and runs past us. We rush after him and into the deserted passageway.

The indicator on one of the elevators chimes and the doors begin to open as we pass. We rush into a cross corridor, almost colliding with a young couple. There's a shout behind us! Run, run, run! My fear's like a vise on my thinking! Hubertus turns into another corridor and shouts, "Laundry chute!"

He's already heaving at a flap in the wall, then he throws himself and the money case into it as I grab the flap. Pearlman shoves at me so I heave myself in and slide, falling into warm darkness.

The air rushes about me and my stomach seems to rise into my throat. I fall into light, into a pile of bed linen, with a jarring thump and then Pearlman strikes my shoulders and I'm half stunned by the impact. Our bodies struggle, there are curses and then Hubertus is dragging me from a large bin. He's saying something urgent, but I don't know what. Pearlman shoves at me, shouting, "Go! Go!" and I stagger after Hubertus.

We run from the room out into another corridor and then Hubertus is at the elevators.

The elevator chimes and the doors open. There's a man in a blue and red uniform, half crouching and pointing a pistol directly at Hubertus. An Enforcer with a Psi-Org badge on his breast.

"Hold still or you're dead!" shouts the man and Pearlman thumps into me as I brace to a stop.

Hubertus, panting, drops the case and wallet and raises his hands in surrender. Behind me, Pearlman curses.

I feel that strange, numbing, almost-painful psi-field

reaching out to us and realize what it is. This man is a Control like those I was aware of last night, a man with a Talent which holds, restricts and defeats other Talents and has no other function. Like Talent which is inverted so that it nullifies.

Inverted? I wonder if—I experience and analyze as the man straightens and gestures sharply with his pistol.

"Against the wall, Outlaws!" he snaps. "Move!"

I reach out into his mind and do a thing, experimenting. It's very interesting—I watch him fall sideways like a loose-jointed doll. Hubertus gapes and Pearlman says, in an hysterical way, "What—? What—?"

I say, "I removed his consciousness, but he'll awake in a few minutes."

Hubertus and Pearlman thrust me aside quickly to drag the man from the elevator, pick up the money case and wallet and haul me into the box that I hate so much. Hubertus touches the controls, the doors close and the elevator falls in that horrible way.

"I forgot my carryall," I say sickly. "All Yo-Yo's new clothes were in it."

Hubertus laughs in a way that borders hysteria and says, "If we get out of this I'll buy you twenty carryalls of clothes for Yo-Yo! How, just how, did you do what you did to a Control?"

"I don't know," I say. "I can't explain. I folded myself into his psi-field—"

How can I explain? I felt the possibility and did it, that's all. And I was frightened, which helped me to do it.

I wipe perspiration from my face and then the doors are opening. We move out briskly. The reception area is crowded and we push between people carefully, then head toward the main doors. Moments later we are on the outside and a siren begins to wail. I hear the doors click as they seal and can see people standing, as though frozen, through the glassite.

Pearlman grasps my arm and drags me after Hubertus to the carryway. We step on it and rise towards the main junction of the complex where all the shops are. There aren't many people about at this early hour and we have no difficulty in walking briskly to the further carryway that leads to the outside of the building. The air is cool, full of human scents, the aroma of food and the sweetness from a flower stall.

Some alien minds brush my awareness and I retract myself.

"Investigators," I say and Hubertus says, "Where?"

I say, "Two ahead of us, one behind. Some distance away."

He says, "That trick of yours, that psi-field retraction, can you do it on others?"

"I don't know," I say. "I never tried."

"Try now," he says. "The two ahead of us must be at the entry."

"I need a quiet place where I can look," I say.

There's an eating place, gaudy and pleasant, with little booths. We go in quickly, find the furthest booth and slide into it. Pearlman puts coins in a slot with hands that tremble and coffee comes out in mean little cups. They eye me nervously and I extend myself and see if something can be done that I've never thought of doing before.

I look and think and look again, then say, "I can't help you to retract your psi-fields, but I can impose a kind of shock to repress the fields for a short time. You won't like it. You'll feel disoriented and confused."

They look at each other, then Hubertus clips the

money case to his belt and gives me the wallet. He says, "Do you know the way to the aircar pool from here?"

"Yes," I say. "If you tell me where we're going I'll hire an automatic and then, when we're away from here, I'll remove the shock."

"The coordinates you ask for are 23-C2-801 North," Hubertus says grimly.

So I quickly do the thing I have to do. They look at me blankly. I retract my psi-field.

"Come along," I say and stand up. They obey.

Hubertus moans and begins to cry quietly, the tears filling his eyes and running down his hard cheeks. "Mother?" he whispers, "Where are you, Mother? It's cold here."

I put an arm about him and take Pearlman's hand in mine. Pearlman is scratching and squirming. "They're crawling all over me!" he hisses.

"Mother?" says Hubertus, "I'm frightened."

"Mother's here, Huby," I say. "Stop scratching, Pearlman! Ignore them and they'll stop crawling!"

People stare as we move from the restaurant. Hubertus begins to sob loudly, Pearlman hisses and squirms as we walk. I take them to the carryway at the junction and haul them onto it.

An elderly man moves aside and says, "Drunken louts!" as Hubertus begins to sob without restraint.

"His mother died," I say unkindly and a woman clucks sympathetically. The elderly man turns away, embarrassed, and sweat runs down my ribs. A man in a red and blue uniform appears on the walkway as we come to the end of the carryway—but he has no badge. I manhandle Hubertus and the wriggling Pearlman off at the stop-plate and hurry them past.

Two more uniformed men stand at the exit and stare at us as we pass by. One has a badge.

We are in the open air and the chill and the breeze are wonderful. Enforcers stand in a group near some aircars, so I drag my two charges along the promenade as quickly as I can and find the ramp to the car pool. Hubertus is now crying hysterically and Pearlman is moaning, "They're biting me! I can't bear it! Filthy things!" in a desperate way.

I all but carry Hubertus to the line of aircars. Two Enforcers—no badges—are standing at the top of the rank, looking grim and suspicious. I quell my fear and make a decision before they grow too suspicious.

"Please," I say, "could you help me? My friend has had a terrible shock and I must get him to a med-center."

They looked startled and one moves to open the aircar door. Pearlman scrambles in, hissing, and I heave the sobbing Hubertus into a seat, banging my head painfully on the door opening.

"Thank you. I'm most grateful," I say to the Enforcer and climb in quickly. He closes the door for me, nodding and looking concerned.

I tap out the coordinates on the console, take money from the wallet and feed it into the slot when the car calculates the cost, nod gratefully to the staring Enforcers and then the car is moving. Oh, the relief!

I rub my head and then pat Hubertus. Pearlman is thrashing about in his seat and tearing at his clothes as the car soars up the ramp and begins climbing into the airlane. I avoid looking out the window because flying terrifies me. I risk opening my psi-field enough to put Hubertus and Pearlman to sleep and they subside.

I wait until the aircar is well into the airlane before opening my psi-field properly. I attend to my aching head, remove the imposed shock from my charges and give them a moment of pleasure-pulse.

They awake.

"Chaos!" says Pearlman. "What happened? Did you have any trouble?"

"Not really," I say.

It's better they don't know.

"Barbier mouthed us to the Enforcers," Hubertus says. "It had to be him."

"But why would he do that?" I ask.

"He wants the Clan out of the Faith organization. He thinks he can handle Diam and take over the whole organization," says Hubertus. "He and Jonaas have been arguing about the money for some time. I suspected he might try something—but I didn't think he'd go this far!"

"But what about me to make the miracles?" I say stupidly.

"The Faith doesn't need you to make money any more," he tells me. "It's Diam who believes that you're some sort of divine. Barbier would have organized this raid through the Enforcers he has on his secret payroll. We have to put a stop to him quickly."

"Dijon?" says Pearlman.

"Yes," says Hubertus. "He has to go there to wait for Diam. We have to get there before Diam arrives."

"But," I say, "what if you're wrong? What if Barbier didn't betray us?"

"And who else could have done it?" Hubertus asks. "Barbier was the only one who knew where we were."

(*The investigation raid which Saulus describes was recorded as a "false alarm." One investigator was found unconscious in a corridor but remembered nothing. Five Sensitives and three Controls combed the area without results. See Reports C504-60 and C504-61. The Enforcement Bureau gave the alarm after an anonymous call from someone who understood procedure.*

—J.T. Semantics Division)

We leave the hire-car at a little waystation near the outskirts of Lyons and get into another aircar which I recognize as being the one we usually travel in. Hubertus sets the coordinates and we soar once more.

"Saulus," says Pearlman, "did you realize that the man in the elevator had a laser pistol?"

"Is that different to the kind of pistol you carry sometimes?" I ask.

"I carry a stunner," he says. "A laser kills, Saulus."

I must ask Hubertus about laser pistols sometime.

Pearlman looks at me so strangely that I ask if something is wrong.

"Yes," he says, "you are. I've never heard of any Super who does the things that you toss off so lightly. You scare me. I'm glad you're not against me."

"But," I say, "you're my friend. And apart from that, I've never knowingly hurt anyone. Apart from one time with Jonaas—and he wasn't really hurt."

"It's your potential that scares me," he says.

That annoys me.

"That's what Auria told me the Psi-Orgs would terminate me for," I say. "But anyone, anyone at all, can be potentially dangerous! It's like saying 'Yo-Yo might take a hammer and hit someone on the head with it.' But he won't and you know it. So don't get spooky about me, Pearlman, because it's insulting!"

I settle to sleep.

I awake as the car bumps down.

We're in the countryside and it's very stark-looking,

with no leaves on the trees and the sky dark with cloud. The chronometer that Hubertus gave me indicated 14:50, so this must be near Dijon where we have the next meeting. Behind the trees, half-hidden by leafless shrubs, is an old but imposing house. It looks very bleak.

"You wait here, Saulus," Hubertus tells me. "We saw Barbier's car from the air and it could be dangerous for you in the house."

"May I walk in the woods?" I ask.

"Over that way. Don't go too far," Pearlman says, pointing. He has his pistol out of the door pocket so I don't ask any more questions.

So I walk in the bleak woods for an hour. It's interesting, despite the cold, but I can't stop myself from wondering what is going on in the house and how I wish I didn't know as much as I do. It's a relief when I see Hubertus and go to meet him.

I ask, "Was Barbier there?"

He says grimly, "Yes."

I ask, "What happened?"

He scowls and says, "Nothing you need to know about. But he was the traitor for certain, if you still feel squeamish about it. Could you make Jubal look like Barbier for a while? You'll have to work from photopics in the Faith brochure."

"Yes, I suppose I could. I know his face fairly well anyway—but do you need Barbier?" I ask.

He says, "Diam can't handle everything and people know Barbier. And Jubal understands enough to manage for a while."

I don't like Jubal. I don't trust him, although I don't know why.

"Come and eat," says Hubertus. "Diam and Jubal

will be here in an hour or so and you'll have a busy evening ahead."

Seen closer, the old house looks more pleasant. There are gravel paths and white verandahs. From the upper windows some of the tall buildings can be seen in Dijon. I have a very good meal of fruit and vegetables in a much-used, old kitchen. Pearlman comes in with his shoes muddy and soil stains on his clothes.

"How did you get so dirty?" I ask.

"Planting something in the garden," says Pearlman and I realize that I've asked a very silly question.

(Following this statement of events, Investigation Teams searched for and found the house in question. The house was leased to Barbier Fugerio for some months during that period. The badly decomposed body of a man, identified by his dental records as Barbier Fugerio, was found in a shallow grave in a rear garden. His neck had been broken. Records and testimonies can be found which claim that Barbier Fugerio was very much in evidence for a further month before he handed his duties over to the Solar Faith Trust and disappeared without fuss.

—*J.T. Semantics Division)*

Diam and two of his assistants, Jubal and Osmund, arrive at 16:20 and there's a discussion—from which I'm excluded—between them, Hubertus and Pearlman. I hear Diam shouting in distress at one stage but, when I see him later, he's as serene and calm as usual.

Jubal isn't unlike Barbier in size and coloring so I have little difficulty in rearranging his features to suit, working on Barbier's pictures in the brochure and my memory. Jubal doesn't like any of it, but doesn't argue. By 18th hour even his fingerprints are identical, being copied from a bank-identicard. No one will notice that his height is a little less since he's slimmer than Barbier. Hubertus is very pleased, particularly with the voice which was so distinctive.

Diam and Jubal, who is now Barbier, leave at 19:15 while Hubertus, Pearlman, Osmund and I eat.

"I need an usher's uniform," I tell Osmund and he agrees to procure one for me.

Osmund drives me to the Dijon Recreational Center in Barbier's car which is very luxurious. We drive right into the complex with a special pass. Outside there are huge crowds and the stadium is packed with excited people, some praying and singing already. All the pennants and glo-signs are up and subsonics are being played to soothe the crowds.

I follow Osmund into the dressing room where Diam's scarlet robes are laid out and his gem-encrusted staff is being polished by Adreana and Phillipa. I've heard Hubertus sneer that Diam is too theatrical, but the staff and robes look very attractive to me.

Osmund gets me a red and purple uniform which is a little too baggy but will do. Diam comes in and kisses my hand in his unctuous way and Osmund tells me to meet him at the main gates as soon as the meeting is ended. The routine never varies now.

I walk out into the packed stadium. Through the clear roof I can see the stars and that reminds me of the Love Palace.

I walk past the rostrum and up into the huge seating area, then look back at the color and the lights which attract the eyes of the crowds. It's all simple, garish and striking.

The affirmations are painted with something that

affects the retina and makes them seem brighter, pro-
claiming "Purity Of The Body Through Purity Of The
Mind," "Strength, Health, Happiness—The Mind
Directs, The Body Obeys," "Discipline Of Thought
Means Perfection Of Physical Function" and so on.
The banners, with their formalized sun signs, are bril-
liant and seem to radiate light.

As I move up higher, passing other ushers who have
already done the work of seating the noisy crowd, the
music begins. It's low, vibrant and sweet, with several
almost-illegal subsonics which have a stimulating
effect on the nervous system. I hate it.

I look about at the crowd. Some faces are excited
and eager, some composed and serious, many simply
alert and curious. Most clothes are sober and the few
bright, fashionable costumes are moderate in style.
The Solar's lectures and exhortations on moderation
and sobriety in all things seem to have struck a
responsive chord. And yet, when I look at the gaudy
lights and banners, I'm amazed that no one sees any
contradiction of principles.

Here are the sick, the maimed and the old. Most
are fools who could be treated at any medcenter
instead of luxuriating in their illnesses. Many merely
seek sensation, many are hypochondriacs. Why do
such people need impediments to prevent them from
enjoying their lives? I don't understand their attitudes.
I begin scanning with my Secondary.

Ah! There—a young woman, unsuspecting of the
tumor in her womb. I activate processes which will
remove it and the cause of such a condition.

There—a middle-aged man with mild but increasing diabetes. An adjustment and it'll be gone within
the hour. There—a child with poor eyesight. A

moment of planning, a delicate rearranging and it'll correct itself.

Ah! And there a candidate for a "miracle," a man with damage to his spine so that his legs are partially paralyzed. Some surgery is evident but I see why it hasn't helped. I dull the necessary nerve pathways, begin stimulation which will cause regrowth of the atrophied areas and speed the cell activity. The man wriggles at the uncomfortable sensation as I remove the nerve blocks. I place an electronic marker on the arm of his seat so that Diam will be able to "call down a miracle" later.

A prostate problem takes a moment of adjustment. A woman with an unsightly skin condition—balance anew. An elderly man with a leg ulcer—change conditions and heal. Another electronic marker here.

Ah, another "miracle candidate," a young girl with cerebral palsy—I make connections, rearrange motor controls minutely and place the marker. A bladder infection—adjust and arrange balances. An epileptic—tricky, but the brain pathways can be persuaded. A blind eye—discipline nerve centers, regenerate tissue, place the marker.

Now I move to the next aisle. An arthritic condition, the beginnings of a cancer, digestive problems, haemorrhoids, a sufferer from migraine, ah—another marker for a severe lung condition, a marker for a subcutaneous cyst, another one with poor eyesight—

A fleeting moment of psi-field brushes my awareness! I retract and enclose my field, moving casually but quickly up toward the rear, my heart beating faster.

A man with an intent look and a tunic of plain but expensive make comes quickly down the aisle and I know he's "listening." I step aside for him and move on. A psi-Org Investigator? It seems likely. More of Barbier's meddling? Or chance? No more "miracles" of my making tonight. The people will generate their own with hysteria and encouragement from Diam. I'm too afraid to take more risks.

I look back and see that the man has been joined by a woman and they are both scanning the crowd intently. And now I see that there are Enforcers at the exit doors.

The subsonics in the music have increased and the lights on the rostrum are fully up. The trumpet theme for the Solar begins and the crowd tenses expectantly, the noise of conversation ceasing. The choir, singing as they come, begins to file onto the levels above the main rostrum, their white robes shining.

I move quickly past an Enforcer to the exit and through, nodding to the attendants, who hardly see me. I can hear the hymn, "Hail, Divine Humanity," as I walk into the deserted service corridor. I start running and quickly reach the door to the corridor leading to the dressing rooms. As I enter this, I can hear Diam's voice boom suddenly and then the crowd's answering roar, then Diam again. The choir begins to chant to the background drumming. Down here the noise pounds through my head.

"Hail the Mind!" I hear Diam shout and the crowd roars. "Hail the Body!" he shouts and another roar replies. "Through the Mind comes Perfection of the Body," Diam begins.

I go into the room where Diam dresses and close the door. The sound is mercifully softened, although I can still hear the pattern of the meeting. I look for my clothes and begin pulling off the usher's uniform in haste.

Diam has reached his opening harangue about the

disciplines and the self-denials necessary in order to become enlightened. He has a marvelous voice and the convictions of a true fanatic, really believing in what he preaches. But he's not so blinded by ideals that he can't appreciate the money and the fame which are now his. He's an actor with a real calling, playing his audiences superbly and never losing sight of the practicalities.

I haul my trousers on, pull my tunic over my head and look for my boots.

The dressing-room door opens and a man in a red and blue uniform, complete with Psi-Org badge, is there, staring. It's the man who was in the elevator this morning, the Control! For a moment we are both frozen, recognizing each other!

"Outlaw!" he hisses and reaches for his pistol.

I open my psi-field for a moment and he staggers, falls sideways. In those moments I'm aware of other psi-fields very close! I retract my field and am aware of an alarm pipping piercingly. It's from a device on the Control's belt! I run to him, rip it from his belt and crush it beneath my stamping heel. I crouch and gather him up with desperate strength, heave him over my shoulder and stand, then stagger out into the corridor. The fresheners are close but not suitable. I need a place where he won't be found. There's a waste-disposal chute that goes down into a great container outside. With difficulty, I shove him into it and listen as he slides from sight.

I run into the fresheners and into a booth. Can I climb into an air duct? No, the grille is too well-fitted. I daren't open my psi-field to find out whether the others are coming . . . What to do? What to do? I must be a victim, an unsuspected casualty! I must brazen it out!

I can hear the clatter of feet in the corridor. I kneel by the basin, take a deep breath, and bash my face against it. Ah! The pain! My nose is broken and the blood begins to run. I bash my face against the basin again and the pain is sickening! My lip splits and blood runs. I stagger to my feet, smear the blood about my face and reel out into the corridor, moaning.

There are Enforcers in the corridor. One grabs me.

"A man—an attendant—hit me—" I burble, blood dripping onto my tunic. I fall against the wall and slide downward.

"Which way did he go?" the Enforcer shouts and others are running to join him, three—four of them.

I point to the dressing rooms and sag in a simulated faint. There's a noise of running feet and shouting. I open my eyes enough to see one of the "listeners" from the stadium bending over me.

Diam's voice comes faintly, shouting, "Deny the base instincts to indulge! Reach for Truth!"

Arms grasp me and Enforcers are hauling me to my feet.

A voice shouts, "Hey, fellow, are you still with us? Howah! What did he hit you with? Someone get a med-unit!"

I'm half-carried into a dressing room and helped to sit on a bench. A face comes close to mind—the "listener."

"This attendant," he says. "What did he look like?"

"A stranger—" I mumble, "Not with the Faith staff—dark hair—"

He goes and there's more movement and thumping of feet. My face throbs, my head throbs. I begin to feel genuinely faint and drift into a gray state, only vaguely aware of people about me. I hear Adreana's voice protesting from somewhere—

Someone lifts my head and a hand, cool and smooth, covers my eyes. Something is sprayed on my face and the pain fades. The hand is removed and I see a man and a woman in med-unit uniforms.

"You'll be all right," the woman says. "A little plastic work and you'll be as good as new. We'll get you to a medcenter. Can you walk?"

They heave me to my feet, my arms about their shoulders, and half-carry me out, past some Enforcers and along the corridor. In the stadium, the choir is singing and the world floats about me. More time must have passed than I realized because I hear Diam bellow, "He walks! He walks! Witness the divinity of the Mind!" and the crowd roars.

A door opens and we go outside. The air is chill. I'm being assisted into the back of a tall, white vehicle with a medsign on it. They lift me onto a stretcher and the doors close. A blanket is drawn over me and the woman sits beside me, taking my wrist to feel my pulse. The car begins to move. There's the scent of antiseptic and my face is sprayed again. I can hear a high-pitched electronic wail.

"Relax now," says the woman and pats my arm.

What to do? What to do? I mustn't go too far or I'll be lost! I don't know Dijon or its landmarks! The car swings left and then the speed increases. Are we airborne or is it a groundcar? I lift my head and peer through a window. A groundcar. There are buildings and streetlights passing. Are we far enough away from the Psi-Org people for me to risk opening my psi-field? Oh, my head throbs from holding myself in! I open a little—ah, the relief of being aware again! No psi-fields close—none at any distance I can judge.

I open my field fully. I put my attention to the woman and she slumps over me. I sit up, pushing her aside gently. Oh, the dizziness! I increase adrenaline, quicken heart rate, feed muscles and cut off pain centers. My head clears.

The car travels so fast! I drag the blanket from about my legs and get up, seeking the driver. I clutch the stretcher as the car slows and turns a corner, then I put the driver out of action. The car slews wildly and stops with a jarring thump!

The door—where's the handle? Ah—turn and push—cold air. I climb from the car and close the door, my senses singing. The car has mounted a walkway and is against a building. The woman is already stirring within. I move quickly, feeding energy to my muscles and taking control of myself fully.

Have we come far from the stadium? The streetlights are bright and there are groundcars moving, slowing. I walk briskly, adjusting my heart rate and glandular system. Is there enough useful tissue and basic material to become Prime Mode quickly? There are people about, staring at my bloody face as I pass. Must change the face first. I apply myself to repairs and changes. Cartilage to begin, then the blood vessels. I use my hands to assist shape.

There's a crossroad and I turn left. There aren't so many lights here—repair split lip now. Activate patterns to become Prime Mode now and hair begins to fall out. Brush it away. Ah, there's a carryway and few people on it. I walk to it and step onto the sliding surface. Rising above the street now, toward higher galleries. Must find a freshener to wash my face. Skin color now. Hair begins anew but won't bother with beard. My tunic is covered in blood at the chest. Must wash that, too.

Where's the stadium from here? So many big buildings blocking the view—I step off the carryway to the gallery and pause to look about. Down there, a long way down the street, is a dome all lit up. The stadium? Must be. I walk along the gallery. So many bright lights and people staring. Where is a freshener?

I see an elderly man pausing to stare at me.

"Please, sir," I say, "I've had an accident. Where's a freshener?"

"You need a med-unit, lad," he says.

"No," I say, "a freshener."

He points and says, "Along there."

"Thank you, sir," I say and walk quickly.

Ah, a freshener—I go in. Deserted. I go to the basins and wash my face, strip off my tunic and wash the blood from it as best I can. Put the wet garment back on and stare at myself in the mirrors. New hair coming along well, features almost complete, skin color right. I drink water greedily and smooth my hair. I readjust balances until Prime Mode is complete, then leave the freshener. Nobody stares as I make my way along the gallery and seek a carryway to the lower level. Ah, there it is—

I've utilized tissue for energy and not replaced it, so I feel somewhat weak, but I walk briskly in the direction of the dome, closing my psi-field again. The streetlights tend to haze in my vision—

(*Psi-Org Investigators attending the Solar Faith meeting that evening found no trace of unusual psi-activity. At 20:25, an alarm was set off by one of the Controls in the dressing-room area but Enforcers found no sign of him. He reported in later in a very confused state (See Report C504-82). At 20:58, a med-unit was called to attend an assault victim in the dressing-room area. At 21:16, Dijon Medcenter received a report from Unit 12, claiming that an accident had occurred and that they had lost a patient*

from their service-car. Enforcers called to the scene
searched the area, but found no patient.

                                        —J.T. Semantics Division)

I've used up too much energy to maintain warmth
and I'm very cold despite walking briskly. Weariness
affects my vision still. There are still crowds and
Enforcers in front of the stadium and I look for
Osmund anxiously. My chronometer says 22:09. It was
a long walk and I feel very tired.

No sign of Osmund and the meeting is likely to go
on for some time yet. I'm so cold! I go into the reception area which is jammed with people. It's warmer,
at least. I see Phillipa through a haze and struggle to
her. Will she remember Prime Mode from Genoa?
She stares and nods and pushes her way to meet me.

"Why the change?" she asks.

"Psi-Investigators are here. Get me away, quickly,"
I say.

Her eyes roll in fright. Being a non-Talent, she
regards the Psi-Orgs with superstitious awe.

"Wait here," she says. "I'll find Osmund."

I wait, shivering, until Osmund comes.

We go out to where the special cars are parked and
he shows his pass to an Enforcer. We get in and I
settle in my seat to doze and save energy—

I awake as we arrive at the house. Osmund lets me
out, I thank him and he departs again. The sky is
ablaze with stars and a sharp breeze whistles slightly
through the bare trees as I walk to the house. I can't
stop shivering.

Inside, I go straight to the kitchen and find food.
I'm still eating when Pearlman and Hubertus come in.

"What happened?" Hubertus asks. "I thought you'd
be another hour at least."

I tell them verbally since Pearlman doesn't mind-speak. I tell every detail. Hubertus listens and analyzes while Pearlman boils water with his small Talent, one of his few tricks but a useful one now. He makes coffee and I'm very grateful for it.

When I've finished explaining, Hubertus sits thoughtfully in silence. With food to restore me I'm feeling much better now.

Hubertus says, "If the Psi-Orgs are interested in the Faith we'll have to take further precautions. Perhaps you could miss a couple of meetings—"

"Not Rheims," says Pearlman. "They're cynical about miracles in Rheims."

"I'll consult with Diam," says Hubertus. "We can't fold up yet. After the tour, Diam wants to go on with the Faith and the Clan will be out of it. Can you manage a few more meetings, Saulus?"

"Yes," I say, "if some provision is made to get me away should the Psi-Org people be about."

"I'll organize something," says Hubertus. "It's only a few more, Saulus, and then the Clan can get on with the move to that island with money enough to keep us for a long time to come."

So the island is definite. I feel ill. I go out into the cold garden. I need to talk with Auria because I feel trapped. Barbier is dead and I'm as much to blame as anyone for that because I did nothing to stop it. I feel I should stand by the Clan and do what I can for my friends, but I don't want to leave the valley. Will Jonaas agree to lave Yo-Yo and me behind?

I go inside and bathe, then go to bed. But I can't sleep. I'm still abuzz with thoughts when Diam and his people arrive at 23:50. I get up, wrap a blanket about myself and go into the living area.

Diam and Hubertus are exchanging information.

Diam is excited by the success of the meeting and his own performance.

He complains about the director of the choir and about the sound technicians, but is pleased by the flood of new members. They talk of Hoskins, Perrimi and Borosov who handle the donations and other finances, of the publicity system which Barbier set up and which Jubal must handle until the Faith Trust is set up, and of the venues for the meetings to follow.

The setting up of permanent Faith Temples is already planned and Diam has people interested in studying his teachings to become Solar Ministers. I don't understand much of it, but it seems to involve a lot of people and a lot of money. The murder of Barbier seems not to concern them at all.

Diam is very concerned at hearing of my experience this evening and I leave them working out a way of removing me quickly if something similar happens in the future.

I get into bed wearily.

❊ EIGHT ❊

(At this point there is a jump of 18 days before the narrative resumes. According to Auria Shasti's reports, Saulus returned to the valley on the 8th of the 9th month after touring through Euroasia with the Faith. Between the 23rd of the 8th month and the 7th of the 9th month there were twelve meetings and the establishing of the first Temple of the Faith in Moscow.

—J.T. Semantics Division)

I awake. The calendar says 10th Day of the 9th Month, 2280 A.D.

I slide away from Yo-Yo, feeling the onset of that old excitement. The sun has not risen yet but the East is full of light as I go into my garden. With no Jazalu to worry about, I dance and dance until the sun has risen and my body is wet with sweat!

I'm tired but satisfied with the violence and wildness of my dance and I drop onto the moss banks, breathing heavily. I feel wonderful and life is good. Silver beetles rush out, prepared to attack and destroy but, at my scent, they run about my body briefly and then return to their nests.

Here in the valley it's midautumn and chill but it

has its own special glory. I see that the roses still have
a few blooms and that Red Tree's Daughter is laden
with her first real crop of fruit. I go and allow her
the token sample of blood in exchange for several of
the ripe globes. She has grown and is very beautiful.

I start as a voice says, "Is that Red Tree's Daughter?"

It's Auria, blue gowned and with her dark hair
flowing down her slim back. She stands on the path,
uncertain about entering my garden. I reach out with
my mind for direct contact, but she refuses the joining, as though shy.

"Yes. Come in," I say, delighted to see her, but
puzzled by her refusal to contact minds.

She comes, saying, "I heard that this garden is
strange and dangerous. What should I avoid?"

"Damaging it," I say. "Red Tree's Daughter and
the roses don't harm humans. I made a taboo,
remember?"

She comes in warily. I go to her, take her hand and
lead her to Red Tree's Daughter which ignores her.

"Touch," I say.

She touches the deceptively delicate-looking leaves.
They curl but don't grasp. Auria smiles nervously at
me.

"She's very pretty," she says, hoping to please me.

"But created by a man who makes horrors," I say.

She refuses to look at me and I feel badly about
my jibe.

"Come inside and have breakfast," I say and she
nods.

I lead her in and cut some of the fruit for her. She
tastes of it cautiously. Then I leave to pull Yo-Yo from
the bed and take him to the freshener. He squeals,
"Sollus! Sollus!" when we bathe, which is an exciting
thing to me. I dress him in his new baggy trousers,

woolen shirt, warm jacket and the boots that I bought in Moscow. He loves those boots. I wear my brown kaftan and sandals.

Yo-Yo is pleased to see Auria but more pleased to see his breakfast. I slice fruit for him, pour him some milk and then make real coffee that Hubertus bought for me in Rome yesterday.

"The fruit is delicious," Auria says. "I've never tasted anything quite like it. What kind of fruit is it?"

"Those are fruit from Red Tree's Daughter. She'll bear a great deal of fruit and it's very nourishing," I say.

She slices another ripe globe.

She says carefully, "Some things you helped to create are obviously very good and valuable. I was watching you for a while before I came into the garden. Were you exercising?"

"I was dancing. Once I used to do it every morning and evening," I say. "Some people say prayers, but I dance. I suppose it must look amusing to you. Jazalu thought it very funny and primitive so I stopped."

"I don't find it funny," she says. "Are you sorry that Jazalu has gone?"

"No," I say. "I hope she'll be happy with Cassim and the money and the jewels she took. It was a relief to find her gone and the other things weren't important. We weren't close in affection. We were bed-partners, that's all."

"She stole from you?" she says, frowning.

"I'm not sure that you could call it stealing. Jonaas always gave her my cut of the money. Everyone has the idea that I don't understand such things very well," I say. "But Diam gave me money as a gift, not as a payment, for every important meeting and I understand it very well. It's hidden away safely."

She finishes her fruit. I wipe Yo-Yo's face and send him out to play.

Auria is strange today. She speaks with her voice and she alternates between looking at me intently and avoiding my eyes. There is an appeal about her manner although she doesn't cast her lure. She's contained and slightly defensive. She's the most beautiful and desirable woman I've ever known and this morning I'm very aware of it.

"You've never been to the Blue Place before," I say. "I'm very glad you've come."

She blushes. I've never seen her blush before.

"When I was with Hubertus I knew he was jealous of other men," she says quietly. "And when I went with Jonaas I didn't dare to be too obviously friendly with you. He truly hates you. It's fear that makes him hate."

"So?" I say. "What's changed that you're here now? And so early."

"I'm no longer with Jonaas—and I wanted to thank you for what you did for me," she says.

I think of those terrible burns which she endured for nine days and shudder within myself.

"You already thanked me," I say. "It's Noni and Christina you should be grateful to for looking after you so well and keeping infection away. Without them you could easily have died."

"I'm grateful to them and they know it," she says. "They were wonderful. And so were you."

"I did what I'm good at doing," I say.

"Saulus," she says, "are you angry with me?"

"Angry at you?" I say in surprise. "Why would I be angry with you? You know how I feel about you. I've always made it plain. It's Jonaas I'm angry with! When he gets back from Paris I'll have it out with him—"

"No," she says. "You mustn't confront him. I want no trouble between you and Jonaas. You must promise me that you won't do anything."

"No," I say, "I won't promise."

"Please, Saulus. I was the foolish one," she says. "I made him angry. I refused to be his lover any more and I was cruel in the things I said to him. I was too angry to be sensible and he was outraged. I misjudged my influence with him and brought trouble on myself."

"For Jonaas to do what he did to anyone—it was an evil thing!" I say. "Even supposing you'd survived without me to help, you'd be sexually crippled and perhaps even unable to control your natural functions! If it had been Meriem or Cecile or anyone it would be just as evil! How can I not be angry? I'll make you no promises! It was a wicked, wicked thing and I won't forget it!"

I pour the coffee, trying to calm the anger which burns in me.

She suddenly casts her lure.

"Don't do that!" I shout at her. "You've no need to do such a thing with me! I'm already yours for the taking, a fool without pride before you!"

She withdraws her lure and, trembling, I finish pouring the coffee. We sit down in silence, she as remote and untouchable as the goddess on the ceiling in the Love Palace.

"What makes you think that I'm unable to look after myself?" I ask. "You're as bad as Hubertus who thinks me so ignorant, so helpless, that he hovers over my every action—or thinks he does. I'm no longer a child, nor am I stupid. I've learned more than I care to know since I've been involved with things in the Outside. I've learned to face realities and I don't need mothering by you or anyone else."

"I hadn't intended to mother you. You're important to me," she says. "and it hurts me that you might become as the rest of the Clan are—criminal and vicious."

"I do what I have to do," I say, "but I see things differently than the Clan. I always have. You, of all people, should realize that."

She sips her coffee and her eyes are fixed on me strangely.

"Are you lonely without Jazalu?" she asks.

"No more than I was with her," I say. "We had nothing in common but bodysharing. I don't miss her. It's a relief to have her gone, to be honest."

She's very intent on me now.

"Would you accept me as a companion, Saulus?" she says. "As your woman?"

I'm so surprised that I gape at her.

"I can't live near Jonaas and I don't have any feelings for Hubertus," she says, "so I wondered—"

"Am I the only alternative then?" I interrupted. "Carolus has the entire North Wing to himself and there are quarters where Meriem lives."

"Don't be angry with me, Saulus," she says. "I come to you because I care for you."

I don't know what to say.

"A woman like me needs to feel secure," she says. "Hubertus is weak and Jonaas is strong. Don't despise me for that. And Jonaas was good to me at the beginning. But I never cared for them as I cared for you."

I say, "Why didn't you come with me when I first asked you, then?"

"You're so young, Saulus," she says, "and a year ago you were an unknown quantity to me. And someone like me, dependent on goodwill to live here, can't always choose what she cares to choose. You hadn't asserted yourself then. You were a half-savage child. And I thought you and Jazalu were truly lovers."

"Auria," I say, "I always cared for you, wanted you—I never attempted to hide that. But I'm not clever about women and I don't understand intrigues if that's what this is all about."

"Trust me," she says. "It's you I care for."

(I have deleted part of the narrative here out of respect for Auria Shasti. As a Psi-Org Operative in a difficult situation, her motives for allying herself with Saulus seem clear enough.

—J.T. Semantics Division)

I go down to the West Terrace to see the Red Trees. They are as high as my knees and "recognize" me. There are bones on the moss banks about them already but how much of those is due to Red Trees and how much is due to silver beetles is impossible to know.

Old Red Tree is quite dead and the beetles are already removing his drying body little by little. I'll miss him. I know that's foolish, but nature created part of him and I created the rest and I had joy in his life and his usefulness.

All the golden trees on the other side of the Crack and on the slopes are leafless, but the evergreens in the valley are as luxuriant as ever. I must direct the beetles to neaten the thickets which are becoming untidy and have branches across the path to the Blue Place. A protective barrier is needed but not a jungle which must be fought when we come and go.

Noni and Auria must surely have finished shifting furniture about by now, but I'd better not go back until I'm called.

I find Yo-Yo at the colonnades, showing Meriem

his boots. She says all the correct things to please him. Dear little brother.

More of the pillars have collapsed, but the remains are safe enough. I regret the passing of the colonnades. They were so handsome. Meriem says that Noni had to make a new pathway to the Tunnel because of slides from the steep slopes which lead up to the West Terrace.

I take Yo-Yo to visit Carolus who is back from Paris and tells me that Jonaas, Cecile, Mario and the Twins will return from Paris and Teheran soon. We go to visit Dundas, Lacy and Selene. Their relationship is a good one and I'm glad to know that they've taken young Francois in with them. He's such a bright, lively child now and Yo-Yo loves playing with him.

We visit Christina who now lives in quarters with Paul and Radley. Their relationship doesn't worry her and she plays mother figure to them. They are away in Rome with Cadmus, Mahmud, Guiseppe and Fatimah so she's having a wonderful cleanup of the place. She gives us work to do for the next hour and I have a good talk to her about The Hand and the activities of the Sewer Rats.

It's late when I pick Yo-Yo up and leave the Red Palace to go up the slopes to the Blue Place. The sun has set and there are lights shining at the windows. I can see Noni sitting at the table, so I lift Yo-Yo up and whirl him about until he squeals with laughter. Noni comes out in a fluster.

She mindspeaks, "I didn't realize it was so late! We've made it very comfortable and pretty, Saulus. I'm glad about you and Auria. I hope it works out for you."

I kiss her cheek and she hurries off. Yo-Yo runs in and says, "Oo!" in a wondering way. I follow and pause to stare. Everything has been shifted about, far more attractive to look at and very neat. There are new hangings on the walls and a few pretty ornaments arranged to please the eye. There is a certain elegance. Auria is cooking dinner and looks at me demurely.

"It's very pleasing," I say.

"Peasing!" says Yo-Yo squeakily. He tries so hard to learn.

"Go and wash your face and hands," I tell him and then I go to Auria.

I mindspeak, "I love you," and she comes into my arms.

(A gap of four days occurs here.

—J.T. Semantics Division)

It's the 15th Day of the 9th Month when I look at the calendar. It's well after sunrise and Auria still sleeps in my arms, but Yo-Yo is pushing at my back and murmuring because he's hungry.

I slide away from Auria carefully, pick Yo-Yo up and we go to the freshener, then dress. After I've made our breakfasts and coffee I take Auria's in to her. She stirs so delightfully and is so warm and scented when I kiss her that I'm tempted to stay. She is recovered from the sexual trauma and did not merely pretend to enjoy me last night. That's a very wonderful thing. And it makes me even angrier with Jonaas.

I go to clean up the table and then spend some time in the garden. Yo-Yo says, "Naughty," when I growl at him for poking at the moss banks to make the beetles run about, then he runs off, chuckling.

I go in and Auria is bathed, groomed and wearing her green gown. She doesn't care for it but knows that I like it. I snuggle her until she laughs and pushes me away.

"I've been thinking," she mindspeaks.

"How alarming," I return and she pretends to hit me.

"Jazalu acted as a kind of agent for you but she didn't take that idea far enough," she tells me. "The Clan all take you for granted and that's bad for you. The one thing they all understand is that things have to be paid for. So, from now on, I'll be your agent like Jazalu was and they'll pay for your services through me. I'll negotiate—oh, don't look so alarmed. I'll use my discretion. But it'll give you a position, Saulus. It'll give them respect for you."

"If you think so," I tell her. "And Jonaas must be included."

She looks worried at that.

"But," I tell her, "I won't have you going near Jonaas. I'll handle him."

She looks relieved but asks, "You won't do anything silly? I don't want more trouble with Jonaas for either of us."

"I'll be careful," I tell her. "He needs me to keep Diam happy for these last few Temple meetings so he won't be stupid, either."

This is said to reassure her. I've made my decisions.

"If you're sure—" she tells me. "And we'll keep the money here, so that you'll know where it is."

She shows me the lockable drawer in the big chest.

"I trust you," I tell her.

"No," she states, "from now on you'll have the key. If I need money I'll ask for it."

So I go and take the money given me by Diam from the hiding place in the moss banks and we put it into the drawer. She gives me the key and I immediately put it in her jewel box.

"Are you sure?" she asks.

"Quite sure," I tell her.

I'm tempted to show her the secrets of the Love Palace, but a selfishness prevents me. I want to keep my secret to myself for a time yet.

"I must go down to the meeting this morning," I tell her. "Jonaas came back last night and I want to be there so that they don't make my decisions for me. And I'll negotiate about my cut."

"Are you sure you can do that without bringing trouble on yourself?" she asks.

"Quite sure," I tell her, having made my decisions.

"I'll come down with you," she tells me. "I want to see Christina."

She goes for her cloak because the morning is chill and we walk down to the Red Palace holding hands. I'm so happy that she's with me that all my decisions are strengthened. We part at the West Wing and I watch her go down the corridor before I go into the Long Room.

Hubertus, Pearlman, Carolus, Fatimah and Guiseppe are already there in the Long Room. And so is Jonaas. He ignores me when I say good morning to everyone. I sit next to Hubertus.

They talk on the drug runs before the Faith is mentioned and I say nothing as visits to Rheims, Munich, Orleans and Paris are discussed. These are to be the Clan's last involvements with the Faith. It's interesting to hear of Diam's future plans for training new Solar II Ministers. There are even interested people from the Americas involved in this. Diam is amazingly ambitious.

Jonaas looks healthy and handsome since I treated him last. I can understand why women are attracted to him. It's not merely his Charismatic fascination. It's also a sexual vibrancy in his looks and manner. He has great charm when he wishes. That charm is evident now, as he talks with the others, complimenting them and making little jokes about their work. He manages people wonderfully, preferring to persuade rather than bully. Unless they're very stubborn, of course. Stubborn as I am.

For all his megalomania he's aware that he needs the Talents of the Clan. He likes to be in charge, to manipulate forces, but he's no fool when it comes to making himself liked as a person. Even Hubertus, who is so clear-thinking usually, is willing to be manipulated by him. Perhaps, if mama hadn't grown to hate him so and hadn't infected me with her attitudes, I could have established a better relationship with him when I was young. I've wondered, at times, if producing Yo-Yo was the cause of them souring each other or if it would have happened anyway.

He wasn't unkind to me in the early days. Only later, when I wouldn't fit into the niche he'd designed for me, did he come to dislike me. Too late to repine on that now. Now I have to assert myself with him.

They finish their discussions and rise to go. I remain seated.

Hubertus says, "We need to discuss safety arrangements for the meetings, Saulus."

"I'll come soon," I say. "I must speak with Jonaas first."

Pearlman, perhaps sensing something strange about my manner, rolls his eyes at me as he leaves. This is a warning not to do anything foolish.

The door to the Long Room closes and Jonaas stares at me coldly.

"Is this another form of dressing up?" he says maliciously. "You become more eccentric each time I see you!"

"This," I say, "is Dark Mode. I have three Modes which I use to keep from becoming too noticeable when I'm Outside. Dark Mode is very comfortable."

"Well, Black Man, what is it you wish to speak to me about?" he says and I brace myself, sweat coming coldly beneath my arms.

"You didn't wait for me before you began the meeting," I say.

"So?" he says. "Nothing will be different for you. The work is as usual."

"My cut will be different," I tell him. "I'm worth more than I've been getting."

He didn't expect this and is irritated. I smile at him in the way that he dislikes because I want him angry. This is the time.

"The Faith doesn't need you any longer," he says. "Be thankful for what you get."

"No," I say. "I've ceased to be grateful to the Clan or you. I don't need the Faith either. I'm quite content to remain in the valley and never go Outside at all."

He thinks on this, calculating, for some moments.

"It's only four meetings," he says. "Rheims again, Orleans, Munich and Paris. Temples are to be opened in Paris and Orleans and Diam wants them set off to a good start. I'll add five percent to your cut."

"Ten percent," I say. "What do you care? You'll extract it from Diam if he really wants me."

He's becoming angry. It isn't the money that upsets him. It's the fact that I'm bargaining with him.

"You have more ambition than I credited you with," he tells me. "I suppose I should be pleased that my offspring has some drive at long last. Very well, I'll make it ten percent."

"Instruct Hubertus," I say. "Now."

His anger rises vividly.

"You don't trust me?" he bellows.

I give him my biggest smile.

"No," I say.

Oh, he's angry! Good, good. So am I. But he isn't angry enough. I feel him mindspeak, presumably to Hubertus, before he glares at me.

"I've told him," he growls. "You're an ungrateful son."

"I'm not your son," I say. "My father was—"

"Get out of my sight!" he roars.

I feel a wave of heat hover, but it's withdrawn. I'm ready for him.

I stand up.

"I'll go," I say, "but not before I make it clear that I won't have you near Auria again."

"Auria!" he shouts. "You're welcome to my castoffs, you whelp! She should please you—I used her often enough so she must know something about pleasing a real man!"

"Why did you reduce her to the position of a Clan-servant?" I ask. "She's a Beta Calculator, a valuable Talent."

"She's a fool!" he rages. "Two jobs were botched because of her! Those sources of income were destroyed forever! I could never trust her Outside again! If I didn't know better, I could think she botched them deliberately! You're welcome to her! As far as I'm concerned she doesn't belong to the Clan at all!"

I smile big and make a laughter sound.

"How it must hurt you," I tell him, "that she should see you as such a worthless lover and reject you."

Oh, his anger swells!

The cloth of my kaftan blazes at my shoulder and

my skin sizzles with the heat, sending daggers of agony to my brain. It was only a warning from him. He teeters on the edge of control but his rage is not yet enough. My shoulder is an agony that stimulates me to ferocity such as I've never felt before.

"You're a bullying savage," I tell him. "You can't even face the truth of your own inadequacy with a woman!"

Oh, how his anger flares! Heat sears me terribly for a fraction of a second before I pounce! I seize him with that ferocity which I've nurtured for this moment! I enclose him in a vise of pain which is mine, magnified, and strike him with the power which my own anger gives me! My anger is rich, exultant, glorious and as vicious as his!

He begins to scream, eyes wide and staring, his face livid with anguish, his body writhing!

The pain is a momentary thing. He couldn't stand it for long and live. He's not familiar with pain as I am. I put an end to the pain, but I hold him with my mind, step forward and grasp him beneath the arms. Dark Mode is wonderfully strong and I exult in that strength now. I begin to shake Jonaas with a violence that makes his head jerk back and forth and his limbs flail! I shake him until he's limp and almost unconscious and I'm tired, then I release him and allow him to fall to the floor like a piece of soiled clothing.

I've not done yet.

I shout into his mind, "That was for what you did to Auria! You're filth! To do that to any woman was a vile thing, but to do it to Auria almost convinced me that I must kill you! But I won't kill you—"

I draw his reeling awareness into mine and show him part of myself. His mind shrieks in terror and I'm pleased!

"Look!" I tell him. "See what I've made! See the alarm pattern that I've imprinted over my basic survival instincts! See it! Next time you try to burn me, even if I'm sleeping or unconscious, that instinct to survive will attack you in full reflex so swift that you'll be destroyed totally! See it! There's your destruction! You'll be swept away like a leaf before the gale, a dust mote in the torrent!"

I release him into his own awareness again and keep him in cruel consciousness.

I tell him, "I'm neither your enemy nor your rival, Jonaas. I'm separate from you by inclination, needs and genetics. I have no wish to control the Clan or its activities and I'm prepared to obey you in all that seems reasonable. But I'm not a tool to be used as you please or a weakling to be bullied. From now on I'm an entity to be consulted and respected for my abilities. I don't belong to the Clan. I'm merely allied with it. From now on, I do nothing for you or the Clan without being consulted. And you'll never attempt to harm me or mine again."

I release him entirely and he becomes unconscious.

His wrenched muscles and bruises will be sore for days, but his shock will be worse. I know it's weak of me but my anger has faded so I reach out and touch his mind with pleasure-pulse to ease his trauma a little. Then I manipulate his body's healing capacities so that he'll be physically recovered by tomorrow instead of being incapacitated for days.

I pick him up, aware of my own physical weariness, and carry him from the Long Room, along to his own quarters and to his bedchamber. Cecile, putting cosmetics on her face, shrieks when she sees us. I put Jonaas on his bed. Cecile shrieks again, genuinely frightened of me. She is such a fool!

"Be quiet," I say to her. "Look after your man and pretend to have some sense!"

I go out, down the corridor and out to the colonnades where I sit, recovering and examining the burns which affect my shoulder, my face, my arms and part of my thighs. My kaftan is so scorched that it crumbles in places.

Presently, Auria comes running.

"Saulus! Cecile is making a great commotion! Jonaas is unconscious—" she mindspeaks and then realizes my state. "Saulus—what have you done?"

"Jonaas will recover," I tell her. "I made some things clear to him, that's all. I'll go up to the Blue Place and heal myself. Would you go and tell Hubertus that I'll come to see him later? I'm in no state to consult with him at the moment."

"You fought with him?" she says in alarm.

"I did what I had to do. There will be no more fighting between us," I say angrily.

I leave her staring in horror and walk slowly up to the Blue Place, reaction making me tremble. With food inside me, I repair the damage quickly but I'm tired. I bathe and then rest on the bed.

(This confrontation between Saulus and Jonaas has been verified by Auria Shasti, although her coloring of the event differs. Whereas Saulus regarded it as a venting of anger and vengeance, she saw it as Saulus asserting a new authority and independence, the first crumbling of Jonaas's authority within the Clan.

By this time it becomes quite clear that Saulus has capacities as a Super-Talent which rival those of the legendary Narnia of Syracuse who was, thankfully, killed during the Great Mistake, e.g. his ability to subdue Controls, suppress his own psi-field beyond detectable levels and to control the minds of other

Super-Talents, quite apart from his unusual Secondary abilities. He would have to be classified as a Unique on the basis of his Secondary alone. We must be grateful that his psychology is such as to confine him to self-preservation rather than to domination.

Following this part of the narrative comes a gap of 16 days.

The Solar Faith meetings at Rheims, Orleans, Munich and Paris attracted worldwide attention during the fortnight between 17-9-80 and 1-10-80, particularly for the establishing of permanent Temples at Rheims and Paris. There have been many developmental groups which have enjoyed great success, but I am sure there would be no argument about the growing influence of the Solar Faith as the most successful movement of its kind in modern times. It is not a religious order in the accepted sense (unless one could call it the religion of Humanity rather than the worship of a Divine Presence).

Many of its teachings derive from human-developmental groups and there is nothing very startling about its principles. Yet it is now becoming a worldwide organization and a valuable one since its views on the Medcenters have moderated. It has had a distinct influence on putting down the drug trade and motivating a general trend toward a healthier lifestyle.

Cassim Odemi is a problem which is, as yet, unresolved. If Diam Ennio is indeed Cassim Odemi, it is doubtful that it can ever be proven. He has covered his background expertly. The Psi-Orgs, along with most other authorities, have agreed that it seems most expedient to accept Diam Ennio's value as a social influence to the good rather than cause upheavals in the public sphere. Investigations show conclusively that, whatever the Solar Faith began as, it is now *perfectly legitimate and free of all associations with the underworld.*

Saulus's account of certain events that took place on the evening of 1-10-80 explain occurrences which had puzzled Central Security in Paris for some time. At 19th hour, a call was received from an anonymous source, claiming that the meeting to inaugurate the new Solar Faith Temple was to be influenced by illegal psi-activity. Particulars were given that a certain Hubertus Aanensen and his cohorts would arrive behind the central stage by car just prior to the meeting which was scheduled to begin at 20th hour. Despite previous "false alarms" and fruitless investigations, a Security Unit was sent from Paris Central Psi-Org and placed in position behind the Temple's central pavilion and in the public galleries.

At 19.56, Sensitives reported the arrival of a car containing two psi-positives and an unknown. The car paused at the dressing-room entrance to allow the unknown, a man in an usher's uniform, to alight and then move toward the exit gates. Enforcers and part of the Security Unit closed in on the car, forcing it to stop before it reached the gates. The car immediately exploded and a paralyzing gas of the H272 type was released. The two psi-positives escaped in the ensuing chaos. A large-scale search of Sectors 5, 6 and 7 failed to find them.

Enforcers and Psi-Org Operatives entered the dressing-room area of the Temple and found Diam Ennio, five Temple assistants, a choir of twenty-nine singers and three ushers. The ushers were immediately arrested and the others asked to produce their identi-discs and to submit to a brief psi-probe.

Investigation of Diam Ennio, his assistants and the choir proved fruitless. The ushers were also found to be legitimate and released later. It was not until half-way through the meeting that an observant Enforcer noticed that there were only twenty-eight members of the choir on stage. Subsequent esquires revealed that twenty-eight was the correct number of members and that additional choir uniforms were always kept available. When questioned later, choir members could not accurately describe the missing man other than to say he was negroid and heavily built. No one had queried his presence since several members of the choir had been recruited from other musical organizations for the evening. The matter had to be dropped for lack of further leads.

—J.T. Semantics Division)

* NINE *

I decide that I don't like Paris when the weather is so cold.

Pearlman slows the car and Hubertus says to me, "We'll pick you up at the White Cockerel at about 22nd hour. You know where to go?"

I say, "Main Promenade until I reach Rue Verite."

"About ten minutes' walk. You'll see a park opposite it," says Hubertus as I climb from the car.

I close the door, the car moves off and I start walking down the pathway toward the dressing rooms. It's very chilly. I must get a big coat such as Hubertus wears.

Something isn't right—

Several men suddenly appear from the shadows of the decorative gardens and a sonic alarm begins to squeal! I pause and turn to see that the car is being stopped by other cars near the gates and that two of the men are heading toward me. Too dark to see them clearly—

The car stops, there's a loud, thunderous noise and the car flies into pieces! Huge clouds of white smoke appear from the remains of the car and roll rapidly across a large area! I'm momentarily shocked until I realize that this is the escape mechanism that Hubertus told me of. The men heading toward me have stopped to turn and stare, also.

I'm galvanized into action!

I run to the dressing-room area at full speed, down a narrow passage and into a room where the choir is preparing. Panting, I tear off my jacket, transfer my identidisc, my money and the pretty stone which Yo-Yo gave me to my trouser pockets, search frantically for a spare choir robe and take one from a hook, hoping someone doesn't reclaim it indignantly. I haul it over my head, smooth it hastily and then hang the usher's jacket in its place on the hook. I calm my breathing, try to look placid, stare about and then ask one of the attendants about a gold sash. I'm given one and tie it about me quickly.

A man is handing out sheets with strange marks on them.

"Tenor or baritone?" he asks me.

"Baritone," I say, although I have no idea of what singing voice I have, and take the sheet he hands me. There are the names of three songs that I know, having heard them so often, and I realize that the sheet is marked with the tunes in music-script.

"Are you from the Elysees Guild or the Pigalle?" a man asks me.

I'm about to reply when Enforcers walk in, followed by two people in Psi-Org uniforms. My heart pounds and I fight for calm again.

One of the Enforcers shouts, "Please have your identidiscs ready for inspection! There will be a brief psi-probe! Please remain calm!"

Out in the corridor, some loudly protesting ushers are being removed by Enforcers. The choir, too, makes protesting noises. I'm frightened and sweat runs coldly down my ribs.

From somewhere down the passageway, I hear Diam's voice bellow, "Outrageous! This is persecution! Please don't touch my robe—your hands may not be clean! Are you a member of the Faith?"

The Enforcers begin to inspect the identidiscs while the Psi-Org people "listen." When it comes my turn, I present my disc and feel a mild mental intrusion so I present a mixture of thoughts to do with my terrible headache, my annoyance with the choir director for putting me into the back row instead of the front and how my wife will think this is very exciting. The Enforcer presses my disc against his recorder, which pips sharply, he returns it to me and I move away, looking at my music sheet and adjusting my robe.

The mental intrusion has gone so I move over to another man and say, "Gives you the creeps, doesn't it?" He growls, "Damned Peepers!" and tells me a long story about Peepers being used in psychotherapy for his sister years before and how she's as peculiar as ever, maybe even worse than before. I must ask Hubertus about psychotherapy sometime.

The choir director, the same man who was in Turin, comes in and makes a great fuss about the interference with the inauguration. There's a great deal of discussion among the choir members about what the Enforcers can be looking for. One of the women says, "Shame!" as she passes a Psi-Org man.

Diam's voice is still roaring about persecution and several anxious officials come in to see what the delay is. The last of the choir members presents her identidisc and the choir director begins to group us. He's very agitated and yells, "Places please! We'll never be ready! Where are the tenors? Ladies, stop talking,

please! What a shambles!" We shuffle into lines and
I don't know whether I'm with tenors or baritones or
basses, but no one seems to notice or care.

The Enforcers confer with the Psi-Org people and
my robe is wet beneath the arms. The director says
something about "giving plenty of fortissimo in 'Purify
the Earth' and to watch him more carefully in 'My
Life Is A Flame.'"

I can hear Diam shouting, "We must begin! We
must begin!" and a man runs in and says that the sonic
broadcasters are on and where's the choir? Some of
the choir members do soft singing exercises and the
director gestures at the officials.

We suddenly begin filing out through a passageway
and I follow, clutching my sheet of music and sweating. We come out into the bright lights of the stage
and I find myself entering the third tier of the choir
stalls and staring at a massed audience who all seem
to stare at me. The warmth of the spotlights is
unpleasant. So many faces—I look about carefully but
there's no escape.

The choir being in place, the director appears on
his podium and raises his arms, mouthing at us—I
think it's about fortissimo. This should be no problem.
Most of the songs Diam favors are fortissimo. He
finds the grandeur of noise inspiring.

The music begins, the director waves his arms at us
and we sing the song which I always think is so silly.

> "Oh, Divine Humanity,
> Purity our Goal!
> Discipline must surely be
> The saving of our Soul!
> Help me realize my worth,
> Guide me, guide me to rebirth!

Mind and body one perfection
Travelling in one Direction,
Humanity entire!"

I sing loudly like the others and the music thunders.
We begin to chant the Principles and I don't know
them all because Diam has added to them of late and
I haven't taken much notice. I mouth silently, not
really listening to the words.

I wonder where Jazalu is. She was in the audience
at Munich but didn't know me because I was in Pale
Mode. Are Pearlman and Hubertus safe? Did they
get away? What will I do if they were caught?

The trumpet theme begins and the lights change,
fading on the choir as Diam comes onto the stage in
a blaze of light. We sing "Oh, Cosmic Light" which
is not so silly as "Oh, Divine Humanity." Many of the
audience sing, too.

Diam raises his arms at the end of the song and
begins to talk. His voice is so rich and honey-smooth
with dark undertones. He's such an actor. He's mag-
netic, holding his audience wonderfully. He's trans-
formed from being a mere man and becomes a
fountain of philosophies and entrancing words. He has
such conviction and is so compelling that I almost
forget who he is. But I'm soon bored from having
heard it so often. I look at the audience and wish I
could be part of it instead of being up here. My headache increases from holding in my psi-field.

There are still Enforcers in the galleries and the
two Psi-Org people are moving about on the second
level. Oh, it's unbearable to be standing here not
knowing what's happened to Hubertus and Pearlman!

I can see Jubal/Barbier up on the second level,
quite clear in the soft lighting. Who's that with him?

I know the face—it's one of the men who spoke to me when my face was bleeding in Dijon. He was a Control! But he's not in uniform . . . Why would Jubal be friendly with a Psi-Org man? Hubertus would be interested. They're moving out of the second level now—I'm certain it was the same man. The heavy brows and that interesting nose—Oh, they're coming down to the lower level. It definitely *is* the Control! They're moving out into the reception area now—

Diam has finished his opening harangue. We sing "My Life Is A Flame" which, at any other time, I would enjoy because it has a thumpy tune. We kneel for the first prayer and meditation and the audience rustles to its knees, too. Diam intones the words of the Faith Prayer and then begins the chant which sounds like "Om Pardmi Hom." I like the reverberation of it and find it very soothing.

But then I discover that there's a gap in the choir stall behind me. I can't resist this opportunity to escape. The subsonics are on now, adding to the sonorous sound. I shuffle back on my knees very carefully and look about. There's a space behind the choir and more steps going down. I hitch my robe up carefully and wait. The sonorous, hypnotic sound goes on and on—

The tinkle-bell sounds come and then a silence of brief meditation. Diam, his voice soft, begins the prayer about the Discipline of the Mind. That goes on and on and on—the tinkle-bell sounds come again, the music begins and the choir stands suddenly to sing "As One Truth" in soft voices.

I shuffle sideways on my knees behind the choir and crawl quickly to the steps. I ease myself down them until I'm hidden from everyone, then stand and move to the door at the bottom of the steps. It opens easily and I'm in a corridor. Another door here leads me into the choir room again. No one about.

I haul the sash and robe off and hang them on a hook. My undershirt is soaked with sweat and my head pounds from holding in my psi-field. I risk opening my psi-field a fraction and close it again because there are others not too distant.

I need a jacket or an overtunic. I see a large overjacket which I recognize as the director's and grab it. No—too tight. I put it back. Oh, here's a dark gray cloak! That'll do! I drag it about me and, hastily tie the neck cord. It's a very fine cloak, long and full, with slits to put the hands through. I arrange it and go out into the passage quickly. Still no one about.

Outside, there are still Enforcers in the service area, close to the gate. I flatten myself in the shadows against the building. The remains of the car are being removed and the gates are closed. What to do? What to do?

I edge along the side of the building, eyes on the Enforcers, until I come to the little garden, recently planted with shrubs and trees especially for this inauguration. I hide there for a moment and see that there's a small gate in a metal fence that cuts the service area off from the front of the building. I move quickly. Oh, wonderful! It opens easily and I'm out in the approach to the Temple. And there's the brightly-lit Grand Promenade with the cars moving silently along it. There are people about and I walk by with all the confidence I can muster until I'm on the walkway.

It's a cold night and there are no stars. I walk briskly until I feel it's safe to release my psi-field. Ah, the relief! My headache begins to ease. I saunter along casually. My chronometer says 20:52. Strange how one loses the sense of time during periods of tension. Diam's audience must make its own miracles tonight.

I quicken my pace and soon I see a little park. I cross the busy Promenade on a pedestrianway and look for Rue Verite. Ah, there it is! I turn into a little alley and there's a bright sign that says WHITE COCKEREL in Francaise and Universal. I go inside. It's very pretty and fake-homey and warm. I go to a booth in a corner and slip into it.

Ah, so good to be quiet and still! The sonics are soothing and the servex is one of the simple kind that I understand. I dial for coffee and a flavored carbohydrate which come quickly. I enjoy both and then doze.

My chronometer shows the creeping time. At 21:35, I decide I must change my Mode. I have the roll of money that Diam gave me in Munich so I pay the servex and go to the freshener. There's no one about so I go to a cubicle, lock myself in and begin the change.

I'm quick at it now. It takes me ten minutes and Dark Mode's extra bulk is consumed easily. I flush the wastes and dark hair away and go out to the basins. My blonde hair needs combing, but I have no comb so I use my fingers as best I can, wash my face and drink greedily. My trousers are too baggy for comfort now. I go back to the booth, dial for more coffee and wait.

There are several people in the restaurant now. The 22nd hour comes, but no Hubertus and Pearlman appear. I'm beginning to grow anxious. If only I knew whether they were caught or not! I dial for more coffee and carbohydrates. People come and go, a robomech services the empty booths and it begins to rain lightly outside. At 22.35, I pay for my food and leave the booth, resolved to risk going back to Diam at the Temple.

As I walk through the restaurant, I see that a young woman stands inside at the doorway, staring carefully at those who come and go. She's expensively but showily dressed, wears a great deal of cosmetic substances on her face and her hair is coated with a gold lacquer so that it appears to be an ornate helmet. She's familiar and I pause, trying to remember where I've seen her before. Then I remember. Hubertus brought her to me in Rheims and I removed terrible knife scars from that pretty face. I was in Pale Mode in Rheims.

I move close to her.

"Justine?" I say.

She looks at me suspiciously.

"I'm not for sale, pretty boy," she says.

"I'm Saulus. Hubertus brought you to me to have the scars removed," I say. "Look at my eyes. I never change them."

She looks carefully. She's frightened.

"We talked of gentians," I say. "I'd never seen the flower before and you had one pinned to your coat. I said that the color reminded me of my beloved's eyes."

Her face draws into a strained smile. She's terrified of me.

"Very well, Bogy-Man," she says. "I believe you. You said you liked my blonde hair—"

"No," I say, "I admired your brown hair. It was worn free, pretty and curly."

"Follow me then," she says, satisfied. "Your friends ran into some trouble. You're to come with me."

"Are they safe?" I ask.

"Must be," she says with a shrug. "They got a message to The Hand about you."

She goes out and I follow. The rain has stopped and it's very cold. I shiver and pull the cloak about me.

"Why are you wearing a woman's cloak?" she asks.

"Is it a woman's?" I say. "I had to escape quickly so I grabbed what I could. Is there a place where I could buy some clothes?"

She considers.

"There's a maleserve on the Promenade," she says. "Do you have money, Bogy-Man?"

"Yes," I say and show her the roll of money-slips.

She walks briskly and I follow. Her own clothes are light and impractical and she's very cold. I take off the cloak and swing it about her shoulders. She stops and stares at me.

"It's a good cloak," I say. "You'll be warmer with it on. I'll warm myself from inside."

She ties the cords carefully and smooths the material, then walks on briskly.

Presently, we come to some brightly-lit shops and an arcade. There are very few people about.

"In there," she says, pointing. I look into the shop and it's all mirrored and featureless.

"I've never bought clothes in a shop before," I say. "Will you help me, please?"

She shrugs and walks into the shop. I follow and the mirrors become alive with color.

A computer voice says, "May I help you?"

Justine says, "This man needs clothes."

I say, "Trousers and a jacket and a big overall coat such as Hubertus wore when we met in Rheims. In quiet colors and not too extreme in style."

"Standard fashion trousers," Justine says to the colored mirrors. "Blue-gray."

"Size 48D," says the computer and a picture of trousers in a pale blue-gray appears in one of the mirrors.

"Much darker," says Justine before I can comment.

Oh, it's fascinating! Pictures of clothes appear, colors and styles change in the mirrors and Justine becomes as interested in the articles as I do. We choose dark, blue-gray trousers in a stretchy fabric, a heavy overtunic in rich blue, two shirts—one blue and one scarlet—and a wonderful overall coat in gray, just like the one Hubertus has.

Justine disapproves of my sandals so I bow to fate and get gray, soft boots that come up to my mid-shins. Justine says I need hose and underwear so I ask for two sets of hose but don't order underwear. She peels money-slips from my roll and puts them in a slot, a door in the mirrors slides open and I go into a little room where I put on the fine new clothes that hang from a valet-mech. When I come out, carrying the other things, she takes more money from my roll and buys me a carryall, toiletries and a comb from a little bar.

She's no longer afraid of me, which is a relief. I think this has to do with the fact of me being so ignorant about the clothes and looking to her for help. She counts my money roll and makes me put it in my trouser pocket.

"Do you usually carry so much money about with you?" she asks.

"I don't usually carry any," I say.

She says, "It's a lot to be flashing casually. You'll need to keep a good eye on it where we're going or you'll find it missing."

"And where are we going?" I ask.

"Somewhere safe," is all she says.

We go out and the cold wind sweeps along the Grand Promenade as we enter it. We go to a hire-car rank and climb into one. She directs it to somewhere I don't know and we speed through the streets so fast that I can't look. I put my hands over my eyes.

"What's the matter?" she asks. "Are you ill?"

"How could I be ill? I'm afraid," I say. "I don't like this kind of hurrying."

"That's stupid," she says. "This is quite safe."

"Yes, but I don't like it," I say. "Did you know that you have something wrong with your left hip?"

"Don't peep at me, you damned mindmucker!" she says, suddenly angry and nasty.

We are silent for a time.

"I've had a pain in my hip for a long time," she says suddenly. "Is it something serious?"

"It's what people call arthritis," I say. "It's part of your body condition."

We're silent again for a time.

"Could you fix the arthritis?" she says gruffly.

"Yes," I say.

"Would it hurt " she asks.

"Did removing the scars hurt?" I say. "I try not to hurt people. Shall I fix it?"

There's another long silence. I risk taking a look at her and she glares at me because she's afraid of me again.

"Yes," she says.

So I begin. This keeps me from thinking on other things too much.

The car stops in a dark place and we get out. Water laps one side of the street. A canal? The car moves off and I see that cliffs of brick and stone rise enormously high on the other side. She takes my arm and leads me down some steps, almost into the water, to a big tunnel where water runs and falls into the larger waters of what must be a river.

I adjust my sight and see that there's a narrow walkway along one side of the tunnel. A very strange odor of staleness comes from the stone. She takes my arm and leads me along the walkway which is very narrow and wet.

"This is a stormwater drain," she says and her voice reverberates in the strange place.

It's very damp everywhere and there are unhealthy gases in the air. We come to a cross-tunnel and I can see faint, luminous patches on the walls at intervals. Justine produces a tiny flashlight and we cross a metal bridge over flowing water, walk along another tunnel, cross another bridge and then into another tunnel.

I'm lost now. I don't think I could find my way out of this place by myself.

"Where are we going?" I ask and my voice echoes strangely.

"To the world beneath the world," she says.

It's very cold and the air is horrible. I apply myself to her arthritis and follow closely. We walk for a long way, changing tunnels sometimes and walking up steps once or twice. It's very confusing.

She stops suddenly, shining the torch at the roof of the tunnel. I see that there's a tiny device like the ones in some public buildings that Hubertus calls spy-eyes. She shines her torch back on herself and then me and says clearly, "Justine and the Bogy-Man."

We wait and then a man's voice says, "Acknowledged."

We walk on, around a great curve in the tunnel, then there are steps up and yet another tunnel. She stops before a blank wall.

A door, very cleverly hidden in the wall, opens and we go through. Here there are glo-lamps shining and men waiting, shadowy and menacing. They wear rough clothes and I glimpse fierce eyes taking me in. The tunnel stinks of unwashed humanity, gases and decay. Suddenly we are at steps and go up into a much loftier tunnel. There's more light here and several people who seem to slither away from us as though afraid.

Justine takes my arm again and says, "The word's out about you."

We come into a large, open area where several tunnels meet and a lot of people peer at me and back away. Some are so dirty that they don't look human. Some are maimed, some have minor-Talent psi-fields and some have guns which frighten me. The open area has a vaulted ceiling that rises into darkness and I think these tunnels are very old because they appear to be made of bricks and are very worn about the floors.

"Wait here," says Justine and leaves me suddenly to go into a side tunnel. We all stand silently in that horrible place and the people have eyes like sharpteeth, all staring at me. Fear makes me angry when I see the guns pointed at me.

I say, "Put the guns away or I'll decide you're my enemies. I do very nasty things to enemies."

My voice sounds loud in this place. After a moment, the guns are lowered, but the eyes remain fixed on me. It's a relief when Justine returns.

"Come," she says and I follow her into a side tunnel, then another, then through a door into another huge room.

It's brightly lit and there's clean air. The room is bizarre, tawdry and colorful. There are rich, dirty brocades and bright, silken hangings, a vivid red and yellow carpet, gilt and black furniture, a dusty chandelier and ornaments enough to confuse the eye with their variety. There's a bed, hung on chains like a cradle, so that it swings slowly and gently, and crowded with grubby, brightly embroidered cushions.

And there's a body, obese and grotesque and distorted, supported by the cushions and dressed in brilliant silks. It's a man, his legs and one arm withered and twisted, his bald head huge and lolling. He has eyes like white stones and a pale skin which is clean and smooth. His normal arm has a beautiful, elegant and manicured hand, rings glittering with jewels on every finger. And there's a young-old girl, pretty and slender and exhausted-looking. She sits by the bed and stills its swaying as I come in with Justine. Justine leaves quickly.

The distorted man wheezes, "I'm The Hand. Come forward and let me see you, Bogy-Man."

I move forward to the bed. His perfect hand reaches, grasps my coat and pulls so that I'm drawn to lean on the bed close to him. He smells of a sweet, artificial perfume. The beringed hand reaches to touch my face and trace my features.

"Sit," he says and I sit carefully on the bed. The young-old girl peers at me intently and I'm aware of a psi-field which can only be his since she's unTalented.

"They say that you can make miracles, Bogy-Man, and that you're very dangerous," he wheezes.

"I'm dangerous only to enemies," I say. "I won't harm you."

He chuckles at that and says, "Oh, I'm not afraid of you. I'm your pass to safety. And what could you do to me that birth and age haven't already done? Hubertus sent word that he was having difficulties and wanted you looked after until he could come for you."

"I'm very grateful," I say.

He suddenly offers mind-contact to me. He's an Alpha with something of the Calculator about him. And I realize that he's linked to the girl in such a way that he sees through her eyes.

I meet his contact and feel him draw back momentarily.

"You're a Super," he mindspeaks.

"Yes," I reply.

"I'm told that you heal people, that you can change their identities," he tells me. "I have pain frequently. Pain can be the domination of one's entire existence."

"I can imagine that," I reply. "May I look and see the source of your pain?"

"Yes," he tells me, "but carefully. I'm near death and what little life remains is still sweet."

I touch him lightly with pleasure-pulse and then examine his body. There's a wealth of malfunction and atrophy, but he's not as near death as he imagines. I close some of the nerve pathways in his spine and withered arm so that pain ceases.

"Ah, is it death you give me?" he mindspeaks and I'm aware of his fear.

"No," I tell him. "Only release from pain. I could do much more. I could give you a strong body, sight and health. Shall I do it?"

He's full of terror and suspicion at that.

"You go too fast, Bogy-Man," he tells me. "I know no other existence. I've been like this for forty years. What do I know of the things you offer?"

"I can make you anew," I reply. "But I'd want something in return."

He's agitated. The girl moves to wipe a sheen of sweat from his forehead with a soft cloth. I send him a moment of pleasure-pulse and he calms.

"I think," he tells me, "that the old writings might

be true. You're the Demon of Temptation, come to mock me and bring cruelty."

"What nonsense," I reply. "I have capacities which I use to help, not harm."

He withdraws his contact from me and is silent for a time.

He wheezes, "I'll think on what you offer. Go away, Bogy-Man, and leave me to consider your temptations. Go and sleep. Simone, take him to Honore and Magda and tell them to care for him. Tell Justine to come in to me."

Simone beckons. I stand and follow her out into the passageway and through a warren of places until we come to a small, dimly-lit room which has a bed in it. She leaves me and I undress, hanging my clothes on a chair and arranging my carryall so that I can reach it easily.

There's a basin of hot water on a stand and a receptacle for wastes beneath it. I empty my bladder and am washing myself when Justine comes in. She stands and watches as I dry myself.

"What you were saying about my arthritis," she says. "Will you do it?"

I've already done it, but it doesn't seem wise to say so.

"Yes, but you'll have to pay me for it," I say.

She stares and then begins to undo the catches of her dress.

"No," I say, "not that way."

"What then?" she asks.

"Get a message to Hubertus," I say. "Tell him not to come for me yet. Tell him I'll write a message to the Rome address when I want to return."

"I'll see to it," she says slowly. "When will you fix my arthritis?"

"Tomorrow," I say.

She leaves.

I'm so tired that the bed, hard and lumpy and slightly unclean, feels wonderful as I settle in it. The noise of people moving about and talking in the tunnels fades from my awareness. I think briefly of Serenel, of Auria, of Yo-Yo—

(*The 2–10–80 is entirely edited from this transcript since Saulus talks of little that is pertinent to the narrative. He satisfies Justine that her arthritis is cured, talks of Serenel and discusses "bodychanges" with The Hand, comments rather vaguely on the activities of the "Rats" and rambles on, at great length, about the unhealthiness and dirt of the tunnels.*

From his descriptions of the tunnels, it would appear that they are no part of any sewage system, but are more likely to be old service tunnels for the drainage system, somehow overlooked in the rebuilding of the area.

Psychology Division 2 entertains the idea—not without justification—that Saulus was learning to resolve much that had been confusing and contradictory to him before this period. It becomes apparent that he is no longer a frightened "innocent" from this time on. He seems to have realized his self-sufficiency and it becomes obvious that his reasoning is less affected by his emotions than was the case previously. His moral code, a very individual matter, did not preclude him from being ruthless when the need arose, nor was he so ready to accept things at face value any longer.

—*J.T. Semantics Division*)

✷ TEN ✷

I awake and it's cold and dark. I get up, put on my boots, wrap myself in a blanket and turn on the glo-lamp. I go out into the corridor and along to the latrine. Two of the Rats scuttle out of my way and look surprised. Don't they think I need to go to a latrine?

I go into C-Tunnel and find that Honore and her children are already stirring. I nod to her and take the big container to fill it with water from the spigot, put it over the sonic agitator and adjust the dials as Justine showed me to. When it boils I replace it with another big container so that Honore will have hot water, too.

I go back to my room with the container of hot water and wash thoroughly, dress in my new clothes and groom my hair. I go to empty the water in the latrine and put the container back in Honore's niche. Then I wait for the thick porridge which she's begun preparing. She's none too clean, but her porridge is tempting this morning. I eat a large dish of it, putting on plenty of sugar and butter.

Then I look at the youngest child who was so sick yesterday. He's quite better, but shrinks away from me in terror.

"Why are you afraid of me?" I ask. "I'm the one who took the sickness away."

But I realize that it wouldn't matter what I said. I'm the Bogy-Man and all these people are afraid of me.

I go to see old Alouette, who is stirring among her filthy rags and sits up when I speak to her. She grins at me, showing her strong new teeth, her eyes clear of the cataracts I found there. She's wary of me, but not afraid like the others.

"Are you still certain you wish to help me today?" I ask. "It won't be pretty or pleasant."

"Huh!" she says. "Don't let appearances deceive you! I was a medcenter nurse! I don't mind a bit of a mess!"

I leave her with a smile. I like Alouette better than anyone I've met in a long time.

Going back to my room, I find Valentine, the midget, dressed in his child-clothes and looking frightened at the sight of me.

"Did you manage to get the food concentrates, the chemicals and the plastex sheeting?" I ask him.

"Yes, Bogy-Man, yes," he says and shrinks away from me.

I go back to my room, make my bed and tidy my few things.

My chronometer says 7:30 when I go the The Hand's door and knock firmly. Justine, scrubbed and pink and dressed in a severe bodysuit, opens the door, her hair minus its lacquer and drawn back into a severe bun. She looks much younger and quite pleasant. Simone, still painfully underweight and wide-eyed, is wearing a plain overall and a scarf about her hair. I must do something about Simone.

"You don't need to stay," I tell them. "Alouette and I can manage."

"We're staying," says Justine firmly.

"I want no distractions such as fainting, vomiting or hysteria," I say. "If you get in my way I'll put you out of the room."

"You're frightening me!" The Hand wheezes.

"We aren't as weak as you seem to think," says Simone.

"I know I'll be capable," says Justine. "I know you'll do as you say."

The Hand cackles and wheezes, "Justine regards you as something of a god, Bogy-Man!"

He's a great mound of white skin and flesh, naked and grotesque and freshly washed on his bed of grubby cushions. The room is too warm so I turn the heater off and The Hand sees this through Simone's eyes.

"I can't bear the cold!" he whines. "I want the room kept warm!"

I say, "What you want is unimportant. What I decide is what will be if you wish me to do this thing."

Alouette, surprisingly clean and wearing a white overall, comes in carrying the plastex sheeting.

"Spread it on the table," I say, taking off my overtunic and rolling up my sleeves. "Are the food and chemical mixtures ready?"

"Yes," says Justine, indicating the trolley which is piled with concentrates.

"I need him on the table," I say. "Help me to lift him."

The Hand is like dough and so heavy that it takes the four of us to lift him from the bed and onto the table. He has terrible bedsores despite the care the women take of him.

"I'm cold!" he whines, "And the table's so hard!"

I lift his shoulders and put cushions about him so

that he's bolstered in a half-sitting position. He's very frightened and sweating freely. I send him pleasure-pulse until he calms.

I say to him, "In a few moments I'll put you into a trance state and when you become aware again you'll be able to participate in a whole new life."

"What will I look like, Bogy-Man?" he wheezes.

"Like a man," I say and take his mind, placing him in pseudo-sleep.

Simone sees him become limp and is afraid.

"Don't hurt him, Bogy-Man," she says. "He's my master and my child. He's all I care for."

"Don't be afraid," I say. "Justine, you'll need water and cloths to clean him with and a bucket for wastes. He'll also need water for drinking at regular intervals. Go and get them while I prepare his heart, lungs and digestive system for what has to be done. Simone, you'll feed him as I tell you. Alouette, you measure out the chemical mixtures and concentrates as I instruct."

I put myself into that state which is two-in-one and direct all my capacities to examining, planning and preparing The Hand.

I begin by setting his heart rate and endocrine system as I need, then I manipulate his digestive system. I begin utilizing the excess body fats, liquids and proteins and then Simone begins to feed him as I instruct. He gorges and I help him convert materials while Alouette supplies chemicals and protein pastes at key points. For me, the awareness of time ceases.

Sweat and oils begin to appear on his pale skin, he begins to defecate and urinate. I am dimly aware that Simone weeps and Justine curses from time to time. Alouette murmurs and mumbles at them bracingly, but I don't know what she says.

The frame is a complex matter since it must be developed as the distortions are corrected and the muscles shaped. His body alters slowly, the usual discharges and problems appearing and fading in carefully regulated cycles, the mass of him shrinking.

The frame takes shape, the sinews, tendons and muscles forming about it little by little. I use my hands to assist shapes and direct trends. I talk and instruct with a tiny part of myself, the rest being all directed to this joy of manipulation and re-forming and establishing of balances.

When the basics are done, I realign the major organs and endocrines, rebuilding where necessary and balancing again and again until all is perfection. I manipulate the supportive tissues and build the muscular outlines, dimly aware that the huge lump of doughy flesh has gone. At this stage I begin to model the body to match the exquisite perfection of that one beautiful hand. His torso and hands, his newly shaped skull and body features, his physical characteristics, all become distinct and refined.

I arrange his face, body hair, genitalia, teeth and the newly-formed eyes to become part of the harmony which has come into being. I inspect the results carefully. At last I am satisfied. I return his state to normal function slowly.

He is a no-age adult, unlined and perfect, when I finish. I almost regret the completion because the directing and utilizing of patterns has been so satisfying. I return my own state to normal awareness and reorient myself to the greater world.

Alouette is wearily helping Justine to clean away the last of the mess and Simone is white with exhaustion.

The Hand is a handsome man, dark-haired and pale-skinned, with a solid but compact build and a strongly-boned face in the Roman style which Hubertus envies. Women will find him beautiful and men will admire him.

"It's done," I say and realize that I'm very tired.

The room stinks and it's very cold. I turn the heater on and wait while the women finish washing him. Then Justine and I lift him and carry him to his bed. Simone arranges the cushions and draws the cover over him while Justine adjusts the ventilator fan and Alouette cleans the table and plastex sheeting. My chronometer says 13:35. Almost six hours to do it all. I could have completed it with less time, but the truth is that I indulged myself.

"He'll sleep for an hour," I say to the women. "You were all quite wonderful. I admire you all."

I walk out and go to my own room, asking Honore for hot water as I pass her niche. My clothes are dirty and stink of excrement. In my room, I strip and bathe gratefully when Honore brings the water. She scuttles away as though she really thinks me to be a demon! Fool of a woman!

I climb into bed and sleep for thirty minutes. When I wake, I dress in my old trousers and new boots, wrap a blanket about myself and go back to The Hand's room. Simone is dozing in a chair, Alouette has gone, Justine has changed into a pretty gown and let her hair down. The room smells sweet.

I make minor adjustments to Simone's metabolism before I eat a little from the concentrates still remaining on the trolley. Simone wakes and looks at me with eyes which are full of wonder.

The Hand wakes and I feel his psi-field "color."

I mindspeak to him, "No, don't use Simone. Open your eyes and see for yourself."

He blinks and cries out at the light, one arm coming up to shade his face. I send him pleasure-pulse and place a hand on Simone's shoulder to prevent her from running to him.

I ally my mind with his and our body sits up weakly. Our hands draw back the covers and we look at our body, touch it, stroke it. Our legs move.

"I can't!" his mind cries to me.

"You can," I tell him and our legs swing to the edge of the bed. Justine runs to help us.

"Don't touch him," I tell her.

Our feet meet the floor and the bed sways. We stagger to our feet and sway unsteadily. We look at our body and The Hand cries out in amazement. I give him pleasure-pulse and we stagger to the long mirror that Justine brought yesterday. We look, heart pounding, and our brown eyes blink in terror/wonder.

"Is it true?" he cries aloud, our senses chaotic.

"Yes," I tell him. "You are whole."

We turn, we look, we turn again. Our arms wave, we bend, we stamp, we sway. His emotions are too large to be contained. We begin to shout and weep.

The door swings open and men rush in fiercely. We turn to them, arms wide. I calm him with pleasure-pulse.

"Speak to them," I say. "They come to protect you and now they don't recognize you."

We walk toward them, our arms still wide.

"I'm whole!" The Hand shouts, weeping. "I'm whole!"

They gape and gasp and more crowd in to see. Some cry out, some murmur or curse in wonder. Simone runs to the bed and takes up the cover to sweep it about our body. I'm not sure if this is because of modesty or to protect, but we hold the cover as she wishes. We put an arm about her and stare into her face. She is white with fear or great joy, I can't tell which. Still holding her, we walk back to the bed. We release her and sit.

I remove my control from him and am myself again.

I mindspeak to him, "You'll be weak and clumsy until you learn to control your body. You'll lack coordination until you practice and you'll grow tired until your muscles become used to movement. You'll feel overly sensitive until your senses settle. Keep practicing. And find Torros, the Lifter, for me as you promised."

I collect my overtunic and move from the room. More people are crowding in and they hardly notice me as I push between them. There are many more, dirty and ragged and intent, when I go into the passageway. They shrink away and one lifts a gun at me, but I pass and return to my room.

I sit on the bed and Justine comes in. She's been weeping.

"You made a miracle," she says.

"No, you don't understand at all. Nature is the miracle," I say. "I merely have the skill to persuade and manipulate it. My shirt and trousers are soiled. Where will I wash them?"

She laughs a little hysterically.

"You'll have the finest clothes that money can buy, Bogy-Man! I'll see to it," she says and runs to put her arms about me in a hard embrace. Then she takes my soiled clothes and runs out.

Alouette puts her head around the door and smiles at me. "Come in," I say. "You were a truly wonderful help."

She's pleased at that. She comes in and I notice that she's used some cosmetics discreetly. She hands me a scrip-sheet.

"A message from your friends," she says. "The radio man was too scared of you to bring it."

It's a message from Hubertus and reads, "Do not play games, Saulus. Our friends will bring you to Rome tomorrow—Hubertus."

"Can you get a reply to Hubertus?" I ask Alouette.

"The radio man will," she says, and hands me a stylus.

I write on the back of the scrip-sheet, "I will not be coming. I have things to do. Ask Auria to look after Yo-Yo. Tell her I love her. I will write to the Rome address when I intend to return—Saulus."

Alouette takes the message, looks at it and says, "You aren't leaving then?"

"I want to find Torros, the Lifter," I say.

She says, "The Hand has sent out word to all the Rats about it. Outlaw Talents of big power don't wait about for the Psi-Orgs to notice them, Bogy-Man. He may have gone from Paris."

"He isn't powerful," I say. "He's an Epsilon. I can only hope he's here. Why are you among the Rats, Alouette? You don't belong."

She shrugs and says, "Who's to say who belongs and who doesn't? I killed some people. I used to live in a lovely house, in a good neighborhood, and I was well thought of as a medcenter technician at Paris Central. Times change, things happen, Bogey-Man— I've been with The Hand ever since he organized us sixteen years ago."

"Where does The Hand come from?" I ask.

"Who knows?" she says. "I've heard that he was in a freak show in Marseilles and that he organized the first Rats about him there."

"Are there many Rats?" I ask.

She grins and says, "Hundreds of them, Bogy-Man.

All sorts. But not all here. They're all over the city and elsewhere, up, down, roundabout."

(This last statement is possibly true. Despite improved methods of crime prevention and the cooperation of the Psi-Orgs the problem seems ineradicable. It is a sad reflection on our society that there is still a large percentage of our population willing to ignore social decency and legitimacy in order to satisfy their desire for drugs, sensationalism or unearned luxuries which these criminals exploit so successfully. The service tunnels of which Saulus speaks and which are, apparently, a haven for so many criminals have been searched for without success. Saulus refused to give further details about their location during questioning following the compiling of this transcript.

—*J.T. Semantics Division)*

Alouette comes back from visiting the radio man and brings me real coffee and tasty savory cakes. We sit on my bed and enjoy them. Alouette is shrewd and no longer afraid of me at all. I notice that she's changed her clothes and looks very neat and respectable.

She says, "There's a great fuss going on. Simone's dressed The Hand up and they're all having a big rowdy out there. The word that you made a miracle with him will spread and there'll be a lot of curiosity. Rats will come from everywhere. Not all of them are fools like some of the vermin here. They'd pay to get things done, Bogy-Man. You could make a lot of money."

"Would The Hand allow that?" I ask.

"If he got his cut," she says.

I have a lot of money, but more would be a convenience. I have plans.

"I'll organize it if you're interested," she says.

"We'd have to discuss terms with The Hand and his lieutenants. Shall I talk to them, Bogy-Man?"

"Yes," I say, "but don't promise them too much. There'll be no more big changes such as I did with The Hand."

She laughs, nudges me with an elbow and says, "I won't promise anything! If you make things too easy they don't value them. You've given enough free samples about here. You leave it to me."

We go to the Common Room and look about in the side tunnels. There's a lot of noise and roistering coming from The Hand's room and all about it so no one bothers us. Most of the tunnels are damp or are being used, but Alouette shows me a recess at the top of some steps that lead nowhere. It's dry and gets fresh air, but it's very cold.

"You'll need a heater and a curtain to make it private," she says. "And I'll find some chairs for people to sit on while they wait. Maybe you could burn some incense and I'll find a couple of glo-lamps so it won't be so dark."

I agree.

Prime Mode is convenient but easily recognized. I'll need a disguise.

"Could you find me a mask?" I ask. "Hubertus says that a grain of mystery is more saleable than a large lump of what's known."

"I'll make a mask," she says and we go back to my room.

Justine has brought me some clean clothes and more food. I change and am very fine in heavy silks and brocade.

"Your other clothes are being washed," she says. "The Hand wants you with him to celebrate."

"Yes," I say, "he already mindspoke with me about it."

(I have deleted part of the narrative here since it is not of general interest. Saulus is less disapproving of the excesses at the "rowdy" than he would have been in the past and talks rather sadly of the Rats and their lives which he sees as "wasteful." He worries about Simone and "rearranges weak balances" without her knowing. He puts The Hand to sleep at 19th hour and goes to eat with Justine and Alouette. He then talks, at length, of how he misses Serenel and goes to bed in a state of depression, having politely refused Justine's offer of body-sharing. He omits mention of the next few days and gives no clue as to the date when he resumes.

It may be of interest to note that Alouette, the woman who had been a medical technician at Paris Central and who stated that she "killed some people," is probably Alouette Coltain who vanished in 2263 after killing her lover and another woman with a knife. See the Coltain File 770–161–140, available from Central Files.

—J.T. Semantics Division)

I awake and am aware of the stink of this place and of the cold. I put on the luxurious lounge-robe and slippers, given to me by The Hand, and go to the latrine, then Honore's niche for hot water.

My new chronometer says 6.25 and none of the Rats are stirring as yet. I take the hot water to my room and strip to wash. Alouette immediately sits up to eye me from her bed.

"You're thinner and getting too pale," she says critically.

"That's not true," I say. "My pattern is exactly the same as when I arrived."

"Then it's time you did something about it," she says firmly and snuggles down again.

I have no answer to that. Alouette's logic defeats me at times.

Alouette looks quite handsome and pleasant now that she's clean and takes care of herself. Since I rebalanced her systems and corrected her heart she looks much younger and has far more vitality. Her soft, white hair is very pretty since Justine cut it.

"Why are you up so early?" she grumbles.

I turn the heater on for her and say, "The first marks arrive at 7:30, so stir yourself. You'll need a good breakfast because it'll be a long day."

"And a rich one," she says with satisfaction. "We're doing well, eh?"

I think of the large sum in the account at the Banque Internationale which Justine helped me to open and say, "Yes, we're doing very well. What will you do with all your money?"

This is a game she loves to play. She gets out of bed and puts her new red robe over her red night-gown, then sits on the bed.

She says, "A little villa, somewhere near or in Vichy, comes first. And none of this modern furniture, oh no! Solid furniture that can be polished, that's what I'll have. And a real garden with a little fountain."

She chatters on while I wash and dry myself, then rub my skin with the oil which Justine brought for me. It has a wholesome, woody scent and it helps me to keep warm without burning up too much energy. Alouette, now talking of the carpet for her future living room, gets up to rub oil on my back. She's becoming very motherly towards me.

"Put some clothes on before you catch a chill," she

says and her tone is so like the one Jazalu used to adopt that I smile.

I dress quickly in the bizarre black and yellow robes which The Hand provided and go out to empty the water in the latrine. I get more hot water for Alouette and return to find her looking very depressed.

I put the water down, open my arms to her and say, "What's wrong, little bird?"

She comes to be held close and says, "I will have it, won't I, Bogy-Man? I want to leave this place. I've spent too long skulking in the shadows."

"With your new fingerprints and the new Registration-identidisc you'll be able to do as you please, little bird," I tell her.

"Why did you choose me as your partner, Bogy-Man?" she asks.

"Who else would have the patience and the style to handle the marks so well?" I say. "Besides, I like you more than I like anyone else here. And did I choose you or did you choose me?"

"Will you come and see my villa when I'm a respectable woman again?" she asks.

I say, "I'll try, little bird. Get ready now or you won't have time for a good breakfast."

I leave her and make my way to the Bogy-Man's Niche as they all call it. The smell of incense clings to the yellow and black curtain and I light several sticks of it to dispel the odors of the tunnels. The benches and my chair need a hasty dusting, then I sweep the floor, adjust the music-wheels and the tinkle-bell and adjust the pink glo-lamps. I see that my mask is ready, check that the slop buckets are clean and then go to see the slovenly Honore about breakfast.

It's almost 7th hour when I take the porridge in to Alouette. She's ready in her blue robes and her hair is concealed beneath a glittery scarf which she fancies gives her an "occult" look. I kiss her cheek and give her a bowl of porridge.

Honore makes excellent porridge and I'm very hungry this morning.

There's a tapping at the door and little Valentine pokes his head in.

He says, "Jacques says to tell you that Tonio and Mercier are on their way with the first marks and some of the city Rats."

He's growing quite rapidly now.

I finish my porridge, clean my teeth and go to my niche to turn the heater on. The scent of the incense is everywhere and Lydia and Fernand are readying the chairs in the side tunnel, their robes covering their dirt.

"Comb your hair," I tell them and they glower at me.

Alouette comes at 7:25 with a list and I hear the shuffle of feet as the marks arrive in the side tunnel.

She says, "A nose job, a failing potency and someone balding for a start. They're important Rats, Bogy-Man, so there's no money in it, but The Hand needs their cooperation."

I nod, put on my mask and sit in the chair. Alouette ushers the first mark in with great solemnity, bows to me and departs. The work of the day begins.

It's a day very like the others. Cosmetic changes, sexual problems, balding heads, physical distortions, glandular balances, fingerprint alterations and such. I sip some coffee at 10th hour and resume until 12:30 when I have my rest period.

When I go back to my room there's a healthy lunch of salad and uncooked meat for me and unhealthy fries for Alouette. She looks guilty when I stare at these.

"Just occasionally won't hurt, will it?" she says.

"Not while I'm about to assist your digestion," I say, "but what happens when you continue to eat like this after I'm not here to look after you?"

She eats her fries defiantly.

The Hand comes in, glowing with excitement and goodwill. He tells me that Justine took Simone and him into the Central City to buy clothes and preens for my approval. He looks very handsome and I note that his coordination is excellent now.

"No word of Torros?" I ask.

"No," he says, "but contacts in Sector 12 have promised to help."

"Are you really trying to find him or are you only interested in keeping me here to make money?" I say.

"I keep my promises, Bogy-Man," he says. "At least we traced him to Sector 12."

At 13:30 Alouette and I resume work and are busy with a steady stream of shills until 17:30 when the last one is ushered away. We go to the room and Alouette drinks a little brandy before she changes into her fine, new clothes. She's going to the Residencies and Land Offices to look at pictures of villas near or in Vichy and will then meet with Morian to have dinner at a restaurant. Morian is a minor 'path who makes a living from telling fortunes. I like him and Alouette finds him congenial company.

I change into my ordinary clothes, put on my Hubertus coat and go for my usual brisk walk along the tunnels to the back street where the grille is situated. The watchdog man allows me out and I walk through the back streets in the darkness until I come to the bare little park in the Rue de Saint Marie, once a place where Hubertus met leaders of the Rats. Here, I'm told, old people enjoy the sun on fine days. I sit on the little bench beneath the bare trees and enjoy the solitude for a time. The sky is dark, without stars since it is going to rain very soon.

I think of my mother and wonder who it was she mated with to produce me. I remember her last words about the Paris Central Psi-Org and his Security number.

It seems strange that he's my enemy, living his life with no idea of my existence. Can she have imagined, in some beautiful future which she saw in those last moments that I would find him and say, "Father, I'm your son, Saulus!"? The idea is so ludicrous that it depresses me. I go back to the grille and back to the world of the Rats.

There's a celebration going on, the usual rowdy which follows the weekly division of the spoils, in the Common Room. There'll be hangovers and sour faces in the morning. I avoid the rowdy and go to my room to await The Hand's usual summons. This comes late because he's busy with his lieutenants on spoils night. Magda comes at 17:40 to tell me he's ready. I go to his room.

A great deal of the clutter has gone but the room is still overdecorated and heavily perfumed. The table is neat with sparkling crystal, fine ceramic dishes and silver eating utensils on a pure white cloth. There's the pale, mild wine which he knows I'll have a glass of and a huge bowl of lightly cooked meat and vegetables. There's white, tasteless bread for him and the dark, grainy bread for me, a jug of milk and a large, mild cheese. Simone, now looking much better, serves The Hand, but Justine and I serve ourselves.

The Hand mindspeaks to me, "Eyes of one's own

are so much more satisfactory than looking through the eyes of another and the pleasure of moving my own body is inexpressible! Is it forgivable to adore one's own body and senses? I've reached the stage of such pleasure in mine that I want to show it to everyone and experience every delight of it! I want to be envied, admired, loved for my body! Is that such a very bad thing, do you think?"

"I'm sure you could be forgiven," I tell him. "I notice that plenty of people feel much the same way without the justification you have. Enjoy it while you're able. A few years of abuse, normal neglect and self-indulgence and you'll look and feel like any other man of forty hard years' living."

He protests, "I won't let that happen! I'll take care of myself!"

I tell him, "I doubt it. You've too much of a taste for soft foods and soft living conditions and you're lazy. Your body was designed to be put to good use, not coddled."

He frowns at me, thinking on what I've said. I notice that he doesn't touch the overly-refined bread and has only one glass of wine.

He asks, "Is your life so disciplined that you devote your energies to maintaining your health?"

I tell him, "Of course not. With me it's a matter of inclination and plain common sense. Abuse offends me because it's more obvious to me than it is to you."

He tells me, "If you stayed here with us I'd make it worth your while to look after me. And there's plenty of money to be made from what you do. You could be a rich man, Saulus."

"I have plenty of money," I tell him. "I couldn't live like this for long."

"You don't have to live in the tunnels," he protests.

"There are prettier places to go if you have the contacts and enough money."

"But it would still be a hole-in-the-wall existence," I tell him. "I don't wish to remain a glorified Rat. I want my valley."

He shrugs.

Justine, realizing that we've been communicating, says, "Did he tell you?"

"Tell me what?" I ask.

The Hand mindspeaks, "We found your friend, Torros. He was captured by the Enforcers a few days ago and the Psi-Orgs have him now. He'd been living with a group of Outlaw Talents—nothing big—living like cockroaches in Sector 12 where the amusement parks are. He'd been very ill. He didn't try to avoid capture."

My heart is beating faster. I say aloud to Justine, "Where are they holding him?"

She says, "Our Psi-Org contact says he's being held in the hospital section of the Detention Complex in Sector 2. They'll interrogate him when he's well enough."

"Perhaps they already have," says The Hand in a malicious way, "and they already know about your precious valley."

"No," I say. "Hubertus implants a psychological block in every member of the Clan so that they can't disclose the whereabouts of the valley. I'm the only one he can't do that to. But the Org may learn about this place."

"No," says The Hand, "I implant the same kind of block in any Rat who knows of this place. He won't be able to blab. He's only an Epsilon 'kinetic."

"Where's this Detention place?" I ask.

"Why?" says The Hand. "Do you think you're going

to walk in and take him out? It's a fortress of Controls, guard-Talents and electronic alarms."

"But," I say, "you have a Psi-Org contact. I wish to talk to this contact."

"You're a fool," says The Hand.

I finish my wine, stand up and excuse myself politely. I leave them staring after me and go to my room. The stink of the tunnels seems suddenly worse and the noise is unbearable.

I close the door, undress and go to bed, covering my head and thinking anguished thoughts for a long time.

* ELEVEN *

(There is another gap in the narrative here. What follows occurred on 18-1-81 and further details may be gleaned from Paris Central Psi-Org Files in Reports A902-4 and A902-5.

—J.T. Semantics Division)

I awake and dawn is some time away. I go to the freshener and bathe, then inspect the new face in the mirror. I'm thankful that he's not so very different to Prime Mode, but it's the first time I've changed the eyes and the brown ones make me seem a stranger to myself. It's an interesting face, but one that indicates a certain lack of intelligence.

I dress in the dark trousers, shoes and undershirt, comb the thinning brown hair as he does and put on the Hubertus coat. I check the stun gun, my identidisc, my wallet, the water bag and the little pellets. I remove all signs of my stay in the hotel, which is easy since I have no fingerprints, put my few toiletries in the rubbish chute and leave the room.

At Reception, I present my identidisc, pay my tariff and check that my carryalls are already consigned ahead. There are very few people about at this hour. My chronometer says 5:30.

I go to a small restaurant and dial a good breakfast which I enjoy. I pay for it and leave again. I go to the nearest maleserve and buy underwear, trousers, shirt and a jacket suitable for Torros and leave with a neat parcel. Out in the street there's a cold wind and the sky is dark. I think it will rain later. Few cars are in the traffic lanes and no people are to be seen on the walkways.

My chronometer says 6:10 as I begin walking the now-familiar journey to the Detention Complex. I walk so briskly that it's only 6:20 when I arrive at the pretty little park. The sky is growing very light now.

I stand about, waiting for the passenger shuttle which brings my quarry. He's a careful man and drives no groundcar of his own. It's very cold, but not so unpleasant as yesterday. I practice his voice and his walk yet again and finger the stun gun in my pocket. My anxiety makes it necessary to calm my glandular activity.

Two passenger shuttles arrive and leave again before his shuttle comes. It's a relief to see him step off and walk across to the park. I avert my face until he passes, my psi-field retracted tightly.

Every morning of my study he's followed the same routine. He walks across the grass and strolls beneath the bare trees, looking up at the little birds which huddle there. Then he goes to the same seat near the fountain, sits and puts his carryall beside him. He takes out the bag of crumbs and makes little whistling noises, then he casts the crumbs and the birds come fluttering.

Yesterday, in Pale Mode, I even sat with him while he fed the birds and we talked about them. He loves birds. I'm sure he's a very pleasant man but, more important to me, he's also the convenient Control I need.

He follows the usual routine without change. I wait until he casts the first handful of crumbs. No one is about but another shuttle will arrive in five minutes and there'll be several who get off at this stop. I have to take the risk now!

I open my psi-field, already running toward him, my heart pounding. I'm quite close before he notices the movement and looks at me. The birds rise, fluttering in alarm. His eyes widen, I feel that psi-field of his and then I use my Secondary before he can react further. He falls slowly sideways, unconscious, as I reach him.

I take his carryall and empty it of its contents—his lunch, another bag of crumbs and some sports equipment—take off my Hubertus coat and stuff it in, having removed the stun gun, the bag of pellets and the water bag. On top of the coat, I manage to squeeze the parcel of clothes for Torros, but have difficulty closing it again.

I shove the sports equipment under the seat, then toss the Control's lunch and the crumbs for the birds. I undo his weathercoat and have difficulty getting him out of it, but even more difficulty in getting his uniform sash and jacket off. I'm panting with anxiety by the time I manage this. I put the tunic on in haste, tie the sash and then don his weathercoat.

A quick search of the pockets finds his identidisc, his Control-pass, his wallet and other things which don't matter. I transfer the stun gun, the water bag and pellets to the tunic, do up the weathercoat and take his right hand to examine the fingerprints. Duplication takes precious time.

The hungry birds are descending on the bag of

crumbs and his discarded lunch as I pick up the bulging carryall, hurry to the emergency-call unit at the shuttle stop and press the button.

A woman's voice says, "Name and identinumber, please."

I shout, "There's an unconscious man in the park by shuttle stop twenty! He's been robbed, I think, and he's breathing strangely! Send a med-unit, quickly!"

I walk away briskly, hearing her voice saying something about staying calm and asking my name. The Control, the birds collecting in a great crowd before him, is sprawled on the seat with only a shirt on his upper body and it's very cold. I hope he won't become too chilled for his health before the emergency-call people come to find him.

I tidy my hair as I cross the road by the pedestrianway in great haste. On the other side, I slow down and adopt his walk and manner. I partially withdraw my psi-field and make the pseudo-Control pattern, very aware that it won't deceive if examined too closely. I see the laneway and walk down it. It's exactly as was described by Justine. I quickly shove the bulging carryall under the bushes near the glassite doors and take a deep breath.

The doors slide open automatically and I walk into the staff entrance of the Detention Complex. A chronometer on the wall says 6:40. I'm ten minutes early. There are several Enforcers about. I nod to one and head toward the registration-mech.

"Birds not hungry this morning, Mal?" an Enforcer calls.

"There was a bunch of tourists feeding them!" I call. "Tourists at this hour!"

The Enforcer grins. I take Mal's identidisc and place it in the slot, press my hand against the dull metal plate and wait. There's an electronic pip, I remove the identidisc and walk through as the inner door slides open. I'm sweating so I calm myself as I go through the business of the identidisc and finger-prints on the other side of the door where a sign says DAY STAFF.

I walk along the corridor, getting the Control-pass out of the weathercoat as I near the cage. I come to the grille and present my pass to the Enforcer there. He barely looks at it.

"See you at the handball court at midday," he says as I go into the cage.

"Today I'm unbeatable," I say, grinning as I walk to the other side and present my pass to another Enforcer.

He says, "Early today, Mal?" and I repeat my remarks about tourists. He laughs and opens the cage door for me.

I take the pass and walk along the corridor, looking for the cross-corridor with the sign that says Section 4. I turn right into it and make my way to the third elevator. The doors slide open, I press the button marked 3 and the doors close.

The elevator shoots upward to Level 3, the doors open and I walk out. I turn left as instructed and pass several Controls discussing some sort of duty roster on a notice board.

"Good morning, Mal," someone calls.

I waggle my free arm without looking around, pass the sign that says THERAPY 2, pass the doors marked SECURITY, pass the carryway rising to Files and turn left into the second corridor.

The notice states DETENTION B-RED and there are two Controls at the inspection post, one of them being the contact.

Relief floods me briefly and I register my finger-prints on the plate, grinning. He's looking at me very intently, wondering if I'm Mal or not.

"Plenty of birds this morning, Mal?" he says.

I say, "Too many tourists in the park," and he knows it's me.

His eyes show a moment of worry but he says, "I'm off-duty in a few minutes. I'll see you in the Rest Room—the rosters may have to be changed."

I say, "Nothing drastic, I hope. I like day duty."

The inspection gates open and I walk through, nodding to the other Control. I pass two doors on the left, a barred corridor on the right, turn left into another corridor and left again into what is obviously the Rest Room.

The tables are empty but for an Enforcer and a female Control in the corner. I nod to them, take the weathercoat off, transfer the identidisc and pass to the tunic and hang the coat on a peg. I dial for coffex at the dispenser and find a table, glad to see that the others are leaving. My chronometer says 6:50 and Mal's duties begin at 7th hour.

The contact arrives at 6:55, sits down and mutters, "I must have been insane to get mixed up in this."

"Why?" I mutter back. "You're healthier than you've been in years and you have the increased libido you wanted. And maybe it'll teach you not to double-deal. Tell Jubal that the next time he tries to betray his friends I'll see to it that the Enforcers learn the truth about his activities. You can be grateful that I didn't tell The Hand about your part in it."

He says, "I swear I didn't know that The Hand was involved with the Faith!"

"You do now," I say.

"Are you sure you can handle this?" he says. "Block

B is low Security, but it's not easy. If one of the Controls gets suspicious—"

"Did you get the uniform?" I ask.

"I went to see your friend an hour ago. He has it on under his prison uniform by now. The car's a blue Multi. You'll find it in the street next to the park. Torros has the keys. Leave them in the side pocket when you change cars and I'll collect it later."

He leaves me and I calm my glands once more.

I wait until my chronometer says 7:05 before going out into the corridor and left to the cells. I'm thankful that Torros is only an Epsilon or he'd be in a high-Security section instead of the hospital section.

I go to the office. I remember to call the Control there "Howie" and ask him how his back is. He tells me in great detail while I wait for the changeover med-officer to arrive. She's late. She doesn't arrive until 7:10 and Howie is moaning about his bad leg by then. I pick up the electronic keys to the cells and smile at her. She doesn't smile back but signs the registry book and walks past me with a cold glare.

I take the stun gun from my tunic.

The stun gun makes a "brrrr" sound as I shoot her and then Howie. They fall unconscious, sprawling to the floor noisily. I take the pellets and the water bag from my pockets, break the water bag seal and go through the door into the cell area. The Control on duty at the observation desk looks up and says, "You're late, Mal."

"Sorry," I say. "Got held up by the med-officer."

I drop the water bag and the water splashes out across the floor. I drop the pellets in it.

There's a loud hissing and great clouds of white smoke erupt and billow. I shoot the Control with the stun gun and run for the fourth cell. Smoke covers the ceiling scanners and fills the area with rolling whiteness within seconds.

I fumble with the electronic keys and yell, "Torros, it's Saulus!" as the smoke envelops me. The door swings back and I see him vaguely as he rises from his bed and starts dragging off his prison uniform.

"Saulus," he yells, "how did you manage?"

I yell, "Hurry!"

The smoke, slightly acrid, is a white fog everywhere. I can hear the other prisoners crying out in alarm as I grab Torros by the arm. We run through the acrid whiteness to the office. I open the door and take him through, then pull one of his arms over my shoulder.

"Pretend injury," I say and open the other door. Smoke billows through the office and into the corridor, pursuing us. I bellow, "Fire! Fire!" and two startled Enforcers gape as smoke billows toward them. One shouts and runs by, the other follows. The yells of the prisoners can be heard quite clearly.

More people appear in the corridor as Torros and I move by. "A fire in the cells!" I bellow and Torros staggers very effectively, covering his face as though affected by the smoke. We move quickly to the cross-corridor and turn right toward the inspection post.

The Controls there are looking alarmed at the noise they can hear. Our contact sees us coming and drops his smoke bomb. There is a great thump and smoke billows up as he opens the gates. We run through, coughing at the choking fumes.

There are suddenly people running and colliding in the smoke and the shouts are full of panic. Torros and I reach the elevators just as the doors of one open and two Enforcer-women emerge. I hear them exclaim as I push by and press the button. An alarm begins to wail as the doors close.

Torros is saying, "Oh, shit! Oh, shit!" as the elevator drops and I'm suddenly as calm as I've ever been. The doors open and we walk out. The cage is ahead and the alarm sounds deafeningly.

I open my psi-field and embrace the Enforcers. They collapse. I use the electronic keys to open the cage, fumbling to find the right ones. We walk through and Torros is still swearing.

"Smooth your hair," I tell him, "and straighten your tunic."

I drop the keys beside one of the unconscious men and we go to the outer door. I use the identidisc and my palm on the plate and the door opens. The Enforcers in the reception area collapse as I embrace them with my mind.

We walk outside, I pick up the carryall from beneath the bushes and we move quickly up the laneway.

Torros is very pale and thin. I see that he's dangerously malnourished and still has a fever caused by some virus.

"Are you able to hurry?" I say.

"I feel weak—dizzy," he says faintly.

I stimulate his glands as much as I dare, taking his arm. We walk to the end of the lane and across to the pedestrianway. I can hear the alarm wailing until we cross above the road.

The blue Multi car is where the Control said it would be. There's no sign of Mal in the park. Torros takes keys from his pocket and opens the car as I take off Mal's sash and tunic hastily and put on the Hubertus coat. I put the stun gun in my pocket, drop the garments on the walkway and climb into the car beside Torros. He looks very ill.

I give him the parcel of clothes and say, "Change into these. I'll see to everything."

I take the keys from him, activate the car and put the controls to automatic. I say, "Coordinates 430 and 723, in Sector 5," and the car moves off slowly, choosing its lane and beginning to build up speed. I polarize the windows and assist Torros to change. This isn't easy in the confined space, but we manage. I pack the uniform into the carryall and tuck it into the baggage space, then take Torros by the hands and begin changing his fingerprints to match his new identity.

He asks, "How did you manage all this, Saulus?"

I say, "I'll tell you the story sometime," and put him to sleep. I finish his fingerprints, do what I can to improve him physically—although I can't do much without nourishing him first—and then begin changing myself to Prime Mode.

I'm halfway there when the car slows. I depolarize the windows and discover we're at the Rue D'Or. I put the keys in the side pocket, wake Torros and then help him out of the car. He staggers and looks at me haggardly. I close the car, put his arm over my shoulders and half-carry him along the street until I see Alouette's red car. She opens the door and I help Torros in. She's startled at my half-changed appearance, but makes no comment on that.

She says, "All well, Bogy-Man?"

I say, "All well," and resume the change to Prime Mode as she starts the car and gives it coordinates. By the time I've resumed Prime Mode completely the car is travelling very fast and Torros has gone to sleep without my help. The scenery flashes by and I find this too worrying to watch.

Alouette combs my hair and says, "He looks sick, Bogy-Man."

I say, "He is. When we get out of Paris, find a roadhouse and we'll put up there until I've made him well."

I put one arm about Torros and the other about Alouette and allow myself to doze.

(As some of the Council already know, the escape of the Epsilon 'kinetic, Torros Kinaidy, from the Detention Complex of Paris Central on 18–1–81 caused a major investigation into Security procedures. The breakout was so simply managed that Security has made major changes to its identification management since then.

No clues to the identity of the Control who assisted in the escape have been discovered, due to inefficiency in the recording of roster systems and substitutions made among personnel for their own convenience. Roster systems are now arranged and recorded directly by Paris Central computers.

Another gap occurs in the narrative at this point, but no clue to the duration is given.

—J.T. Semantics Division)

I awake early and go to the freshener, bathe and dress before I go to check on Torros in his room. He's quite restored, so I leave him sleeping and go to the kitchen to make breakfast and coffee.

Through the window I can see trees and the wild tangle of a garden in need of care and it's lovely. The sunshine is weak, but it cheers me.

I've been happy helping Alouette take possession of her house and move her new things into it. There's a lot of work still to be done, but it's a pleasant house and I hope Alouette will be happy here.

My letters to Hubertus and Auria should reach Rome today. I hope they won't be too unhappy about my decision, but I feel I must look about and learn while I have the chance. Money isn't a problem so perhaps I'll buy a car, a small one like Alouette's, if Torros agrees to navigate until I've learned how to manage manual controls.

I hope he'll learn to accept Angelo's death quickly. I'm sorry I told him before he was strong and feeling his usual vitality, but I don't know what else I could have done when he asked so many questions.

Alouette says she'll drive us to Limoges, but this would be silly when we can buy a car in Vichy or take an overland shuttle. My luggage will be there and it'll be pleasant to have some clean clothes.

I miss Serenel, but the prospect of really seeing some new places instead of merely passing through them is very exciting. I know so little of the world. It's time I learned more.

(I have edited the transcript somewhat extensively at this point since it will hold little interest for the Council in any practical way. A precis of the activities of Saulus and Torros Kinaidy seems to be in order here.

Saulus was very distressed at hearing how Torros was forced to scavenge for a living and philosophizes at great length on the iniquities of civilization in general. They left Alouette's home on 7-1-81 and travelled by overland shuttle to Limoges where they indulged in the usual tourist activities and bought a small car. There is a jump of ten days following this and they are in Bordeaux when Saulus resumes. The narrative then jumps to Zaragoza and no date is mentioned. Saulus insists on calling the area "Espana" although where he learned to call it so is puzzling since it has not been called that since the Euroasian Amalgamation in 2173 A.D. References are made to Marseilles and Barcelona so it can be presumed they

passed through these cities before reaching Zaragoza.
The commune he and Torros Kinaidy spent time in
could be any one of several and the casino mentioned
is unnamed. I have included the following sections in
the narrative because they indicate something of the
personal development Saulus was experiencing.

—J.T. Semantics Division)

Torros is still asleep after the religious celebration
last night as I go out into the early morning to visit
the little shrine which so fascinated me yesterday. I
find it surrounded with wreaths of drooping flowers
and strange little offerings of food and small personal
belongings. The Madonna has a chipped hand which
someone has tried to conceal with a garland of daisies
and the paint on her blue robe is peeling, but she
obviously means a great deal to these people.

I like this cluster of dwellings and the simple people
who live here and work together in the commune.
I'm glad we decided not to stay in Zaragoza because
I wouldn't have come to know things that I've learned
here.

All my life I've been with other Talents or people
who were criminals and refugees from the societies
of Euroasia. My ideas were colored by theirs and, in
the back of my mind, I've always tended to equate
the unTalented and all those beyond the valley as
enemies. And, under certain circumstances, they are,
but my biases have been dispelled by much that I've
discovered here. In a small commune, one notices
things which aren't so apparent in a large city. It
seems to me that, no matter where one goes, people
are much the same in their needs and basic interests
and failings.

Here it's the family, religion and custom which are

most important on the surface, but having the opportunity to look around and learn in small places has shown me, for the first time, how highly organized and clever "civilization" is generally.

Governments, politics, the social services, the financial structures—they may not always be ideal but they protect people and bring order where there could be chaos. And then the customs and local rules add to this so that there's security in the future.

The people here seem simple in outlook and rich in the things that make for contentment, living much as their ancestors did centuries ago. There are few signs of technology here but the soil is rich so they live well on their simple agriculture. And, overall, they are very kind. Despite being regarded as rather eccentric tourists, Torros and I have been generously accepted among them.

But, in their way, many are confined by religion, social custom and superstition. The better educated and more successful among them are sneered at behind their backs because they don't fit the accepted mold of the commune. Those who don't ascribe to the accepted religious framework or who dare to break with custom are regarded as undesirables. And yet these educated and successful prevent the rest from ignoring the progress which goes on and which benefits the whole.

The bulk of the Clan are much the same in their narrow attitudes when one thinks about it—and perhaps that includes me—with Jonaas and Hubertus and the cleverer ones dragging the rest in their wake, rightly or wrongly. But I'm trying to learn, at least. As I see it, on the one hand there are those few among humanity who see further than the generally accepted way of things and try to drag the vast majority along with them while, on the other hand, the vast majority create that stability which protects the whole. There are advantages in this system. I wonder if it's always been that way? And where do I belong in such a scheme of things?

The old woman who sold me the big hat yesterday comes coughing and snuffling to the shrine and I nod to her.

"You have a bad chest infection," I say to her. "Perhaps you need medical treatment."

"Ah!" she snorts. "I don't hold with medics and their nonsense! All they do is dole out pills and take my hard-earned money! The Madonna will look after me."

This is the same attitude that makes the Solar Faith so successful. I see that the infection is what they call pneumonia and do a small rebalancing to help her recover from it. A medic could cure her with simple antibiotics. But she follows her biases even though they could kill her. Poor Madonna, she will probably be credited for the woman's rapid recovery. I have no patience with that. Faith healing has its limitations, as even Diam is discovering now that I'm no longer about to provide miracles. He no longer decries the medical profession and even has medics on his staff.

We make our own prisons, some seeking security and comfort in what we know or, even like this woman, in superstition. And I realize that, up until now, I've been much the same. The difference is that I seek experience so that when I go back to my lovely prison, I'll have had experiences and collected knowledge to take with me. I'll understand more and, perhaps, will be able to put it all to use in some way.

Torros wishes to leave tomorrow and I've agreed.

I must force myself to examine new things, to investigate the puzzles which have presented themselves since I've been Outside.

The Law Enforcers seldom come here because there's so little crime and the Psi-Org Investigators come even less. As I walk along the cobbled streets and look at the quaint houses, I remember what the fat man who makes the pastries and the wonderful bread told me at the ceremony last night, after he showed me the street where the family of Talents was clubbed to death almost fifty years ago.

He said, "Mental gifts beyond the normal capacities of our forebears are an aberration, a distortion of nature! We don't tolerate such things and have remained untainted because we follow the teachings of our church and our community without deviation. Those who will not follow these teachings place themselves in Satan's Way!"

I did not dare make a comment. He had a mild psi-field which would have been noted by any Psi-Org Investigator. It had been so self-depressed and self-inhibited that he had lost the ability to use it, even supposing he had ever tried. He had maimed himself. How many others have maimed themselves in a like way, I wonder?

Why must the clairvoyant gifts be so frightening or distrusted by the ungifted? Surely the gifted should be encouraged to develop and be utilized for the betterment of those who are not so fortunate instead of being so rigidly confined by the Psi-Orgs? Education of both the gifted and the ungifted should surely be a priority in this. More and more Talents appear in the societies as the years pass. How wonderful it would be if, someday, every human being could be gifted! What societies humanity would have!

The cafe where the excellent coffee and breakfasts are sold has just opened. As I hesitate, the pretty woman whose breast cancer I destroyed two days ago comes out and begins putting white cloths on the little tables. I decide to stay for coffee and the excellent fruit they serve here.

I feel badly about having scolded Torros so angrily. *Me* scolding *Torros*! But to exhibit his Talent so obviously in the casino was dangerous and foolhardy! He's sulking now because I insisted we leave with the credit he's already won so dishonestly. Someone may have become suspicious and it's a well-known fact, told to me by Hubertus, that the casinos often cooperate with the Psi-Orgs in keeping an eye out for the 'kinetically gifted. And I don't like the idea of preying on the unprotected.

"All very well for you!" he growls at me as we find a robocar. "You seem to have plenty of credit, but I haven't!"

"Then use my credit," I say. "I've enough for both of us."

"I won't be under any obligation to you!" he says crossly. "I've always paid my own way!"

"Then we'll find work," I say, "and you can earn credit honestly. We could work on the cargo barges and get to know the kind of people you found such good company in the wine bar last night. Our identities are secure and it could be very interesting. Or I could give you the credit to make your way home to Serenel alone if you're unhappy with the idea."

"And find myself unprotected from Jonaas?" he snarls. "Not likely! And you wouldn't last for five minutes without me to keep you out of trouble!"

I almost laugh at this last statement. I'm the one

who's been keeping us out of trouble this far. But I won't say so and hurt his feelings.

"Why," he demands, "are you dragging us both about the world like this? Haven't you had enough of adventuring yet?"

"You have nothing to fear from Jonaas if you keep out of his way," I tell him. "And, no, I haven't done with adventuring. I wish to learn about the Outside, about people and the ways of life they follow and I won't learn much of that at Serenel. You used to tell me, 'Don't scoff at experiences you know nothing about,' and I'm storing experiences and knowledge so that I can make up my own mind about things. All my life I've been largely dependent on the teachings of others and it isn't enough. Ignorance makes for bigotry and I may not ever have this chance of exploration again!"

We are silent as the robocar speeds through the busy traffic lanes to the crowded waterfront.

"One of The Hand's agents told me of a barge operator who's looking for men to oversee the cargoes on a short-term basis," I tell him. "The cargoes are going to Afros, to Terhazza."

He looks interested.

"I've never been to Afros," he says, brightening up. "Terhazza? We could get further work picking fruit there if you want."

So we're friends again. I suspect he's enjoying his adventuring more than he likes me to think.

(The next skip in narrative places them near Chegga in Northern Afros. It becomes obvious that not all their travels were made as tourists.

His references to his father in this section are intriguing, but no clue of identity is given.

—J.T. Semantics Division)

I awake and the false dawn is passing to reveal the imminent arrival of the sun. The dormitory is full of snores, sleep-noises, and the slightly sour scents of men who work hard and don't wash frequently. I slide from my bed and walk down through the old trees to where the lake sparkles in the dawn. The water is cool and refreshing. I swim lazily as the sun rises. Mustapha appears and joins me.

"It'll be a hot day," he says.

I say, "All the days are hot."

He sighs and says, "But they seem hotter when you're directing a harvester-mech."

"It's my free day," I tell him. "I'll think of you sweating while I'm lolling about in one of the pleasure-houses in Chegga."

He swears at me good-humoredly.

I go back to find others stirring and Torros sitting on his bed, scratching and yawning. He watches me dress in my new briefs with the lion's head codpiece and my matching blue, sleeveless shirt in silence. I put on my sandals and send him pleasure-pulse.

He shakes his head and says, "They'd never know you in the valley."

"They've seen Dark Mode before," I say.

"Not in those indecent briefs," he says. "I like my butt covered."

"Mine's better looking," I say. "It's a commonplace fashion in Chegga."

He looks at the calendar and lowers his voice to say, "The Psi-Org Patrol comes through in a few days."

"I know," I say, "and as soon as they've been we'll move on. If we go now we'll only have to go through an inspection at the border. It's better to get our inspection-chits here where they aren't so thorough."

I look at the calendar, knowing that it's the last day

of my father's holiday and probably the last time I'll ever see him. I daren't tell Torros. He'd only harangue me about the risk and tell me what a fool I am. I leave him after promising to buy some brandy.

I decide not to wait for the usual revolting breakfast. I clip my money belt on securely and go out to the place where the trucks are loaded.

I arrange a lift with a driver who likes the look of me, an attractive woman who has no family here. We talk small talk and discuss the irrigation scheme all the way to Chegga.

I retract my psi-field as we near the city.

Oh, I'm so grateful to The Hand for getting me the information about my father and the news that he was to holiday here! Poor Torros, he keeps wondering why I was so determined to come to the irrigation scheme instead of to Terhazza and the easier job picking fruit. But, this way, I'll have known my father a little, at least. Will he remember me from our meeting at the Music Festival the other day?

I get off at the White Concourse at 7:50, wave goodbye to the driver and go to look for the Oriol where he said he usually breakfasted. I find it easily. It's a plain, cheap restaurant which caters to manual workers. Most of the men there are as fashionably half-naked as I am, but few have my darkness of skin so I get stares.

I see him sitting at a table in a corner and my heart beats faster. I stroll to him, being very casual.

"Good morning," I say. "May I join you?"

He looks startled, then recognizes me and says, "This is a coincidence! I was thinking of you and about the participation-theater you told me of. Have you had breakfast?"

"No," I say, "and I'm very hungry."

My head is already beginning to ache, but I dial for eggs, fruit and coffee. He watches me eat with eyes that are as vividly blue as Mediterranean skies.

"Do you come from these parts?" he asks.

"No," I say. "I come from a place near Turkey. Where were you born?"

"A place in Greece," he says, "but I haven't seen it since I was a very young man."

I say, "Since you were taken to be trained by the Psi-Orgs?"

He looks alert, suspicious, and says, "How do you know I'm with the Psi-Orgs?"

"Because," I say, "the material of your tunic is so thin that I can see your badge pinned to your undershirt."

He relaxes, but covers the badge with one hand.

"Does it worry you?" he asks. "A lot of people aren't fond of Peepers."

"You're a Peeper?" I say. "No, it doesn't worry me. I doubt if you'd learn much worth knowing if you Peeped me. Have you?"

"No, certainly not!" he says, offended. "Psi-Org Disciplines don't allow Talents to use their gifts outside an Org unless it's required as a public service. You must have heard that."

"Oh, I've heard it," I say, grinning, "but that doesn't mean it's true. Don't be so stiff-necked. I'll take your word for it. You must be an important man in the Psi-Orgs."

"Why do you think so?" he asks.

"Because you're careless with money," I say and hold up his money folder. "You could have lost it to any pickpocket."

I take off my money belt, tuck my money in my

codpiece and put his money in the belt before I hand it to him.

"You money's safer in that," I say. "It has a safety clip."

"I can't accept such a gift," he says, amused.

"Regard it as a bribe," I say.

He takes the belt, considers, and clips it on carefully.

"Thank you," he says. "What's the bribe for?"

"I'll think of something," I say. "Which Psi-Org do you belong to?"

"Paris Central," he says. "Why are you so interested?"

"Because now I can tell people I know an important Peeper from Paris Psi-Org!" I say. "Come and I'll show you the old ruins."

He's interested and I lead the way from the restaurant.

He has such dark hair. My coloring must come from my mother. How I'd love a quick look at his genes! It would be a pleasure to truly see our kinship instead of merely trusting The Hand's information and my detective work.

My headache is pounding.

We walk along and look at the shops, discussing what we see. Then we go and look at what remains of the ruins. From there we go and look at the sculptures in the Circle Plaza. He knows a lot about such things and tells me a great deal which is probably fascinating, but I can't take it in because my head's aching so badly.

I take him to see the hideous fountain called the Triumph of Water and he's very amused, agreeing with me that it's hideous.

From there I take him to the upper galleries of the

Pleasure Dome and he's so entranced by the displays of rock crystals and minerals that I take the opportunity to slip away, go downstairs to the fresheners and risk releasing my psi-field.

Oh, the relief! I've never gone so long with it retracted before. It takes me some minutes before I can restore my calm and retract it again. It's almost midday when I return to the galleries. He barely noticed that I was missing, which is another relief.

We go to lunch at a small restaurant and he tells me about a village he visited three days before. He makes it sound very interesting. He's a very well-educated man and what Hubertus would call "sophisticated."

In the afternoon we go to the mime-theater where they encourage participation. I manage to slip away before it ends and release my psi-field in the freshener again. I feel physically ill by this time, but I rebalance as much as I can and go back to my seat just before the performance ends.

We go out into the galleries in the late afternoon to have coffee.

He says, "You're a nice lad, Big Black, and too bright to remain working as a field hand. Why don't you go to a Vocational Service and see what can be done?"

I say, "Perhaps I did."

"I think you could do better for yourself," he says. "Where's your family?"

"A long way from here," I say. "In a place called Serenel. Do you have a family?"

"No," he says. "I never had the time to devote myself to anything but the Psi-Orgs. They provide me with all I ever needed from life."

"That's good to hear," I say.

"What's your real name?" he asks. "I'd like to keep in touch with you."

"Give me your address and I'll write to you," I say. "Everyone calls me Big Black and I'm used to it."

He writes his name and address on a napkin and I look at it, seeing that it's the same as the one I already have.

"I must get back to the travel lodge," he says. "I promised to meet friends there."

My head is pounding again. I say, "I'll walk back with you."

So we walk to the travel lodge.

"Thank you for a pleasant day," he says and grips my hand.

"Have a good journey home," I say, grinning.

And I walk away, full of frustration, my head pounding as though it'll explode. I take a robocar and wait until I'm almost out of Chegga before I release my psi-field. It takes most of the journey for me to recover.

It's 20:35 when I get back. I go for a swim and then meet Torros for dinner. I remember that I was supposed to buy him some brandy.

"Did you have a good day?" he asks.

"Oh," I tell him, "it was so-so."

(I have left this section unedited because it demonstrates how easily Saulus was able to deceive a Psi-Org Operative over a lengthy period.

Another gap in the narrative occurs here. Saulus begins the next part in Rome.

It is interesting to note that the Rome-Paris-Stuttgart drug run organized by a variety of criminal organizations is reported by the Enforcement Bureau to be no longer in existence.

Investigations have also shown that the vines in

some areas about Montpelier appear to have mutated and seem to bear out what he claims.

His mention about "watching the shuttles rise to go to Moonbase" does not indicate the particular shuttle port.

As to the opium fields, it is also difficult to be sure since their whereabouts are not mentioned.

The orange groves around Valencia have produced a record crop this year and have, apparently, developed a remarkable resistance to disease and insect-pests.

The "desert weed" is exactly as he described and appears to be one of the most important influences on that whole barren area.

It remains for time to bear out his other claims.

—J.T. Semantics Division)

* TWELVE *

Rome is as busy and as ugly-beautiful as ever. I stare out through the window and blink away the last of sleep, then I shake Torros.

"We're almost there," I say.

He groans and rubs his changed face. I wonder what Noni will think of his new features? The sun has just risen and the city lights are going off slowly as the shuttle passes through the outer suburbs.

I pull our carryalls from the racks, put on my sandals and go to the freshener. It's good to be in Prime Mode again after so long spent as Dark Mode. I comb my hair and feel better for the wash. Torros goes to the freshener while I check my money. It seems strange to finish my travels with so much more money than when I began them.

The shuttle whines into Rome Terminal just as Torros returns. We grab the carryalls and join the other passengers in the exodus to the platform, then through the inspection-gates and out into the concourse. Hubertus won't be at the live-unit until 13th hour, which gives us seven hours to fill. I climb into the nearest robocar and Torros follows.

"To the Appias Baths," I say.

Torros grumbles, "Why there?"

"You wouldn't ask if you could see and smell yourself," I say. "We'll have a bath and massage, you'll have your hair and beard trimmed and then we'll do some shopping. Where's a good place to go for clothes?"

He brightens at the mention of clothes. Torros was always a smart dresser.

"Donicelli's," he says. "But it's expensive and I don't have much left."

"I have money," I say, as he knew I would.

The bath and massage are very pleasant and Torros looks better for a haircut and beard trim. We take a robocar to Donicelli's.

Donicelli's is so expensive that there are real people as well as mechs to serve the customers. We spend a long time in the viewing rooms. I dismiss the erotic and the outrageous and Torros follows my lead. How times have changed. I always used to follow him.

I choose a clinging bodysuit, all dark gray and severe, without decoration except for the discreetly featured codpiece. I find a black overall-coat to go with it and black half-shin boots with high heels. Torros chooses a dark, multicolored bodysuit with voluminous trouserlegs and sleeves, a sunburst codpiece and heavy belt, worn with platform-soled shortboots. He looks very fine.

I put the clothes I was wearing, including the much-used Hubertus coat, down the rubbish chute and, after a shocked moment, Torros follows suit.

"Breakfast?" he says hopefully, but I lead the way to the nearest credit exchange and check my account. Torros is impressed with my credit rating and needs little persuasion to accept money from me. We go and enjoy a substantial breakfast, then wander about the shops buying gifts. The time flies by and my chronometer says almost 12th hour when I look. We carry our parcels out into the street and I hail a robocar to take us down the coast.

The spring sunshine is lovely and the greenery burgeoning everywhere beyond the city is so wonderful that I long for Serenel. Torros is more interested in the pavilions, the pleasurecraft and the sea.

"Hubertus will probably harangue me very fiercely," I tell him. "Don't attempt to argue with him. Leave the talking to me."

"Pah!" says Torros. "Hubertus doesn't frighten me!"

"He should," I say. "Don't forget that you don't belong to the Clan any more and that Hubertus is Jonaas's right hand. He takes that seriously."

Torros becomes gloomy so I send him pleasure-pulse and say, "Noni will be pleased to see you."

He smiles at that and says, "Noni's an idiot," but he's excited at the thought of her.

The live-unit is already open. Hubertus has arrived early.

He lets us in and I drop parcels as he embraces me, his square face beaming. It's very good to see him. We follow him into the living area, put our parcels down and I remove my overall-coat.

"Torros," I say, "would you make us all some coffee, please?" and point to the kitchen. He goes quickly, unwilling to face Hubertus's lashing tongue.

Hubertus has a wonderful way with words and I do admire that. He can think of ways to put words so that there isn't a Clan-member who wouldn't dread his tongue in a telling-off. But his mindspeak can be even more blistering and cruel. Once, I would have been frightened and shamed, too, but now I can sit and take in his mindspeak at its most vivid without becoming at all upset. I admire the phrasing and concepts as he lashes me.

He becomes increasingly annoyed when I don't respond as he expects and soon begins to repeat himself. There's condemnation of my idiotic wanderings, my lack of responsibility toward the Clan, the warnings of what Jonaas will do and say when he sees me and a lot about the worry and upset I've caused.

When he's run down somewhat, I mindspeak, "Quite right, Hubertus. I'm a thoroughly ungrateful fool. But I don't think the Clan will starve after all the money it made from the Faith. I'm surprised that the big shift to this marvelous island hasn't taken place yet. What happened? Isn't Diam/Cassim tired of his religious phase yet? Jonaas said he'd be the ideal front man for the Clan."

Hubertus is a little taken aback by my attitude.

"Diam!" he tells me. "He's so involved in that fanatic-stirring movement that he's opted out of all his old connections now! The Faith got him like it seems to be getting half the world these days! It's like a disease!"

"Perhaps," I reply, "it's a cure for the worst diseases. How are those of the Clan, my friend? Are they well? Is everyone happy?"

He looks suddenly sulky.

There's distress in his mind as he tells me, "You should have come with me instead of jaunting about, Saulus. There wouldn't have been any trouble if you'd been about to keep an eye on things."

"Tell me," I invite.

He looks sulkier than ever, regretting having to tell me bad things.

"We had troubles," he states.

"Caused by Jonaas," I supply gently.

"There were arguments," he tells me unwillingly. "Hero and Mahmud were very difficult—he killed them. And Mario lost an eye and part of his face because he supported them. You should have come back with me."

"Jonaas is insane," I supply.

He protests, "He had to keep order and discipline!"

"Hubertus, my dear friend," I tell him, "admit it. Jonaas is insane."

He won't look at me. He's very distressed, but he won't admit the truth. Jonaas has been his source of authority for a very long time and Hubertus always finds change difficult to adapt to.

"The Clan are like sheep," I tell him. "Jonaas roars and all obey. He was once a clever man and a great organizer, a man worthy of being followed because he ensured survival and a measure of security. Now his megalomania destroys the Clan from within. And you continue to support him, Hubertus."

"What else can I do?" he asks and he's anguished. "Without Jonaas we'd have nothing!"

"That may have been the case once," I reply, "but times and people change. I've seen something of the world and learned a great deal, Hubertus. The Clan has money now and I've seen places and possibilities that would keep them out of the Psi-Orgs' hands. But I have little respect for the collective intelligence of the Clan and that includes you, too, Hubertus. Jonaas found a hiding place, set everything to work to make money and security and now everyone's so set in their little grooves of obedience that they can't see any alternatives. Old motives have become blind habits. And those who question them are destroyed."

"Chaos, but you've changed, Saulus!" Hubertus tells me. "You know you could take over the Clan if you wished. You must have realized that I had it in mind for you if things got too bad with Jonaas!"

"You did?" I query, surprised.

"Why do you think I became involved in educating you?" he tells me. "I realized, when Auria began to get such amazing results from her teaching of you, that you were a possible solution to the Clan's increasing problems with Jonaas. I was convinced of it after you disciplined him that day when you claimed Auria. Now do you understand why I've been so concerned at your disappearance?"

I tell him, "Then you were wrong, Hubertus. I don't wish to lead the Clan. They wouldn't accept my alternatives for their future! What would you say if I took over and then told you that the Clan needed very little that wasn't already there in the valley? The valley, Hubertus! We could build what we needed, provide ourselves with power-units and anything else required for our comforts, cultivate the land, enjoy its produce and live our quiet lives without any threat from Enforcers or Psi-Orgs. That doesn't mean we couldn't venture forth into the great Outside when the need arose. But not as criminals, Hubertus. We could live quite comfortably within the law. You'd never accept that and neither would they!"

He's shocked at that. He tells me, "But the valley would become a prison!"

"The Clan makes its own prison now," I tell him. "You all go about in terror of Enforcers and Psi-Orgs, you prey on others, you connive and fight, you risk your lives and you have so little to show for it! You exist like vermin, you appreciate nothing but what you can struggle for, you're proud of being criminals with everyone hating you! Is that living free? Have you ever considered a peaceful existence, living on your own resources, restricting your boundaries to develop the things you're sure of? We could provide the valley with all it ever needs to support ten times the amount of people who live there now!"

"You say that," he tells me, "and yet you sit there in your civilized finery, having just returned from the biggest jaunt of your life in civilized society!"

"Yes," I tell him. "I did it to see and learn and to have fun. But I don't need it. I lived in the valley for the greater part of my life and had all I ever wanted or needed. Don't begin an argument about my requirements, Hubertus, because you'll find yourself out of your depth. However, I do understand that those of the Clan have other requirements and I'm certain there are ways of satisfying everyone if we put our minds to it."

"I don't understand you," he tells me. "It sounds as though you hate the Clan!"

"I don't hate it. I simply don't care for it," I tell him. "I never cared one way or another for the Clan as a collective thing. I love many of its individuals, including you, Hubertus, and the rest I tolerate or ignore."

He stares at me, suddenly full of distrust toward one whom he thought he influenced so completely.

"You don't want me as head of the Clan, Hubertus," I tell him. "You want another Jonaas figure. Otherwise you'd all have deposed him years ago. Do you remember why Torros was pushed out of the valley? Do you know why Angelo was killed?"

"Angelo ran off—" he begins.

"No," I tell him. "Jonaas killed him as he killed Hero and Mahmud. As he killed those before them. I know this because I was there when it happened. I thought Angelo wanted to escape Jonaas and the Clan, but Torros knew better. Torros was thrust from the valley because he wanted an end to dangerous and often pointless forays into the Outside. He saw that the valley could provide for the Clan and tried to show Jonaas how it could be done without cutting ourselves entirely off from the Outside. Angelo wanted that, too, and argued the case as his brother had. They didn't talk only to Jonaas about it, but few of the others could accept their ideas. Jonaas could never accept such ideas because, to him, it's the criminal existence and his own influence over others that counts. But Torros talked to a half-aware Saulus about it and I had no difficulty in accepting that the valley was all we needed. Mind you, I'm biased. The Clan don't know the valley at all! They know a few crumbling buildings and the bits and pieces they've brought in from Outside! They see it as a temporary hiding place. It's been 'temporary' ever since Jonaas found it twenty-five years ago! I've learned a lot during the past few months, mostly things about myself. But the really important things in my life were learned in the valley! I'll come back and calm Jonaas down, but forget me as a leader of the Clan, Hubertus. I'm not interested. I don't fit the mold you require."

He looks suddenly so unhappy. I wish I could help him to see things as I see them, but he's too fixed in the ways that habit has made.

"How are Auria and Yo-Yo?" I ask.

"I don't see much of them," he tells me. "They don't come to the Red Palace when Jonaas and I are about. Jazalu is back with the Clan."

"What of her and Diam?" I ask.

"Diam couldn't accept her ways and she grew bored with his. And he was angry about the child. So she abandoned him and came back. She's almost eight months pregnant and is as sour as a lemon about it," he tells me.

We have coffee and something to eat with Torros and I give Hubertus the gold bracelet I bought him. He's pleased with it, but is so unused to being given a present that he doesn't know what to say.

(Saulus breaks off the narrative at this point. LeMaitre records that he was distressed and introspective for some minutes after. There is no clue to the day on which they returned to the valley when he resumes.

—J.T. Semantics Division)

The sun is setting when we reach Serenel. There is nobody to meet us.

Hubertus tells me, "Jonaas wants a meeting at 10th hour tomorrow. Will you see Mario before you go up to the Blue Place? He's in a bad way."

I say to Torros, "Noni is waiting for you," and he runs off with his carryall dragging at one arm.

I go with Hubertus to see Mario and am shocked by his suffering. I do what has to be done and it's after 21st hour when I bid Hubertus a good night, heave my parcels and carryall to my shoulders for easier carrying and start up the slopes to the Blue Place.

The stars are ablaze, the singing of insects in the grasses is like the sweetest music and the breeze coming up from the valley is full of exquisite spring scents. The thickets need trimming again. I wonder how the Red Trees and the Crawlies fare? I can smell the scent of roses long before I reach the garden and a garland of starflies is dancing over the shrubs which were only seedlings last spring.

The lamp is on in the courtyard. Red Tree's Daughter stirs and brushes me as I pass, the night daisies are white and gleaming and the silver beetles are making geometric patterns on the moss banks.

The door is closed but there's light in the windows. I push the door and it opens. I walk into the lovely-familiar room, push the door closed and put my carry-all and parcels on the table.

There's a soft sound. I turn to see Auriä, clutching at her nightrobe and with her hair streaming over her shoulders, at the bedchamber door. She's so lovely that tears prickle my eyes.

"Am I welcome?" I ask.

She runs to me and we lock our arms and bodies together in an ecstasy of emotion, kissing and murmuring and weeping.

There's a shriek from the bedchamber and Yo-Yo comes running, naked and chubby and lovable. I scoop him up with one arm and we all hug and kiss together.

Auria pulls away, tidies her hair and goes to make a meal for me. I sit with Yo-Yo on my lap and cuddle him until he grows curious about the parcels. I give him his parcel and he burbles joyfully at seeing the new red ball of tough plastex.

"Red ball!" he says distinctly. "Put in box?"

"Yes, put it in your box," I say, delighted with his progress.

He rushes off and I hear him gurgling over his ball. Auria brings me fruit from Red Tree's Daughter and some tasty savory cakes. She sits to watch me eat.

"Your letters were so short," she mindspeaks. "You seem to have travelled a great deal."

"Yes," I reply. "I travelled and learned. I discovered I like people, that I can live among them without difficulty and I learned to admire much that I found here and there."

So I tell her of The Hand and Alouette, of Torros's escape and of the travels.

I tell her of the car we bought and then sold at a profit, I describe Bordeaux and what I did to improve the vines, I talk of Toulouse and Montpelier where I also improved the vines.

I describe Zaragoza and tell her how I made changes to the orange trees about Valencia. I talk of Murcia, Malaga, of Tindouf and Chegga and the work in Algeria.

I don't tell her of my father or of the weed that I encouraged to spread over the sands of that terrible desert.

I tell her of Benghazi, Alexandria, of the isle of Crete, of Ghadames and Tunis.

But I don't tell her of our work in the poppy fields where I altered the plants so that they produce perfume but no narcotic.

I tell her of how we worked on a cargo-floater to Marseilles, of our walk to Aix and Arles, of the work we did in Cannes, Savona and Turin. I tell her about watching the shuttles rise to go to Moonbase.

I don't mention that the locusts won't swarm this summer because of what I did.

And I tell her of arriving in Rome and about our shopping spree.

She's pleased with the rose-colored gown, the pearls and the locket.

It's very late—or early, depending on the point of view—when we go to bed. Yo-Yo has fallen asleep on the floor, still clutching his red ball. I tuck him into bed, undress and turn out the lamps. Auria's body is like warm silk against me.

*   *   *

I awake and the sun has risen. The calendar says
3rd day, 3rd month, 2281 A.D. I slip out of bed and
go to the freshener, bathe and put on my brown kaftan and sandals, then walk out into the garden.

Everything has grown within the disciplines I set
all those months ago and to me it's more beautiful
than Versailles. I greet Red Tree's Daughter and take
some of her fruit, then go to ease my way through
the thickets to the West Terrace for the first time
since I came back. These past days have been so busy
with the Clan's needs that I've neglected looking at
my own concerns for too long. Today is mine.

The young Red Trees are splendid, singing their
breeze-music and swaying gracefully. They recognize
me and writhe ecstatically as I come to offer the token
drops of blood. The moss banks have thickened and
spread blue, green and purple to the very edges of
the Terrace and the Crack.

There are new cracks along the blocks of the Terrace's retaining wall and tiny daisies have grown in
them. The Crack seems wider, too, and I notice that
the Crawlies have moved out and up into the crevices
of the rocks on the mountainside. There's a strong
chemical smell coming up from the depths, obviously
the reason for the Crawlies' emigration. Far below,
the Red Palace shines dusty red and half the colonnades have shattered and collapsed.

I go down to the Red Palace to see my old friends
but things are still very wrong there. I go back to
the Blue Place and discover Auria and Yo-Yo getting
breakfast ready.

"Those at the Red Palace are still behaving oddly,"
I mindspeak to her. "And so many of them wanting
to change faces and fingerprints and have illnesses

corrected! It seems as if almost all of the Clan is here. And Jonaas barely spoke at the meeting yesterday, as though he sulked! What's been happening? Everyone I ask questions of makes excuses and murmurs of other business."

"There's been a lot of trouble while you were away. Has Hubertus explained about Jonaas and Hero and Mahmud?" she asks.

"Yes, and Mario. I've restored his face and the eye, but he won't talk of it," I tell her.

"Everything's been difficult," she tells me. "We had an earth tremor and there's something wrong with the Palace's power supply now. All the refrigerated food went bad and there was no heating during the last part of winter. Things like that have upset people. No one dared to investigate the computer beneath the West Terrace because of those dreadful spider things and you weren't here to tell them what to do as you always have before. So they resent it that you went away. I know that's foolish, Saulus, but people aren't very sensible at this moment, what with the big shift being in the wind."

"But they could have brought in heaters and portable freezers such as we have here," I tell her.

"They did, but things like that added to the general discontent," she explains. "There was also a flood that half-filled the Tunnel for days. The Clan want to leave here as soon as possible, Saulus. The deaths of Hero and Mahmud happened because they agitated about leaving here immediately, before the island was assured. Have you been told about the island? It's near Naxos, a place called Arih."

"I'll see what can be done about the power," I tell her.

Let them have their island, the fools. I'll stay here

with Yo-Yo. Perhaps Noni and Torros will stay, too. And Auria? I daren't ask.

I eat breakfast in silence and then leave them to see about the power. It may be too dangerous to take Torros down into the Crack.

I make my way to the East Terrace and the Love Palace before attempting to do anything. The computer may have information I can use. The sphincter-door sheds adventurous vines as it opens for me and the air is cool and musty in the entryway. As I walk in, the air circulators and the soft music are activated and a cleaner-bug scuttles out to clean dust from the doorway. I walk through the halls and courts to the Master's room. The goddesses and their erotically worshipful slaves are as exquisite as ever and the colors of the mosaics, hangings and furnishings are still as fresh and lovely as when I first saw them.

"Computer," I say, "are you an auxiliary of the big computer in the Crack? Do you share the same power source?"

"I am self-contained and limited to the Love Palace," it tells me. "My power source is solar and separate from any other."

"Can you tell me about the Big One?" I ask. "I need to know about the power for the Red Palace."

There's a pause.

"Perhaps," it says, "you refer to the Controller of Defensive Functions which is situated beneath the Garden of Meditation."

"Perhaps," I say. "Can you tell me about it?"

"I am aware that it exists and that its auxiliaries provide power for the Great Palace and the Fort," it says.

"The Fort up on the East Ridge?" I ask.

"There is no Fort on the East Ridge," it says.

"There is an Observation Post on the East Ridge. The Fort is also beneath the Garden of Meditation. Access to the Fort is available beyond the figure representing Thought in the Great Room. I have no further information."

I remember the goddess of polished stone reclining pensively in the Great Room. I go out and walk to the corridor which leads there.

The goddess has one hand raised to her forehead and the other is pushing away an ardent half-beast lover. She frowns slightly and has eyes made from blue sapphires. I go into the space beyond her and there's a soft sighing as part of the wall slides open. Steps lead down into darkness.

"Light the passageway for me," I say.

"I have no function beyond the Love Palace," says the computer.

"Then leave the door open until I return," I say.

I start down the stone steps. They lead down a very long way, the darkness growing more and more solid as I descend. I adjust my sight, but it's very dim when I reach a flat place which I soon discover is a corridor. I feel my way along one wall for some distance until I come to a dead end in the blackness. I feel about and realize that there's a metal door here. Further feeling about discovers a doorplate to which I press my palm hopefully. I hear the door open and feel the air move and then the lights come on so suddenly that I'm momentarily blinded.

When I can see again I discover that this is a small complex of rooms and passages cut from the solid stone. Some rooms hold supplies of food in dust-covered vacuum boxes, one room has guns of a kind I've read about and the rest are empty of all save for dust.

I walk down more steps to another door and, when

it opens, the corridor is littered with the skeletons of men. Their uniforms are still intact but crumble at a touch. There are signs that they died very suddenly, but from what I can't tell. Perhaps a deadly gas? I climb over them carefully, reluctant to disturb them, and make my way along the corridor. Here the glo-lamps are very dim and, at the far end, I can see daylight. As I walk closer to it, I realize that I'm coming to the Crack. A few abandoned webs and an old nest tell me that the Crawlies had begun to invade the passageway at some stage. The chemical fumes are terrible and catch at my throat.

Then I'm at the Crack, the passageway shattered and split apart. Below, the darkness is impenetrable, above me the light filters through dusty webs and opposite is the continuation of the passageway where I've been before. Over there is the Controller of Defensive Functions, the Big One.

I judge the distance across the Crack, hoist my kaftan and move back. A speedy run, a great leap and I'm across, blundering into thick webs in the dimness. I tear the webs away and make my way to the big door which is always half open.

The lights come on very dimly and I immediately understand what the chemical odor comes from. Water has run down the walls and is still gathered in dirty puddles on the stone floor. Some bags of powdered metal and chemicals have fallen, broken open and become very wet. The fumes they give off are very toxic. I hold my breath and go through the further door to the Big One. Here the air is musty but breathable and I close the door to keep it so.

Big One's panels are dull and lifeless except for a few specks of light and some dials and gauges that show tiny movements.

I put my hand to the recognition-plate and say, "Are you still able to speak?"

"Yes, Master," says Big One.

"Then," I say, "describe your present functions and capacities."

I don't understand much of what it tells me, but I gather that it no longer supplies the Observation Post with power and that power to the Great Palace has become limited to a something-or-other factor. Something to do with compression forces and malfunction. The dissolution capacity is maintained but the projectiles can no longer be fired and are possibly damaged. Utilization of energy banks 3 and 5 is no longer possible and reserves are low.

It mentions displacement once or twice and I wonder if this could be because of the earth tremor that Auria mentioned.

"Can you restore the power to the Great Palace?" I ask.

Big One says, "Possible to cut power banks 1 to 8 and redirect power to Great Palace, close baffles on tanks 2 and 3, place alerting screens on lower power."

"Do that then," I say.

"Due to malfunction there is danger that closing baffles on tanks 2 and 3 will institute self-destruct and dissolution mechanisms due to distortion of dampers," it says.

Alarmed, I say, "Don't close the baffles then! I don't want you to self-destruct!"

Big One says, "Self-destruct mechanisms on hold, automatic destruct at Red Alert. Suitable power banks redirected to Great Palace. Closing off extraneous function now due to inefficient communication leads."

The lights go out. That seems to be an end to it.

I go out to the store room and begin dragging the

fuming bags to the Crack and pushing them over the edge. They fall a long way before I hear any sound of impact. I tidy up what can be tidied and see to it that no more bags can fall down. The air is already clearing slightly. Coughing, I hoist my kaftan and jump the Crack again.

All the lights in the corridor have gone out, too. I adjust my vision once I've negotiated the corridor where the skeletons are, but it takes a long time to feel my way back to the Love Palace in the darkness and I'm very glad it's sealed off from those fumes by two metal doors.

The door beyond the Goddess of Thought closes as I come in and I realize I'm filthy with dust and webs. I go back to the Master's room and bathe, put on a plain blue kaftan and dispose of the other in the room where the mech washes and dries clothes so efficiently.

It's after 10th hour when I get back to the Blue Place. Auria is cleaning it unnecessarily and Yo-Yo is singing a strange little song as he helps her. She puts the kettle on to make coffee and I swing him up for a cuddle before I kiss her.

"Come play?" Yo-Yo asks.

"I have to go down to the Red Palace and tell them that some of the power is on again," I tell him. "You play with your new ball in the meadow."

He runs off and Auria and I settle to drink coffee. She seems worried about something and takes a long time to broach it.

"Saulus," she mindspeaks, "Hubertus has been talking to me while you were gone. He and some of the others have some idea that I might be able to persuade you to take over from Jonaas. It's not a new idea. They discussed it with me several times while

you were away. They think that, with their backing
and Hubertus's organizing abilities, you could act as
the leader—"

I interrupt with, "I won't become Clan leader
under any circumstances. I want nothing to do with
it and I've already told Hubertus so. I'm not the least
bit interested."

She displays relief, as though she feared the
prospect.

"Good," she tells me. "I was afraid you'd want it.
Don't go their way, Saulus. Don't become corrupted."

I have to laugh at that. Auria's ideas on corruption
are peculiarly her own where the Clan is concerned.
I wonder, not for the first time, how she ever became
involved with it in the first place.

"And," she tells me, "Jonaas has called a meeting
for 11th hour. It's to do with the island. Will you go?"

"No," I tell her. "I'll go and see Torros."

We drink our coffee and then I kiss her before
going down to the Red Palace to tell them about
the power.

❊ THIRTEEN ❊

It's 12:30 when I get back to the Blue Place. I'm surprised to find that Jazalu is there, because she's kept well away from me since I got back. Auria looks enigmatic and is busy making a meal, while Yo-Yo sits under the table, gurgling at his red ball.

"I heard you were back," Jazalu says. "Noni told me."

"I've been about the Red Palace frequently," I say.

I don't like her being here. She upsets Auria.

Jazalu gives me an artificial smile and says, "I came from the meeting. You should have been there, Saulus. It's all set. We leave the valley by the end of the month."

I knew this would come but the news upsets me. I won't go! I won't! But what of Auria?

"Jazalu has been telling me of the plans the Clan is making," says Auria in a strangely quiet way.

"Such plans, Saulus!" says Jazalu. "We'll be closer to the center of things and the island's a perfect place to use as a headquarters! Jonaas and The Hand have planned some big operations together already. Drug-running's becoming too dangerous to handle from Rome but, in the north, there are big opportunities.

And, by pooling our Talents and The Hand's resources, we can establish operations that'll make us richer than we've ever been! The lottery scams, bond forgeries, some truly profitable robberies—"

Jazalu goes on talking, but I hardly hear her. For all Auria's outward calm I can tell by her glandular activity that she is distressed. Is she afraid to leave the valley or is it anger at something Jazalu said?

I interrupt Jazalu, saying, "Did you wish to see me on business or is this only a social visit?"

"Oh," she says, "I wanted you to have a look at the baby. It won't be more than a month now and I'd like to be sure that everything's as it should be."

"It's a boy," I say, "and very healthy. But you shouldn't be too active at this stage. Live quietly and don't take drugs."

"Oh," she says, "are you sure it's healthy?"

"Of course I'm sure," I say.

She chatters on for some time but I hardly listen. It's a relief to see her go.

Yo-Yo, Auria and I eat.

"Is the power in the Red Palace working?" Auria asks.

"Some of it," I say. "There's enough to make life comfortable down there."

She finishes her meal in silence and then blurts suddenly, "The Clan will never change, Saulus! They won't live quietly on their island! They're habitual criminals, incapable of thinking any other way! It'll all go on as before!"

"I suppose so," I mindspeak to her, "but I won't be with them. I intend to stay here with Yo-Yo."

She doesn't respond to this.

"Will you stay with me?" I ask.

She looks at me with expressionless eyes, but I feel

her emotions swell. She comes to put her arms about me and her eyes are suddenly wet with tears.

"Saulus," she tells me, "I have no choice but to do as Hubertus decides! I have the directive he planted in my mind! I would have run away long before my confrontation with Jonaas if I'd had a choice! I can't make those kinds of decisions for myself!"

I think on that for a time, drawing her onto my lap and stroking her beautiful hair.

"I could make it possible for you to make your own choice," I tell her. "If you decide to stay I want you to be willing, not because you're a captive. You don't wish to go to the island?"

"No, Saulus. I want to be free of the Clan," she tells me.

"If you're willing to open your mind to me," I say, "I'll remove the directive."

She hesitates. Why does she fear?

"Saulus," she queries me, "can you really do that?"

"Yes, it's not difficult," I tell her.

She thinks, her eyes fixed on me.

She tells me, "I have secrets that are precious to me. Secrets I wouldn't want you to know."

"Have I ever tried to take your secrets?" I ask. "I won't look at them. I'll simply remove the directive that holds you captive to the Clan. But you'll have to show it to me."

She does not reply but after a moment, I feel her open to me like a flower opens to the day and draw me to the directive. It's a precious thing, willing and trusting. Oh, how I love her.

The directive is very strong. Hubertus is clever about such things. I examine carefully, afraid of damaging her should I do something wrong. And, after a time, I see the way. I put her into pseudo-sleep and she rests against me, then I fold myself into the directive and dissolve it slowly so that there will be no trauma. It takes time and I am very gentle. And it is gone. I remove myself and give her volition again. She blinks at me, resting against my shoulder. She has such beautiful eyes.

"Now you have your own right to choose," I tell her.

She kisses me and then pushes away to begin clearing the remains of the meal from the table. She's quite closed off from me and as enigmatic in manner as the goddess on the ceiling in the Love Palace.

I help with the tidying up and then Yo-Yo says, "Come play?" so I pick him up and go out, down past the West Terrace and down the long slopes to the meadow. The long grasses are rich and healthy so we play with his ball for a while, then play Bob-Up Bob-Down until he tires of it.

I lift him onto my shoulders and go down into the valley. The little lakes are full and the water is pure. All the trees are covered in new leaves and some are thick with blossom. The groundcovers are robust and some have little flowers or berries. A sharpteeth scuttles away and Yo-Yo squeals. I look about at the valley and the mountains and it's all so beautiful that I'm ecstatic with wonder. The only poisonous radiation is high beyond the West Terrace near the Peak and, with Torros and Noni to help, this could soon be buried and harmless. The rest is very fertile and there's food in plenty for the looking.

I see the beginnings of the old mountain road that leads toward the land they once called Syria. It's almost covered in tiny daisies which follow the sun with their pretty white faces. And, up on the East Ridge, the old Observation Post is almost hidden with vines. In my mind I can see how easy it would be to cultivate the valley and have all that one could possibly need.

I swing Yo-Yo down and we walk back to the slopes, holding hands. Some of his chatter is quite unintelligible but, occasionally, he speaks quite coherently. I must explore and find out what else can be done to improve his thinking. I've already learned so much about the brain from examining his.

We pick some of the scarlet and white flowers which grow so thickly on the slopes and Yo-Yo says, "For Auria?"

"Yes," I say. "You take them to her and give her a hug from me."

He rushes off, up the slopes and beyond the thickets, squealing happily. I go to visit Torros and Noni and admire their new arrangements in the apartment they have decided to move into. It's very attractive and overlooks the old White Court where the stone nymph holds a large bowl that was once a fountain. Torros and Noni are obviously very happy at being together again.

It's almost 16th hour when I get back to the Blue Place. Auria is out somewhere. Yo-Yo has toys from his box spread everywhere, so we put them back in it before I give him some milk and biscuits.

Then I discover the note from Auria on the table.

It reads, "Saulus, you have given me the ability of choice and I must think some things out before I make decisions. Please indulge me in this. I am going down to see Meriem and I may stay the night with her. Do not come for me. I need time away from you so that I may see you more clearly.

—Auria."

I take Yo-Yo out and we walk around to the East Terrace and the Love Palace. I'll show this to Auria tomorrow. Perhaps it'll help her to think more kindly of a life in the valley. Yo-Yo likes it and runs about, shouting at the "pretties."

"Computer," I say, "tomorrow I'll be bringing some people here, perhaps to live. I want them to be able to come and go as they please."

"Free access programmed," says the computer. "Is it your wish that I open the storage compartments and have food available?"

"Food?" I say. "What food?"

"Food stored in the vacuum freezers," it says.

"Is it still good after all this time?" I ask.

"Storage is maintained at maximum efficiency. The food is unimpaired," it says.

"How much food is there?" I ask.

"Storage is 86.8% full," it says.

"Make the food available then," I say.

So there'll be food for a while and we could get busy with cultivation in the valley for more food to be ready when the storage runs out. That's very reassuring to plan on. Torros will approve. He likes to plan ahead.

I take Yo-Yo back to the Blue Place and wash us both, then make an evening meal. Yo-Yo is tired so I put him to bed early, then go out into the garden.

The stars are very bright and the night-scents are wonderful. I play with the silver beetles for a while, say goodnight to Red Tree's Daughter and take some of the roses to put in a vase for Auria. I tidy the Blue Place as she likes it to be kept and am very aware of her absence.

When I climb into bed I can smell Auria's faint fragrance. This is pleasant but depressing, too.

*   *   *

I awake and the sun has already risen. The calendar says 4th Day, 3rd Month, 2281 A.D. and it's already 6th hour.

I take Yo-Yo to the freshener, dress us and get breakfast. Yo-Yo goes to play with his red ball so I decide to go down to the Red Palace to see Torros and Noni and then to find Auria. I'll take them to see the Love Palace and they'll make decisions, perhaps.

I go down and through the remains of the colonnades, then into the main corridor. Few are about at this hour. It's only about 6:30 so I hesitate to wake Torros and Noni yet. I'll find Auria first.

I go to Meriem's door and knock. After a long time, she comes, bleary-eyed from sleep and the alcohol which is still evident from last night. She scowls at me.

"I want to see Auria," I say.

Meriem curses and says, "Well, you won't find her here! What time is it?"

"Didn't she stay with you last night?" I ask.

"Why would she be staying with me?" she asks. "Did you two have a fight?"

"No," I say. "Go back to bed."

That's very puzzling and makes me uneasy. Where can she be? I go back to the colonnades and open my psi-field to seek without politeness. I feel the 'paths stir, am aware of the 'kinetics, but I find no Auria. Hubertus mindspeaks a curse at me for disturbing him. I bring my psi-field back to normal.

No Auria. Not anywhere in the Red Palace.

A terrible worry begins to needle at me. Where is Auria? I think on it anxiously for some moments, then I spread my psi-field large again, demanding strongly.

"Where is Auria?" I mindspeak.

They stir, protesting. Jonaas mindshouts at me,

Hubertus curses again, Noni queries and the lesser
'paths show fear at my demand. I draw myself in to
normal again. No one knows of Auria! No one!

Fear seizes me. I run to the Tunnel. The monorail
car has gone!

I know then.

I run up the slopes to the Blue Place. Panting, I
go to the locked drawer in the big chest. It's still
locked. I run into the bedchamber and find that all
her clothes and belongings are still there. No, not all.
Her carryall and what she calls her "work clothes,"
the red bodysuit and her light boots, are missing. And
her overcloak with the fur collar.

I calm myself and go into the other room. She has
run away from the Clan and from me! I made her
free to go and she has fled. I sit at the table and try
to think about what I should do. My thoughts go
around and around in confusion. I need coffee. The
indulgence will make me feel better and keep me
occupied. I'm about to fill the kettle when Yo-Yo
comes in, chuckling.

"It's good that you're happy," I say. "What makes
you laugh?"

"Auria," he says. "Present."

"What present?" I ask.

"Present," he says. "For you."

He has his red ball in one hand and a folded scrip,
somewhat grubby, in the other. I take the scrip from
him hastily and unfold it.

It reads, "Saulus, I leave this with Yo-Yo to give to
you in the morning. I hope, I pray that he will remember. By the time you read it I will be in Izmir. What
I am doing is something that should have been done
a long time ago, but I was a prisoner of Hubertus's

directive and could not. And, now that I find it possible, I must do my duty as I know is the only thing left for me to do, despite the agony it causes me. There are greater directives than the one Hubertus imposed, my dear one, though I doubt you will understand. The criminal minds and attitudes of the Clan will never change. And you are, though you may not realise it, as guilty as they are for helping them to continue their nefarious schemes. Personal considerations must be put aside and the Clan must be put an end to. I am a Psi-Org Operative. I hope the Psi-Orgs will be kind to you, Saulus. I will speak to them in your defense. I'm weak enough to want you to know that I loved you.

—Auria."

I read it, then read it again. Auria has betrayed me! And the Clan! The blood pounds in my temples. Sweat wets my armpits. An agony seizes me.

I open my psi-field large and project to Hubertus, "Wake up! Auria has betrayed us to the Psi-Orgs!"

He begins to curse me. I mindshout at him to take in my knowledge! I tell him of removing his directive, of the note, of the monorail car missing, of Auria being gone for at least fourteen hours. Suddenly Jonaas is mindspeaking and I'm aware of Noni, Carolus and the Twins. I tell them, too. They begin broadcasting to the others.

I break off contact, calm myself forcibly, grab Yo-Yo and run into the bedchamber. I change his clothes and mine for practical ones, stuff money and my identidisc into my pockets and grab a carryall.

"Is game?" Yo-Yo asks excitedly.

"Yes," I say. "It's called Hurry, Hurry, Quick, Quick!"

He follows me, picking up his red ball as I throw

fruit and bread and his warm coat into the carryall. I
run outside and his short legs pump busily as he pur-
sues. I pick him up and run heavily down the slopes.
From high above the Red Palace I can see some people running for the Tunnel, clutching belongings. I
am almost at the colonnades when I realize that we
have a perfect hiding place in the valley itself!

"Hubertus, Noni, Carolus, Twins!" I mindshout.
"Go up to the East Terrace by the old path near the
thickets! There's a hiding place inside the mountain
where nobody will find us! Tell the others!"

As I reach the colonnades I find Meriem, the
Twins, Carolus and Mario emerging from the Palace.
I direct them to the East Terrace and almost collide
with Noni and Torros who follow, laden with belongings. Some of the 'kinetics redirect their flight after
Torros and Noni. I see Paul and Radley vanishing into
the Tunnel and old Gino following them despite my
cries. Such panic is ridiculous and has become an
unthinking drive. What difference will a few minutes
make?

Jazalu comes from the corridor, staggering under
the weight of her pregnancy and two carryalls full of
goods, screaming at others who pass her to run toward
the slopes. She hesitates at the steps and then Christina and young Francois blunder into her. She teeters
and falls heavily, thumping down the steps with her
carryalls. I put Yo-Yo and my carryall down and run
to her. She's half-stunned with shock and will have
painful bruises. I try to lift her but she's heavy.

Hahmed, Fatimah and Guiseppe almost knock me
down as they thrust by. I shout to them but they don't
hear me. I try to drag Jazalu to her feet, but she grips
her carryalls with fanatic strength, screaming at me,
and I can't manage her.

Cecile runs by and then Jonaas appears, carrying a jewel box and clothes, his face a mask of fear and rage as he moves down the steps. Yo-Yo squeaks in terror at the sight of him.

"Help me!" I shout to Jonaas.

"You imbecile!" he rages at me. "This is all your fault! You're a Psi-Org Judas goat!"

Yo-Yo, frightened, runs toward me and, as Jonaas strides forward, cannons into his father. Jonaas staggers and I see his face distort with madness.

Yo-Yo, staggering from the impact, is suddenly a ball of fiercely blazing, searing flames! He screams, tottering backward, and falls over the edge of the colonnades! Yo-Yo, beloved Yo-Yo! No! No! Not Yo-Yo!

I spiral into Jonaas's mind and he shrieks! I see him fall and then I abandon Jazalu and run to leap down to Yo-Yo.

Yo-Yo! Oh, poor, dear little man! Dear little brother! Burned horribly, inside and out—his skull—and the brain within—beyond my capacity to restore—I can't breathe—he's dead! Dead! A horribly burned little body with, mercifully, a broken neck from the fall and still clutching the remains of his beloved red ball!

I cry out! I bellow with rage and grief! Everything seems to darken in my vision . . . He was learning, becoming whole little by little, a thinking creature who could have developed further—Yo-Yo who never harmed anyone and who loved me, trusted me, is taken from me!

I climb back to the colonnades and my vision clears. I see sharp and clear—so clear!

Jonaas, helped by Cecile, is struggling to his feet, still clutching his belongings. My rage consumes me!

I shout at him with hatred and anguish, preparing myself to strike! This is the time!

"Killer! Jonaas the Killer!"

He turns, bellowing his madness and gathering himself to burn me with his mind-fire! But I am quicker! I feel a momentary heat as I spiral into his mind again, this time to destroy, to sweep away, to cleanse, to obliterate! I hear him screaming!

I am the flood, the storm, the irresistible force! I spiral ferociously, destructively, through his brain, becoming part of each pathway—each synapse—each chemical/electrical carrier—invading each cell cluster and erasing, unravelling his senses/conscious volition/ instinctive memory/motor function/identity of self— tracing every neural connection—wiping clean and destroying and removing all that makes Jonaas himself a sentient and a living creature!

His screams are those of an animal already dead and jerking as muscles and nerves release the last of their energies! I am swift, strong, clean, cruel, ruthless and thorough, erasing and destroying without mercy until all that remains is worthless brain matter!

There is no more to destroy! Jonaas is gone! Jonaas, my enemy for so long! And my rage still consumes me! I withdraw from what was once a living creature and stare at him through a haze of fury! He sprawls, without dignity or grace, on the stone of the colonnades, his belongings strewn about him! And Cecile is screaming in terror and . . . What? What? What's happening? The Psi-Orgs—Auria—Hubertus is suddenly there, shouting at me! Jazalu!

I run to Jazalu, tear the carryalls from her clutching hands and heave her up clumsily, to stagger across the colonnades and up the slopes with her. I hardly see or feel, I'm a machine, an automatic creature, running, staggering up the slopes! My breath come in great gasps, my body aches, but I am unable to give in to physical weakness!

Yo-Yo, oh, my beloved Yo-Yo, the most harmless and innocent of creatures!

Someone shouting . . . What? What? Hubertus is shouting . . . helping me with Jazalu. But what's the water from? Oh! Oh! Jazalu is having her baby! But it's too soon, too soon!

My head clears slowly. The baby. Must see to the baby.

I realize I'm nearly to the Love Palace—here's the door—people milling about—I run into the corridor—so tired, tired—to the Master's Room—Hubertus is shouting to the others. Ah! The Master's Room! To the bed—I begin scanning her. Too late to prevent the birth without damaging both. Must continue and correct the processes quickly, quickly!

She cries out.

"Be calm," I say. "Take deep breaths—push—yes, push—"

Noni is with me, helping. I stimulate healing processes for the bruising. Balance and rebalance Jazalu's glandular system, haul her clothes away. Ah, Noni's assisting the passage with a delicacy which draws my admiration.

There—there—ah, it comes, the precious new life! There, Noni takes it—gently, gently—assist Jazalu's physical recovery, erase trauma—pinch cord, tie it—Christina comes to help—

Noni wraps the baby in something. I hear it crying in a strange way. I put my attention to Jazalu—

It's done. Now she'll sleep—Christina is cleaning her.

Noni shouts, "Saulus, the baby!"

I put my attention to the baby. Born too soon, too quickly . . . Clear the lungs carefully, carefully, assist the heart rate gently gently, adjust the metabolism slightly—there—there—oh, wonderful! How he cries! Such a sound of protesting life!

Hubertus takes the baby—I'm so tired—

Torros is there! I must tell him of the workings of the Love Palace! I babble at him and he listens, nodding.

"The others," I say. "How many others are here?"

"About twelve, I think," he says. "Saulus, your skin is burned, your clothes are scorched—"

Regenerate myself, begin the balancing, tiredness fading—

"Take charge," I say. "Keep the door closed. They can't find us here if we stay inside. I'll see if I can find any more out there—"

He's talking but I don't listen. I run to the sphincter-door and out onto the East Terrace, run down the slopes. Down in the valley I can see a woman, her arms loaded with belongings, staggering toward the Tunnel. Cecile? Difficult to be sure—

I run down the slopes toward the colonnades— Oh, Yo-Yo!—Poor little man!—dearest Yo-Yo!— Can't leave him for the sharpteeth to devour—

A piercing siren sounds shrilly as I reach the colonnades. An electronic computer voice begins to shout, amplified many times over. I look up toward the West Terrace and realize that it's the voice of the Big One reverberating across the valley!

It booms, "Red Alert! Red Alert! Enemy sighted in the west! All systems impaired! Self-destruct coming into effect!" It keeps repeating the message, over and over, the echoes resounding and the siren shrilling penetratingly.

Red Alert? Self-destruct? Enemy?

I look up at the Peak and see something small and high come over the Ridge! And another! Aircars! The Psi-Orgs! The enemy!

There is a great rumble, a huge booming sound, a heavy vibration through the earth and an immense spray of flame, smoke and debris shoots into the air from the West Terrace, from the Crack!

The smoke rises and rolls in a great, gushing black cloud and the earth continues to shake beneath my feet! There's a terrible sound like the groan of a giant, like the groan of the earth—the Big One has self-destructed and destroyed the Fort as it was programmed to do!

But something horrifying begins to happen, so horrifying that it takes me a moment to recognize what it is! I gasp and cry out as I take in the terrible thing that is happening!

The whole of the slopes, the whole of the West Terrace and part of the mountain beyond has begun to slide toward me! The sound is terrible, a groaning of immense agony, so loud that it hurts my hearing! The movement is so slow, so huge, the vibration is so terrible—!

The earth is shaking beneath my feet as the immense giant moves, sliding so ponderously! I turn and run across the colonnades as the last pillars begin to topple, across the rocks which are trembling violently, up the steep slopes toward the Northern Ridge! I run as I've never run before, the earth buckling and shifting beneath my flying feet! The sound of that sliding, groaning earth behind me is deafening, a roar that vibrates through me!

I risk one look back over my shoulder—the earth is like an immense black and brown and green wave!

I run, run, run, the earth shaking so violently that it jars my legs as I mount the slopes! I hear the roaring impact as the Red Palace is crushed beneath the wave and then the earth heaves mightily! I'm tossed, pushed, swept away, tumbled and thumped and beaten by the earth which heaves and rolls about me! I roll and scrabble, wrap my arms about my head, draw my knees up to my chest as I'm caught up, engulfed, hurled with the rolling earth! I'm pounded, beaten, crushed. . . .

It's dark—I look up and the stars are so beautiful— I'm so heavy— Ah, my body pains— Half buried— Must move, struggle, make efforts to free myself— Ah, the pain!— My legs?— No, not broken, only bruises— Covered in dirt— Must get up!— Must fix the pain— Ah, better—

What place is this?— Where?— Fresh earth, clay, debris of grass and trees— Ridge up there— Perhaps I can see from the top— Oh, so tired— Walk slowly, reenergize muscles, stimulate endocrine system— Step by step— A road?— Which road?— Pretty daisies— Yo-Yo, where are you?— Auria?— Step by step—

(At this point the narrative becomes increasingly disjointed and deteriorates into gibberish and aimless singing of the Faith song, "My Life Is A Flame." Later, this becomes merely a tuneless noise.

Saulus was found on the Plains of Harere, better known as the Plains of the Warlords, two days later and taken to Grenoble-Psi for treatment.

Since completing this narrative he has been kept in the Security Wing of the Complex. He has not been allowed to communicate with any but the Security

Controls and certain of the Therapy and Administrative personnel.

He has remained approachable but cautious, is cooperative and willing to comply with any orders or treatment deemed necessary and seems content enough to remain where he is at present.

He seems fully intelligent and recovered from trauma but makes no attempt to communicate in any real way.

Petitions from Louise Vestos, Callios LeMaitre and the Heads of Staff indicate a strong desire for clemency and a demand for further investigation into the powers of this extraordinary young man. It must be noted, however, that he comes under the Red-Line Classification Rules, which makes any decisions about his future dependent on full Council agreement.

It may be of interest to the Council that, in the investigation of the so-called Love Palace, twenty-two days after Saulus was brought to Grenoble-Psi, it was found empty of any members of the Clan—as might have been expected after all that time.

Several priceless artworks from the pre-Warlord era, said to be the work of Abelard Andissoro, were discovered there and have since been removed to the Louvre. The Love Palace has been sealed intact. The valley has proved to be of great interest to horticulturists and biologists from Central Research and preservation orders are, at present, in force.

—J.T. Semantics Division)

✱ FOURTEEN ✱

Memo:
23–8–81
To: Louise Vestos, Director, Study Center.
From: Central Council Advisory Section.
This is to advise you that, after careful consideration
of the petitions from yourself and other interested
parties, it has been decided to allow the subject of
case 113L ("Saulus") to continue working with the
Research and Development Sections. In the light of
his past cooperation and the remarkable results
achieved during the past two months, it has also been
decided to place him in the category of S1-Unique
(Probationary).

—Miles Roche,
for C.C.A. Section

Louise Vestos was noted for her dominating person-
ality. She possessed the authority of long experience
and was used to managing people. With Saulus, however, she was more cautious than was usual.

She took the memo back from him and said, "So
now you're an official member of Grenoble-Psi. I'm

really pleased for you. Are you enjoying the work you've been given so far?"

The light shone on his dark blonde hair and his eyes seemed particularly luminous this morning. She had always found his eyes disturbing and, judging from what she had heard, so did most of those who met him. Quiet, polite and restrained in his manner, he nevertheless managed to emanate an attraction that could not be attributed only to his psi-field.

"It's very interesting," he said mildly. "That was kind of the Council to give me S1-Unique Probationary classification—especially considering the bribes I was offered by three of the Councillors and five of your top Security people."

Her brows rose at this.

"Are you making accusations?"

"No, but I thought you might be interested."

"I'm sure you must have mistaken their intentions. What do you class as bribes?"

"Their support in my case for certain physical changes."

She was shocked at this, but tried not to show it.

"And did you succumb to these bribes?"

"Of course. I'm not a fool."

She decided against delving further. It was better to accept that he had been saved from Termination.

"Be thankful that the Council and others value your Talent despite its potential danger. Do you understand how close you were to Termination three months ago?"

"If I don't there have been plenty of people anxious to tell me so. I also understand how much I owe you and Callios LeMaitre for your support."

She shrugged at that, but was pleased to have her efforts acknowledged.

"May I ask that you pass on my thanks to Callios

LeMaitre? I haven't seen him since my recovery, but I know he petitioned on my behalf. Did you persuade him to do that?"

"Certainly not. He's been genuinely interested in what happens to you, but he's also a very busy and important man and is not a member of Grenoble-Psi staff. He asks after you. I'll be glad to pass your message on."

"I'm very aware that Security made difficulties which you fought. It's good to know that I have your goodwill."

"Security would be less severe toward you if you told them where to find your old friends, Saulus. That Probationary proviso won't be lifted until you give Security reason to feel they can trust you."

He said sharply, "Nonsense. Security will never trust me. No Super is ever completely trusted by the Orgs. By betraying my friends I wouldn't be trusted by anyone!"

"You must be grateful for what you've been given," she said severely.

His face became expressionless and the eyes very cold.

"Grateful? I'm not grateful to anyone. Why should I be? None of this is of my choosing. I don't owe anyone anything. I do what I do because I wish to, not from any feeling of gratitude."

Louise's hair swirled and was rearranged, a sign that what he said disturbed her. She looked at the file on her desk.

"The work you did with Agricultural, Biology and Medic-2 has them clamoring for more and Biochemics is complaining of departmental favoritism. You'd better decide on who you're giving time to before I have a staff war on my hands."

"Medic-1 takes up most of my mornings and I won't drop that just to fit in with Research."

"I'm aware that you're doing wonderful work in the hospital section—"

"Medic-2 and Agricultural I don't mind, although I don't understand some of their technical jargon. But as for Biochemics—! It could be interesting if they didn't become so upset when I ruin their theories and systems by doing what they say can't be done! What do I know of theories and systems? I'm not trying to cheat them, trick them or make them feel foolish! But some things I know in my own way and I can't always explain when they shout and gobble! Sometimes they behave as though I deliberately insult them! I'll give them another try, if you like, but I won't argue about theories!"

Louise decided that another discussion with Lubscholtz and Kenlinson was necessary before Saulus washed his hands of Biochemics altogether.

"I'll see what I can arrange," she said.

She noted that he was wearing a new kaftan and sandals.

"Are you seeing Auria Shasti today?"

"Yes. It's my free afternoon."

"You have no difficulties with Security?"

"Not since she was removed from active Observation duties. And for that I have you to thank. I'm very grateful. Would you allow me to express my thanks by correcting your vision?"

"There's nothing wrong with my vision!"

"No, it's good, considering your age. But I could restore it fully and you wouldn't need to squint at all. Accept it as a thank-you gift and not a bribe."

She considered, her hair swirling again.

"Close your eyes," he said.

She did so. There was a faint "itch" beneath her lids.

"Will this hurt?" she asked nervously.

"No."

The "itch" passed slowly.

"It's done," he said.

He was already moving toward the door. She blinked at him, aware of the sudden change in clarity and definition.

"Saulus—thank you."

He smiled and went out to where the usual three Control guards awaited him and others hovered to engage his interest in small projects proposed by their own departments. Saulus was always kept very busy.

Auria Shasti's reentry into Saulus's life had been at her own instigation. She had applied to see him on several occasions before Security agreed to a meeting. Saulus had seemed reluctant to meet with her but had finally shrugged and nodded after Louise had talked with him.

Auria had entered the Security cell with two Controls observing on the monitors. She had taken trouble to appear at her most attractive and wore a green gown very much like the one she had previously worn for Saulus at Serenel.

Saulus, seated on his bed, eyed her without a trace of emotion as she carefully sat on the only chair in the room and folded her hands demurely. She smiled tentatively and opened her mind to him. The smile faded when he made no attempt at mental contact. She was forced to speak vocally.

"You look very well, Saulus. Are you glad to see me?"

"I'm not sure. Why have you come?"

Her smile vanished entirely.

"Because I still feel as I told you I felt. I wished to see if we could resolve matters between us."

"You betrayed the Clan."

"Yes, that was my task. My directives couldn't be denied. But I regret being forced to betray you with them. I'm sorry about Yo-Yo. I know how much he meant to you."

"Yes, I miss him. But I took vengeance."

"I know."

She sought for another subject, anything that would break down his coldness.

"And the others of the Clan—are they safe?"

"Who asks? The Psi-Org agent or the woman the Clan befriended?"

She looked down at her hands.

"I'm not asking *where* they are. I'm asking if they're safe."

"I imagine the so-called dangerous Talents are. And a few others. Only eight, apart from me, were caught by the Psi-Org. All are minor Talents with no criminal records and they won't suffer too much. They have unrecorded fingerprints and faces that no police force would recognize. Nothing can be proved against them except that they lived at Serenel. They'll probably finish up Registered and fitted into some place in one of the Psi-Orgs for education and vocational guidance, then a life in some kind of public service. As for me, maybe I'll be allowed to live here, working for Research and the Hospital Section, living in my cell and being let out to do as they want at regular intervals. They seem to think I should feel gratitude toward them for the chance to work in a Psi-Org, gratitude for being allowed to live."

"It doesn't have to be like that, Saulus. You'll be allowed to live comfortably and productively—"

He had made a sound of disgust and turned his gaze from her.

She said, "I could help you. If you demanded that I live with you, there's every likelihood that Security would acquiesce. And I think the Study Director would help."

"Why? So that you could keep an eye on my activities just in case I prove too dangerous?"

"No. I could help you, advise you, look after you—you said you loved me."

"Oh, love . . . I loved Auria, the Lady of Serenel. I trusted her. I don't trust Psi-Org agents."

She sat very still for a moment, then rose and moved toward the door.

"Of course," he said, "there is a way. A matter of commitment."

Her eyes were wary as she turned to him.

She said, "A directive such as Hubertus imposed?"

He looked suddenly angry.

"I don't make prisoners."

"What then?"

His mind reached to hers. She returned to sit on the chair, taking in what he wanted.

His contact was carefully devoid of emotion. She tried to emulate him as she mindspoke.

"But, Saulus, if you remove those directives, Security would soon find out."

"I could teach you a little pattern that would deceive them. And they wouldn't find it possible to remove the directive I place, that I promise."

"What do you mean by a directive to loyalty?"

"As I told you, I don't make prisoners. But you'd never be able to betray me to anyone again. That way,

I could trust you. It depends on whether you feel you can trust me. That's the commitment."

She sat very still for some moments, making her decisions.

"And what commitment do I have from you, Saulus?"

"If you don't know how I feel about you as a person and as a woman by now, you never will," he said. "I made my commitment a long time ago."

She eyed him, noting the tension in his body language.

"I trust you, Saulus," she told him finally.

His eyes were brilliant as he turned to look at her. She blushed at the flood of raw emotion he directed at her, then laughed in a half-relieved, half-excited way.

Later, it was the demand from Saulus to security that Auria remain with him which made further decisions regarding his confinement necessary.

With Louise Vestos to assist in the matter, Security found it convenient to have one of their own agents personally involved with him, but were disappointed at finding that Auria was no longer prepared to act as a personal "spy." It took little time to realize that, in fact, they had not gained an advantage but had lost a useful operative to Saulus.

When queried about her own thoughts on the matter, Auria told Louise, "He trusts me and it's my own choice to remain with him. He wants me and I want him. I think we'll form a good partnership. Clever as he is, he's very young. He still needs education and advice and I need to be needed by someone as vital as he is and as important as I think he'll be one day. We'll both gain. And, incidentally, I love him."

Auria Shasti was removed from Security activities in all but technicality and seemed not to care at all.

It became convenient to give her the title of Liaison Officer.

Some weeks later, Auria stirred on the bed and attempted to draw away. Saulus held her. He was far more dominating with her than he had been in the past. She seemed not to mind.

She mindspoke, "Saulus, I must go. Simone will be at the meeting place in an hour."

He released her reluctantly and asked, "You haven't any qualms about it then?"

"No, it's logical enough. Are you certain you can do it?"

"Quite certain. My need grows worse every day. I'll act on the 28th."

"So soon?"

"Why not? If I wait any longer I'll only lose patience with Biochemics again. Would you like to look at my plan again while Security have the spy-eyes switched off?"

"One last time then—"

He drew the somewhat crumpled scrim-sheets from beneath the pillow. She looked at them carefully, noting the additions he pointed out to her and considering them. She nodded and folded the sheets, then watched as he slid them back into their hiding place.

"You're quite determined on this?" she asked.

"Quite. This is no way to live."

"Then I won't see you again until—Saulus, it seems such a gamble."

"I don't see it as a gamble. And I won't go on like this."

He kissed her and allowed her to climb from the bed.

*   *   *

Security Report 557E. Dated: 29–8–81
To: Central Security Investigation Division.
From: Control Head, J. Farraday, Grenoble-Psi.

On the evening of 28–8–81, Case 113L ("Saulus") was escorted to the Central Security Block at 21st hour, his normal retiring time. With him were Controls Boucher, Lauret and myself. After some conversation concerning activities for the following day, Saulus prepared for bed and his lights were out by 21:40.

Controls Boucher, Lauret and myself followed normal procedures and checked the alarms and cameras, finding them to be in perfect order. Control Boucher took first watch and Control Lauret and myself retired to the guard alcove.

At 1:10 Control Boucher woke me to take second watch and I took up my position at the duty desk. Saulus was asleep and all appeared normal. At 4:40 I woke Control Lauret for the third watch and retired again.

At approximately 5:10 I was wakened by the service bell. I heard Control Lauret leave the duty desk and go to the bedroom. He returned moments later and, at my query, said, "All's well. He was having a bad dream, that's all."

At 6:30 Control Lauret woke Control Boucher and myself. He said, "Saulus is getting dressed. I'll check his breakfast order." We did this together and found it to be as usual.

At 6:35 the outer grilles were opened and the relieving guards, consisting of Controls Felichi, Maurice and Tadger took over. Controls Boucher, Lauret and myself left the area and went to the Off-Duty Lounge for breakfast.

Control Lauret then said, "I'll join you in a minute. I want to consult the duty roster for next week." He went out.

At 6:45 precisely, the alarms went off in the Central Security Block. Control Boucher and I immediately ran to the grilles and there we found Controls Felichi, Tadger and Lauret. Control Lauret was dressed only in his underclothes and was very agitated.

He said, "I went to see Saulus at 5:10 when he called. Next thing I knew I was in his bed and my clothes were gone."

I immediately notified Security-2 and Reception to tell them that Saulus was attempting to escape in the identity of Control Lauret. Reception then informed me that Control Lauret had checked out of the Control Section only moments before and that his fingerprints, identidisc and activator card had all been in order.

I notified Security Head Muriettis and waited with the others. I then made this statement in the Presences of Controls Felichi, Tadger, Boucher, Maurice and Lauret with Security Head Muriettis as witness.

(Signed) J. Farraday, Control Head

Memo.

To: Louise Vestos, Director, Study Center.
From: Security-2, Henrique Muriettis.

Further to my previous memo, as nearly as we can ascertain, Saulus was picked up in a dark blue shuttlebug outside Reception at 6:42. The registration number of the car was not noticed. It is thought that a young woman was driving the vehicle, but no description could be given. No further information is available at present.

H. Muriettis, Security Head

*   *   *

(Facsimile of scrip only)
To: Louise Vestos
From: Case 113L ("Saulus")

I am writing this while waiting for contact to be made with certain of my friends. I will ask them to post it to you before we leave.

You have been most kind and helpful to me since I was first brought to Grenoble-Psi and I regret that what I am doing will cause you problems and concern. For this I apologize, but see no other course open to me.

The Psi-Org Council have given me the Probationary Classification but this is not suitable in my view. I would be no less a prisoner with this Classification. I do not care to remain a prisoner.

Therefore, I write to you in hope that you will pass on the carefully thought out solution which I propose and which I enclose with this scrip. I am aware that details will need to be refined, but it must be left to cleverer people than I am to work these out.

My needs are not unreasonable or difficult to arrange, but they are vital to me if I am to remain connected with the Psi-Orgs.

During the past three months I have made it quite clear that I am willing to cooperate with the Psi-Orgs and their allied departments. Of the twelve programs I have worked on in Research and Development I have proved my value in eleven. I do not make claims for Biochemics since I found the people there unreasonable and stupid. That I have been so valuable is not an egotistical statement. It is the truth.

Friends of mine once advised me thus: Give of your abilities, but be sure you receive payment or people will not value what is given. So I propose the bargain which I enclose. I wrote it and hid it in my pillow for many weeks so it is rather crumpled, for which I apologize.

The essence of it is that I want my beautiful Serenel. Let me live there and have my friends about me once more.

In Serenel I will be content to live for all my days. Some form of amnesty could be made for my friends and any other Outlawed Talents who will come to Serenel. I will undertake the work of a settlement with my friends, an open prison in that valley. Then we can all work together and gain a measure of fulfillment in our lives.

I do not know the correct words to make this all sound right so you will find my writing out of the plan showing ignorance of the ways to put it. But I am not ignorant of what I want it to be. I have chosen myself an agent who will speak on my behalf. This agent is Auria Shasti, who is of the Orgs but also close with me.

You will not find me. I have been about in the world and am not so ignorant as I once was. I am experienced and capable of avoiding discovery for as long as I please. Even Auria Shasti does not know of my whereabouts. I will contact her when I decide it is safe and in my own way. Should any harm befall Auria Shasti I will take revenge. This is a blackmail which I regard most seriously.

It is unfortunate but necessary that I trust nobody. I also impose a time limit to the period when the Enforcement Agencies and the Psi-Orgs must give me an answer. That time is 1st day, 11th month, 2281 A.D. Two months is surely enough time to reach decisions, provided that the important people who discuss it do not idle away the time. An announcement of the Serenel settlement must be made in the public media on that day or I will simply vanish and that will be an end of it.

Surely my abilities and my willingness to work with the Psi-Orgs must be worth some discussions and decisions? Would it not be sensible to have socially undesirable Talents limited to a place where they can live useful lives?

I ask for nothing in my plan which will cost the Orgs or the governments great finance or inconvenience. And I could be of great profit to many, I think. I lived in that valley for almost twenty-two of my years without causing difficulties. I was happy there. Remind those who look at my plan of this.

My bargain is a simple one. I am a simple man. But not an imbecile.

—Saulus

(Facsimile of scrip only. Received at private address.)
To: Callios LeMaitre
From: Saulus who was also Big Black in Chegga.
Dated: 29th day, 8th month, 2281 A.D.

This is a difficult letter to write. All letters are difficult for me as I am not experienced with the correct form and manner of them. I say what I mean but, if I put things down that seem foolish or poorly expressed, I hope you will not mind.

I did not get the chance to see you after the Therapists took over when the recordings were finished, but I was allowed to read the transcript of my "trauma breaking." I listened to the recordings, too.

It must have been a distress to you when you realized it was you I claimed as my father. The fact is true, but I will understand if you do not wish to acknowledge it. There is nothing between us except genes and a few friendly hours which we shared.

I liked you when we met in Chegga. You were not as I had imagined and this is a good thing since I had imagined an authority and not a person.

My mother's name was Lorrae Jameson. She was an Epsilon 'path in Administration at Rome-Psi when you were there studying in Psychology-3. She became pregnant by you because you epitomized the ideal man for her, but she had no wish for the relationship to become more serious in an emotional way. She was already pregnant with me when she became involved with Jonaas and drugs and criminal activities. She spent the last nine years of her life in a dream-haze at Serenel as one of his women.

She taught me much and was a good mother in some ways. She bore Jonaas two children. One was stillborn, the other was Yo-Yo. I loved Yo-Yo very much. My mother was gentle and pretty but not clever. She died of drugs and radiation poisoning when I was too young and ignorant to help her.

I do not mean these facts as a confrontation to you. I merely wish you to know because I like you.

I hear rumors that you and Louise Vestos are involved together. That is a pleasing thing to me. She has been kind to me and I like her.

Perhaps we will meet again some day. I would like that. Thank you for helping me when I was ill. I hope you will have a happy life.

—Saulus

Personal.

To: Louise Vestos, Director, Study Center.
From: (Central Councillor) Miles Roche.
Dated: 17–11–81

Just a few lines to let you know that all is going well at this end. Once we plough through the formalities it will be a mere matter of procedure to establish the Serenel Psi-Center.

Auria Shasti certainly knows how to argue. (She reminds me a little of you during our training days together!) A clever woman, always ready with a point and as hard as granite when it comes to ensuring that Saulus gets what he wants.

As it happens, the Council finds this solution to the old problem of Outlaw Talents very convenient. It is proposed to set up a Serenel Authority and the mountains will be ringed with some very nasty, Talent-proof devices to prevent escapes.

The Authority will oversee the internal organization as Saulus and Shasti proposed it. Some of his ideas are surprisingly perceptive when one examines them in detail.

It was interesting to note LeMaitre's claim of parenthood and his stand about his son's rights and privileges, don't you think? Council has suggested that he become Liaison Head between Serenel-Psi and the other Orgs and he seems very interested. He could be a very busy man for a while.

One thing I would like to know. How did all this fuss about the Andissoro sculptures grow so out of hand? Saulus continues his demand and Paris Municipal Arts is up in arms about it! The Louvre Authority gets into the media at every opportunity! Frankly, I don't think Saulus has any hope of getting them back to his so-called Love Palace again!

See you at the Berlin meeting?

—Miles

* FIFTEEN *

Coming in over the low eastern mountains by air-car, LeMaitre experienced his usual thrill of excitement at the view of the valley. In ten years of monthly visits, he had never lost his appreciation of the change from harsh mountains and arid stretches of ugly countryside to this fantasy world nestling so strikingly in its isolation among such areas of devastation. The colors seemed brighter here than in any other place he knew of, perhaps because of the forbidding darkness of the mountains or, perhaps, because he had grown to love it more than any other place.

It was a large valley, seeming only partially cultivated until one examined it more closely. From the air the lakes in the basin were blue and shimmering, surrounded by thick copses of graceful trees, huge rock formations and lush groundcovers which drew great interest from visiting horticulturists. The slowly growing groups of buildings on the southern slopes of the valley hardly intruded into the viewer's awareness unless one knew them as well as LeMaitre did.

Although there was no dangerous radiation to be found in the valley it was still dangerous to venture into some areas of the basin without adequate protection because of the mutated rodents known as sharpteeth.

In the east, the waterways became obscured by thick forests of trees which often puzzled visitors because of their mixture of unknown species. The remaining radiation patches in the valley had been removed with great care and at enormous cost, but the mutations caused by Saulus's long-ago experiments could still be found here and there. The waterways coming from the western peaks had been corrected by Noni and Torros several years previously and no contaminated water was to be found within Serenel now.

Birdlife in the valley was plentiful and exotic, but the killer-birds had long gone, as had the Crawlies and the stinging-moths, due to the decision made by Saulus concerning them some ten years earlier. He refused to eradicate the sharpteeth because he claimed that they were part of the complex ecology of the valley, but their numbers had decreased considerably compared to what they had been ten years before. It was suspected that he retained a small population of them because they were good to eat.

Toward the western end of the valley, on the broad terraces of the northern slopes, huge orchards of the famous Red Trees waved their luxuriant foliage and brought considerable revenue to the valley because of their fruit. They would grow nowhere else in the world and it was suspected that Saulus had arranged this, too. He was, in some ways, jealous of sharing the things in his domain with the outside world.

Lower on the northern slopes, huge vegetable gardens had been established and these were another fascination to horticulturists. These gardens were protected from insects and other non-human predators by huge green and purple moss banks and immense colonies of silver beetles which nested beneath them.

Where the Red Palace, the colonnades and the Tunnel had been was now a large hill, partially forested and partially covered in eyecatching gardens. The scar left on the mountainside where once the West Terrace had been was now covered by robust vines and a particularly unusual type of purple fern that produced small white blossoms.

The Love Palace was invisible from the air, but the gardens which grew about it and over it were spectacular. The East Terrace and the land about the Spur in which the Love Palace was hidden was supported by solid rock and had been fenced since Noni's children had been born. An elevator shaft had been built up the sheer cliff-face to the East Terrace from the valley floor, although it was possible to walk up by the southern slopes if one had the energy and the inclination.

The Serenel-Psi Complex was an orderly collection of buildings among orderly gardens and trees on the lower southern slopes and the valley floor at the western end. The Complex was growing steadily as more and more research projects were established. Eventually it was thought that the buildings would have to be built upward since Saulus refused to have the greater valley intruded on.

At the moment, the Complex housed some three hundred people. It was far larger than the area where the Outlaw Talents lived in what was known as the Serenel Village, a small collection of charming dwellings below where the Observation Post had once been. This was also growing steadily. Not all those who lived in the Village were classified as Outlaws. Many were students from other Orgs who came to

refine and develop their own abilities with the help
of greater Talents or people who had managed to
establish permanent residency because they enjoyed
Serenel and its people.

The Love Palace housed only fifteen Talents and
the Village was set directly below it, hence the need
for the elevator shaft, since social life was usually
very active.

The small hospital where Saulus worked on a con-
stant stream of special cases, the Research and Development Division, Biomedics, Biochemics and the
Agricultural Laboratories dominated the higher buildings of the Complex on the southern slopes. In
between were quarters for Controls—a very minor
influence in the valley—and visitors, several large
workshops utilized by the Talents and an extensive
entertainment/recreation area. In the workshops,
many of Serenel's Talents produced pottery, jewelry,
fine machine equipment and electronics, craftwork
and clothing.

Despite its slowly increasing complement of Talents
classified as Outlaws or Uniques, Serenel-Psi was
becoming "respectable," its activities drawing interest
from other Psi-Orgs and governments as an increasingly valuable resource and research facility.

Most of the Talents who had come to Serenel with
Saulus were actively involved in the work of the Complex in one way or another.

Hubertus Aanensen was Special Advisor to the
Serenel Authority, Torros Kinaidy was in charge of
the workshops and The Hand (he had never admitted
to any other name) was Staff Liaison Officer. The
Foster Twins worked in Biochemics Division when
they felt like working and Meriem and Christina, still
spry despite their ages, headed the Catering Division

with Fatimah and Mario. Jazalu had joined Carolus and several of the minor 'kinetics in Maintenance, Noni was occasionally involved in engineering projects and Francois was in charge of the Complex gardens. Pearlman and Justine and several helpers who had once been among the Rats were in charge of the orchards and vegetable gardens on the northern terraces.

Saulus was usually busy, but worked when and where he pleased. He was too valuable to be pressured in any way, but when he devoted himself to a project the wait was always worthwhile.

It was said that only four people could influence Saulus against his preferences—Auria, The Hand, Torros and Hubertus—but there were times when even they wondered if this was so.

Quiet and pleasant-mannered as he was, Saulus could be very determined and very stubborn when he chose. His authority, never too obvious and seemingly mild, was never questioned. Even Hubertus, who took his position very seriously and maintained order and discipline, consulted with Saulus.

LeMaitre's aircar landed at midmorning, but it was late afternoon before he could escape the Complex and officialdom. With a folder of schedules, petitions and suggestions for future projects beneath one arm, he walked through the Village and down into the gardens about the elevator shaft.

Noni and Torros had produced two daughters, now ages three and five, both now playing near the little ford over the stream which flowed down to the small lake known as the Lotus Pool. The little cave where Saulus had once lived was nearby, vines half concealing its opening.

Both little girls were robustly healthy and, at the moment, incredibly dirty. Neither showed any signs

of Talent, but they were charming children who, like
Jazalu's ten-year-old son, would be educated beyond
Serenel but visit the valley regularly when they were
old enough. LeMaitre exchanged polite greetings with
them and decided not to inform Noni of their present state.

The elevator ascended rapidly and he stepped out
into the enchanted gardens of the East Terrace. Slender, blue-foliaged trees spread delicate canopies over
purple and green moss banks, large clusters of pink
and white daisies and a variety of blossoming shrubs.
Ferns and groundcovers of several strange but exquisite varieties crowded the edges of walkways and grew
over rocky areas.

An animal, not unlike a golden leopard, sprang toward
him playfully and butted his thigh to have its head
scratched, bees hummed busily in the afternoon warmth
and two rainbow-scaled pythons poked enquiring
tongues at him as he passed their perch in a dark-
leafed plum tree close to the sphincter-door.

The door opened at his approach and he walked
into the cool entryway. The computer recognized him.

"Good afternoon, Callios LeMaitre, Saulus is in his
garden. Will you take refreshment?"

"Later, perhaps," LeMaitre said and made his way
along the corridor.

The interior of the Love Palace remained very little
altered in its internal structure from the way Saulus
had first found it, but there were some divisions to
make the apartments more convenient and some
rooms had become work areas. The apartments were
still beautiful and the tenants knew better than to
spoil them if they wished to remain in the Love
Palace.

LeMaitre called out to the Foster Twins as he

passed a room where they were busy with a semi-abstract sculpture of rather disturbing design. He spoke to Hubertus in the small but excellent library area and he waved to Simone and Justine as he went through the vast living area known as the Great Room.

The now-famous Andissoro sculptures had been returned after a three-year battle between Saulus and the Louvre and there was an older sculpture of a charming nymph, salvaged from the West Terrace collapse, which hid the door to what was now a storage area—the remains of the old Fort which had been sealed off at the outer end by Noni and Pearlman.

The Master's Room and three large, adjoining rooms had been joined to the Blue Place to form an extensive apartment for Auria and Saulus. Beyond this, the old garden remained largely unchanged but, where the path to the West Terrace had been, there was now a large and airy pavilion and, further on, a high and decorative fence bordering the sheer drop where the Crack had once existed.

As LeMaitre walked past Red Tree's Daughter, now a huge tree, she brushed his shoulders lightly and the rose vines slithered slightly against the wall. The moss banks were as beautiful as ever and huge clumps of white and scarlet daisies sent faint perfume into the court. The pavilion was covered with white, scentless jasmine (Saulus found the jasmine scent too cloying but liked the blossoms) and the decorative fence beyond was covered with blossoming vines.

Auria, slender and youthful, dressed in a soft blue gown, was sitting at a table in the pavilion, an old book before her. Saulus, in Dark Mode and wearing what appeared to be a silver bodysuit, was talking with Alouette Coltain.

Auria exclaimed at seeing LeMaitre and came to

kiss his cheek. Saulus smiled and the silver beetles which were his "bodysuit" suddenly ran downward to expose his arms and torso, but did not leave his hips and legs as he came forward to embrace his father.

Saulus mindspoke, "You look very well. How is Louise?"

LeMatre replied, "Very well, too. We signed another marriage contract last week— How can you bear those things crawling all over you?"

"They say 'hello' that way occasionally," Saulus told him. "I'm pleased about you and Louise. Not that I thought it would be otherwise."

He walked to the moss banks and the silver beetles began running from him in a stream, seeking their nests and revealing him dressed only in a codpiece. The codpiece was because Auria insisted on it. When he went down to roam the valley basin he seldom wore anything except sandals.

Auria rarely interfered in the activities of the valley people. Since, officially at least, she remained a member of Grenoble-Psi Security, she travelled from Serenel regularly but briefly, Saulus and his surroundings being her main interest. She was not unpopular with most of the Talents of Serenel, but there remained a slight caution between herself and them which Auria seemed content to do nothing about. Her two closest friends were Noni and Alouette.

Alouette had come to be known as Saulus's assistant and "organized" him when he was willing to be organized. She had sold her home near Vichy nine years before and come to the valley with some management by Hubertus and The Hand. "I was so bored!" she had told Saulus. Now she looked as youthful as Auria and LeMaitre did and had formed an unexpected and warm alliance with Hubertus.

"For how long are you staying?" she asked LeMaitre.

"Permanently," said Saulus. "He and Louise are retiring here and becoming members of the Serenel Authority."

"You might have told me!" said Alouette. "I'll have to organize a decent rowdy to welcome them. Where are they to live?"

"In the new villa being constructed near the ford. They'll stay in one of the visitors' apartments in the meantime."

"Why aren't they to live here? There's plenty of room."

"Living with the Clan would drive Callios insane in no time at all and I have enough bossy women about me as it is," said Saulus, smiling. "You and Auria and Noni and Jazalu living close to Louise? What a frightening thought!"

He ignored the protesting exclamations from Alouette and Auria and took his father's arm to lead him inside.

"It's true, you know," he mindspoke to LeMaitre. "They get on very well as it is, but with Louise about they'd all squabble. She wouldn't approve of our free-and-easy ways at all. Her administrative skills should be valuable here."

"I should warn you, Saulus," LeMaitre said, "that Louise is still very doubtful about living here. It's because of the odd rumors that are inclined to circulate. It took me all my time to persuade her to give it a try."

"She'll be content here, I promise. What rumors are circulating?"

"Well—it's that very thing about being content. There are so many criminal Talents living here, people with very positive personalities, competitive people who must have found it very difficult to adapt to the confined conditions and the discipline. And yet they're all content. They've been content for a long time."

Saulus slid a glance at him.

"So?"

"But it puzzles people that they *are* so content. So few arguments, everyone cooperating, everyone enjoying their lives here and regarding your word as law. The rumors are that, well—I don't want to upset you."

"Tell me."

"It's because of the results you've achieved with patients who were mentally handicapped. Nobody expected such remarkable results. Tampering with physical matters is one thing, but tampering with the workings of the brain makes some people uneasy. So rumors tend to circulate that, perhaps, you might have tampered with the brains of criminals here and that's why they're all so happy to stay. I argued with Louise, but she's still uneasy."

There was a silence between them until LeMaitre said, "You wouldn't do such an immoral thing, of course."

But there was something of a question in his statement which was not lost on Saulus.

"You'd have to define 'immoral' and 'criminal' for me if we're to get into arguments about such things. I would never do anything damaging to anyone, Papa."

"Yes, but—"

"You and Louise will both be content here because it's a good place to be content in. Don't you trust me?"

"Well, of course, but I'm biased."

They moved into the garden where Auria and Alouette were staring out at the valley.

"I have a lot of new petitions for you to consider," LeMaitre told Saulus. "Agriculture-2 is delighted with the new seed oil. And Biochemics are very pleased with the success of their latest projects."

"They should be. I had to listen to hours of pointless theorizing. They never change! What's happening about the desert weed?"

"They're harvesting the weed now. Something to do with antibacterial enzymes in it. I also have a prayer sent to you by Diam Ennio. Remember him?"

"How could I forget? They tell me that the Faith is more popular than any other religion now. Strange when you consider all it stole from all of them and a lot of human-developmental movements besides! But it seems to be a good thing on the whole. What's the prayer about?"

"The Americas developments. He prays for your secret influence in his work."

"He doesn't need my influence. People seem to regard him as a demigod if what I hear is correct. But perhaps I'll write and wish him well. How have you and Louise adapted to renewed youth?"

"We had no difficulty with anything but the questions. We tell everyone it's merely cosmetic. But sooner or later someone is going to notice the perpetual youth of a lot of your friends."

"It's already been noticed. I ignore the questions. Obeh will be awake. Come and see him."

The nursery room was brightly colored and light. A naked, rosy-cheeked child was sitting up in his cot, blinking at them as they came in. He was almost three years old, a sturdy and golden child with Auria's dark hair and fine features and Saulus's gray eyes. He smiled hugely at sight of LeMaitre.

"Granpa!"

"Yes," said Saulus, "and you may say hello after you make pee-pee."

He picked Obeh up and whisked him off to the freshener. He returned presently and handed Obeh to LeMaitre.

"He's Talented," Saulus said casually. "He makes minor broadcasts every so often."

"That's wonderful!" LeMaitre exclaimed. "Another 'path in the family!"

"Auria and I decided to have another. It's a girl, already three months on the way. She'll be blonde like me and she'll have Auria's eyes."

"Saulus, I am pleased! A real family! It's all working out beautifully, isn't it?"

"Maybe. We're happy, anyway. Come along, Obeh. Let's go out and see the big shadows creep across the valley."

They went out to see the sun set.

Saulus did not tell LeMaitre that Obeh also showed minor signs of having the same remarkable Secondary as his father.

Only Auria knew that as yet. There was time enough to prepare for the future when Obeh was older. And there was the daughter to come. If he had calculated correctly, she would be quite as remarkable.

He had long been aware that his children would need more freedom than he required. By the time they became active Talents, the restrictions imposed on all Registered clairvoyants would have been eased considerably if the influences he had begun among the authorities who came and went so frequently caused them to respond as he wished. And they *would* respond. Already some of the major Talents at Serenel were being allowed to participate in activities with other Psi-Orgs, some of them even travelling about as specialists under supervision. There was even talk of involving Serenel Talents in the new space experiments.

He had no compunction about imposing gentle mental influences where they were most useful. The trick was to remain subtle, undetectable. He would, it seemed, have to be more careful.

His gentle influences were not only imposed on the visiting Psi-Org authorities. With The Hand and Alouette's help he had a regular stream of important clients who came as governmental or social advisors to inspect Serenel and who paid handsomely for illicit body-changes and enhancements. And there were the scientists who came to participate in the research and the general staff of the Complex also available to him.

Bribery and hidden influences were very useful tools and he wanted his children to enjoy lives beyond the confinements of Serenel if they wished to. He hoped they would see some of the fascinating places he had seen and participate in activities he felt no need for. Perhaps they would even travel to the stars.

And, in the meantime, there was the new hospital for mentally and physically afflicted children to be built high on the southern slopes. Research and Development were very interested in such an ambitious project and it would be enjoyable to teach his own children the things which had taken him so long to learn and perfect. They might have new ideas to add to his. The human brain was a remarkable thing and the barriers between what most people regarded as normal and what the unTalented called paranormal were so very thin, so easily influenced—

"Do you still do your dance to the sun, Saulus?" LeMaitre queried, still carrying Obeh.

"Every morning. And Obeh has been joining me of late. He's very good at it, aren't you, Obeh? We prance about together and then we say hello to Red Tree's Daughter and the silver beetles."

"I brought Obeh a present," LeMaitre said, drawing the red ball from a loose jacket pocket.

Obeh squealed at sight of the ball and clutched it happily.

A momentary shadow passed across Saulus's face, but he smiled, slid an arm about Auria and turned his attention to the valley as the shadows of the mountains crept toward the eastern end.

LeMaitre had already forgotten his doubts.

"Beautiful Serenel," he murmured. "What more could anyone wish for?"

"Quite so, Papa," said Saulus.

Hard SF is Good to Find

CHARLES SHEFFIELD

Proteus Combined
Proteus in the Underworld
In the 22nd century, technology gives man the power to alter his shape at will. Behrooz Wolf invented the process—now he will have to tame it....

The Mind Pool
A revised and expanded version of the author's 1986 novel *The Nimrod Hunt*. "A considerable feat of both imagination and storytelling." —*Chicago Sun-Times*

Brother to Dragons
Sometimes one man *can* make a difference. A Dickensian novel of the near future by a master of hard SF.

Between the Strokes of Night
None dared challenge the Immortals' control of the galaxy—until one man learned their secret....

Dancing with Myself
Sheffield explains the universe in nonfiction and story.

ROBERT L. FORWARD

Rocheworld
"This superior hard-science novel of an interstellar expedition is a substantially revised and expanded version of *The Flight of the Dragonfly*.... Thoroughly recommended." —*Booklist*

Indistinguishable from Magic
A virtuoso mixture of science fiction and science fact, including: antigravity machines—six kinds! And all the known ways to build real starships.

→

LARRY NIVEN, JERRY POURNELLE & MICHAEL FLYNN
Fallen Angels
A near-future cautionary romp by two *New York Times* bestselling authors and the award-winning Michael Flynn.

VERNOR VINGE
Across Realtime
Two Hugo-nominated novels in one grand volume.

ELTON ELLIOTT, editor
Nanodreams
Welcome to the world of the *micro*miniaturized future where with virus-sized self-replicating machines all things are possible—but only human wisdom stands between us and unspeakable disaster.

If not available from your local bookstore, fill out this coupon and send a check or money order for the cover price to Baen Books, Dept. BA, P.O. Box 1403, Riverdale, NY 10471. Delivery can take up to ten weeks.

Proteus Combined	87603-1 $5.99	___
Proteus in the Underworld	87659-7 $5.99	___
Brother to Dragons	72141-0 $4.99	___
Between the Strokes of Night	55977-X $4.99	___
Dancing with Myself	72185-2 $4.99	___
Rocheworld	69869-9 $4.99	___
Indistinguishable from Magic	87686-4 $5.99	___
Fallen Angels	72052-X, $5.99	___
Across Realtime	72098-8 $5.99	___
Nanodreams	87680-5 $5.99	___

NAME: _____

ADDRESS: _____

_____

I have enclosed a check or money order in the amount of $_____